# Prais

MW00474732

"In *Incomplete Sentence*, Kennedy takes well-drawn characters, puts them into situations that keep the reader turning pages, and ends with an unexpected but satisfying ending."

—RICHARD L. MABRY, MD, AWARD-WINNING AUTHOR
OF MEDICAL THRILLERS

"There is nothing incomplete about *Incomplete Sentence* . . . a plethora of unexpected twists and turns . . . what delectable fare for mystery aficionados!"

—ANN AULT, ACTRESS, SINGER, AUTHOR, SCREENWRITER

"*Incomplete Sentence* is a complete delight! This time Amelia gets thrown into a murder investigation while her best friend and crime buddy is MIA. Worse yet, where's the cat?"

—VANDI CLARK, ACTRESS, FORMER ENGLISH TEACHER,
AND AVID BIBLIOMANIAC

"Grabs your attention on the first page and doesn't let go . . . If you enjoy a good old-fashioned whodunnit with plenty of action and humor . . . you'll love *Incomplete Sentence*."

—LYNNE WELLS WALDING, AUTHOR OF *Pastor McAlester's Bride*,
*Winnoby Cabin*, and *Ian's Song*

# Incomplete
# SENTENCE

A Miss Prentice Cozy Mystery

Book 4

## By | E. E. Kennedy

Elkhart, Indiana
46514 USA

*Incomplete Sentence*
Copyright © 2016 by Ellen E. Kennedy.

Published by Sheaf House®. Requests for information should be addressed to:

Editorial Director
Sheaf House Publishers
1703 Atlantic Avenue
Elkhart, IN 46514

jmshoup@gmail.com
www.sheafhouse.com

Library of Congress Control Number: 2015955217

ISBN-13: 978-1-936438-40-2 (softcover)

Cover design by Marisa Jackson.

Cover image props courtesy of Susie Kauffman.

Back cover image from Shutterstock.

MANUFACTURED IN THE UNITED STATES OF AMERICA

# Acknowledgements

Many thanks:

To Joan Shoup, editor extraordinaire.

To Harold Kennedy, for his patience and encouragement.

To Donald A. Edwards, former acting director of the NYS Thruway System, for his sage advice about roads and snow removal.

To Louise Sowa, for her prayers.

To John M. Edwards, for his input on North Country colloquialisms.

To Kate Edwards Trussler, for her expertise in French.

To Captain Mike Branch of the Plattsburgh NY Police Department, for an important set of initials.

To the Cary Alliance Writers' Circle, for listening to my work-in-progress.

To James Lewis, retired Louisville PD detective, for his law enforcement expertise and for the sleigh idea.

To the Greater Adirondack Ghost and Tour Company for being part of the story.

To that long-ago absconding wedding planner about whom I promised to write one day.

And especially to the Lord Jesus Christ, who gives me the whole armor of God.

# Other books

# by E. E. Kennedy

Miss Prentice Cozy Mystery Series

*Irregardless of Murder*

*Death Dangles a Participle*

*Murder in the Past Tense*

"The Applesauce War"

in the anthology *The Farmer's Bride*

from Barbour Publishing

"For me, to live is Christ and to die is gain."

PHILIPPIANS 1:21 KJV

"For we do not grieve as those who have no hope."

1 THESSALONIANS 4:13*b*

# Prologue

Tracey Parish sat at the red light and refused to fume, as she often did, over the time she was kept waiting in traffic.

Today she was glad for the wait. She wasn't looking forward to reaching her destination and enduring the hostile reception she would surely receive. Still, if she wanted her things back, her grandma's heirloom quilt, her silver-backed hand mirror, even some of her underwear, she'd have to see Greg one final time.

She blinked back tears. Losing the beautiful quilt that Granny had so lovingly hand-stitched for her would be heartbreaking.

She remembered the day the old lady had pulled it from her own ancient hope chest. "See here?" she said, pointing with a bony finger, "There's your initials, Sugar. When you get married, you can embroider your groom's next to 'em."

Wherever she went, Tracey had taken that quilt with her. It still bore the fragrance of Yardley's English Lavender, Granny's favorite soap.

During that last terrible phone call, Greg had threatened to throw it and all her treasured possessions out or burn them. He'd do it too. She'd seen him do much worse.

A man in a neighboring car smiled at her, but she kept her expression neutral. Her flirting days were over now that she and Johnny had found each other again.

The light changed, but her own lane was still red. As the cars in the turn lane streamed past, she pulled the scarf from her head and let her long blonde hair cascade over her shoulders. It felt good to have the rental car's top down. Greg had never let her put the top down in his car.

How could she have ever let him run her life so completely? How many times had he demeaned her, cheated on her, even hit her, and then assumed everything could be made right with a handful of flowers or a love song murmured in her ear?

She tossed her head. He'd hate it when he saw that her hair was down. He had only wanted her to wear it loose in private, for him.

Her left hand rested on the steering wheel. She held it up and looked at the diamond ring on the third finger. The stone wasn't very big, but the love behind it was. She'd promised Johnny that they'd be married as soon as she got back from California, even if it meant going to city hall. Mom and Dad would want a church wedding, but they could do that afterward.

Why had she ever left Texas? What on earth did California have that Texas didn't?

"Absolutely nothing!" she said aloud.

She smiled grimly, thinking of how out of place Greg had looked in her tiny hometown, where nobody knew what a great celebrity he was supposed to be. He'd acted like a jerk, looking down on everything: what her family wore, their ranching life, even the blue ribbons that lined the walls of the horse stalls. He hated the food her mother served and snorted when the family bowed their heads to say grace.

Worst of all had been the fistfight between Greg and her brother Hank. She'd never forget the image of her long-haired boyfriend, blood streaming from his nose into his beard, demanding that she leave with him immediately.

She rested her forehead against the steering wheel. "Stupid, stupid girl!" she chided herself. "Why did I go back with him?"

She'd left, despite her mother's tears and her father's angry words. Her brother had stood on the porch, out of breath, with the saddest expression on his face. He had always understood her, but this time, she could tell he was totally bewildered.

*If it hadn't been for Johnny's letter, I'd still be here, under Greg's thumb.*

Hank had contacted her former high school boyfriend, who offered to drive out to L.A., pick her up and bring her back to Texas. And she'd accepted, being careful not to let Greg guess her plans.

It was on that trip home that she and Johnny had realized there was still something special between them, and within one month of arriving back home, she'd accepted his ring.

As she drove past the old familiar Los Angeles land-marks and made the old familiar turns, her heart began to beat faster. This would not be a fun encounter, but maybe it would be okay. Maybe he'd be away, out of the apartment.

*I don't have to do this. There's nothing stopping me from turning around and going right back to the airport.*

She frowned. *But I can't let Greg win. I have to show him that I'm my own boss now. He's not going to burn my wedding quilt. I have a much better use for it.*

The light changed. Resolutely, she shifted into drive, merged into traffic, and was never seen alive again.

# Chapter | One

I t was spring in the Adirondacks when the figurative ice jam finally broke.

Early that evening, Gil and I were at our lake house. Baby Janet was fast asleep in her crib. We had built a fire in the fireplace and settled into the sofa with a bowl of popcorn and our respective books when there was a knock on the front door.

Interruptions at odd times weren't unusual for us, since Gil was editor of the local newspaper. Important news doesn't keep nine-to-five hours, but an unannounced in-the-flesh visitor this late was a little out of the ordinary. We lived seven miles from town, down a dark and inconvenient gravel road. Furthermore, tonight wasn't a good time. Gil had been on edge and rather secretive lately and I'd hoped to get a chance to talk with him about it.

I sighed and looked through the peephole. "It's Vern!" I said, startled.

Gil's nephew had considered us *personae non gratae* ever since the taxi-driving grad student had gotten himself into trouble with the law and we'd declined to cover it up. The incident had a happy ending, but Vern still nursed a grudge.

It was painful, but over the ensuing year I'd gradually accustomed myself to his snubs during our encounters about town.

"Hi, Amelia," Vern said when I opened the door. His gaze avoided mine. "Gil here too?"

"This is a surprise." I stepped back. "Yes. Come in."

He didn't reply, just plunged his hands in his pants pockets and ambled down the hall into our rustic living room.

Gil stood, frowning. "What's up, kid?" he asked, his tone kindly, but reserved.

Vern's long arm waved in the air. "Sit down, please, both of you."

We sat.

So did Vern. His long legs seemed uncertain where to place themselves. He looked around.

"The house looks about the same." Vern had lived with us during the first few months of our marriage.

Gil reached for the bowl of popcorn on the coffee table and jerked his head toward a door down the hall. "Janet has your room now. She keeps it neater than you did." He offered the bowl to Vern, who shook his head.

"Can I get you something to drink?" I said.

He fidgeted with his hands. "Nope. Um, thank you. I better get this said: I'm sorry."

Gil and I looked at each other. I'd been earnestly hoping, indeed praying, for reconciliation with Vern for over a year, but this abrupt apology was a bit of a shock.

Gil leaned forward. "For what, exactly?" he asked sternly.

A little too sternly, in my opinion. My first instinct had been to jump up, run around the coffee table, and wrap the boy in a big hug.

Vern ran his hand through his floppy blond mop. "You know, all that stuff about the lunchbox and the police and everything. You were right. Melody helped me see that." Melody was Vern's girlfriend.

"She did, huh?" Gil's face was unreadable.

"Yeah, she pointed out that I'd probably be in jail right now if you hadn't made me, well, do the right thing. So I'm sorry." He held his palms upward in entreaty.

"So now you're sorry." Gil stood and looked down at his nephew. He pointed at me. "Do you know what you have put this woman through, mister? Do you know that she has tears in her eyes every time she speaks of you?"

Vern looked over at me, his own pale blue eyes wide. "Really?"

"Wait a minute. No, not really. Gil's exaggerating." I got to my feet and looked at my husband under an arched eyebrow. "Yes, you are." I turned back to Vern. "We both felt bad that you were so angry with us, but we managed to soldier on. Now, though, I am just so very, very glad that we can put this behind us. I think the occasion calls for a hug."

Vern stood, his arms extended towards me. "Then you forgive me?"

I embraced him. My nose came in line with his second shirt button. "Yes, of course we do, don't we, Gil?" I looked back over my shoulder.

He shrugged. "If she can, I guess I can." Smiling, he extended his hand and Vern shook it.

My eyes did well up at this, and I gave a little silly laugh.

Gil noticed. "See? Tears."

"I have something else to say, but I can't say it alone."

It only took Vern a few long strides to reach the door and step outside. In seconds he reentered with Melody, who gripped his elbow tightly, her pretty brown eyes holding a quizzical expression.

"How did it go?" she asked out of the side of her mouth, nervously tucking a dark curl behind one ear.

"Fine. We're friends again." He turned toward us and with his arm around her shoulders. "Here's the announcement: We're—"

"Engaged?" I cried.

Immediately, a blush began at Vern's neck and flowed upward. My gaze traveled to Melody's left hand.

Her hands were a bit red and rough, an occupational hazard for a student nurse who has to wash them often. There was no ring. She looked up into Vern's face.

"Yes," she said tenderly. "And we wanted you to be the first to know."

"As you can see, she doesn't have a ring yet." Vern picked up her hand and kissed it. "I'm giving her my Mom's, but I have to get it from Dad first." Vern's late mother was Gil's sister.

Gil smiled. "That's a great idea, kid. I know she'd be pleased."

It was a night for hugs. I hugged Melody, then Vern, then Gil for good measure. I stifled more tears.

Gil hugged Melody, too, and shook hands with Vern again. "You've picked well, kid," he said gruffly.

"Thanks, Gil. And thank you, Auntie Amelia." He leaned down and kissed me on the cheek.

*Auntie Amelia.* I sighed happily. The funny, affectionate Vern I knew and loved was back.

"When is the big day?" I asked as the four of us sat down.

The couple exchanged glances. "We'd like it to be fairly soon, before Vern finishes up his Master's at the end of the summer," Melody said. "He's got a job lined up already in Virginia, and—"

"That's great!" I said, thinking of the current tight job market. Then the sad truth dawned on me. "But wait! That means you'll be moving away! A long way away!"

Vern shrugged apologetically. "About five, six hundred miles."

Gil put an arm around my shoulder. "We'll both be sorry to see you go."

"We're not gone just yet."

I could see Vern was uncomfortable with the subject so I changed it by turning to Melody. "I imagine you'll be getting married in your hometown."

She stirred in her seat. "Not exactly. You see, most of my friends—and Vern's, too—are here. We thought we could get married at my church here in town and—"

"Have your reception at Chez Prentice?" I finished for her.

She nodded.

"Of course! It's a great idea!" My old family house was now a B&B and I was part owner. "I'll call Marie and Etienne tomorrow and get them started on it right away. Oh, this is going to be wonderful!"

Gil chuckled. "Give them some breathing room, Amelia. They only just got engaged."

"No, I appreciate it," Melody said. "I'll need all the help I can get, especially once my mother gets here. She's, well, she's kind of strong-minded and has a tendency to . . . um . . . take over."

"Have you met her, Vern?"

"Me?" I could have sworn his ears lay back like a distressed dog's. "Uh . . . no, not yet. Just said hi to the whole family on Skype. Her mom seems, er . . . nice."

"Have you told your dad yet?" I remembered with a faint pang that Vern's father struggled with alcoholism.

Vern shook his head. "Can't catch up with him. As usual."

"He has that new job. That's probably what it is, pal." Gil didn't often make excuses for his brother-in-law, but it was clearly a time for tact. "I'll try to call him myself and let him know."

Later that night, as I gave Janet her eleven-o'clock bottle, I gazed at her beautiful little face and sighed. "Ah, well."

Gil frowned at me. "What's wrong?"

"I was just thinking, if only they'd wait a little bit to get married. A couple of years, I mean."

"What? Why?"

"Then Janet would be big enough to be a flower girl."

Gil guffawed and turned a page in his book. He brightened. "Hey, think about this: We could decorate her stroller and give it a shove down the aisle!"

I laughed. "And instead of flower petals, she could throw handfuls of Cheerios like she did this morning." I glanced at a large spot of dried milk on my bathrobe. "Honestly, though, it's a little bit like our eldest child is leaving the nest, isn't it?"

"He left the nest over a year ago, honey, remember? Him and that idiotic lunchbox."

"*He* and that idiotic lunchbox," I corrected absently as I burped Janet. "Well, at least we're friends again."

# Chapter | Two

"Gil, how long is this going to go on?"

My husband maintained his customary wry aplomb as he pulled our car into the driveway of the Chez Prentice B&B. "Honey, I'm the wrong person to ask. Talk to Etienne. He's your business partner."

"I know that. I'm just sick of all this mess. How long are they going to keep this up? They've been at it for over a week now. It looks terrible!"

Indeed, the generous front yard of my family's ancestral home on Jury Street had been reduced to a vast patch of dirt by a crew of workers, supervised by Manuel Esperanza, a jovial, barrel-chested man in a grimy baseball cap who was fond of playing loud salsa music on a portable radio.

The elegantly lettered sign, "Chez Prentice, a Victorian Bed and Breakfast," had been relegated to the front porch, where it leaned dejectedly against the railing. The lawn in front of my family's lovely hundred-year-old house looked like a wasteland.

Hurriedly I heaved a diaper bag over my shoulder and retrieved Janet from her baby seat before shutting the car's back door. Gil leaned out of the driver's window.

"Want me to help you with that?"

With the heavy, basket-shaped baby carrier in my hands, I braced my legs and smiled at him. "No, thanks, I'm used to it by now. You go on to work."

With a wave, he began backing out.

"Write something positive today!" I called after him.

We had a running debate over the popular "If it bleeds, it leads" philosophy of journalism. Lately, Gil's newspaper had taken on a decidedly sensational slant.

Janet was just beginning to wake up from her nap, and the loud music and shouts of the workers didn't do anything to cheer her. She whimpered and struggled to get out of the carrier as I step-dragged my load around the dirt and tried to make use of the soil-dotted sidewalk.

"She's getting too big for this thing," I grumbled under my breath as my business partner, Etienne LeBow, dashed out of the front door and skittered down the steps.

He reached out. " 'Ere, let me take 'er," he said in the French-Canadian accent I usually found so charming.

"Etienne, what are you doing now?" I demanded, "And how much longer are we going to have to put up with this mess?"

"*Du calme*, Amelia, *du calme*," he said as he ushered us into the front hallway. "As I told you, Manuel Esperanza is wonderful with lawns—a genius with a tiller—and I was lucky to get him." He confidently patted my shoulder before setting Janet's carrier on the floor. "The result will be *magnifique*, you'll see."

"I don't care if he can split the atom. When's he going to be finished?"

By this time, Janet was vigorously demanding to be released. I extracted her from the carrier and hefted her on one hip. At the sight of Etienne, the tears stopped. She smiled her enchanting gummy grin and reached for him.

"Sorry, *ma petite*, I 'ave no time." He shook his head at the baby, adjusted his expensive tie, and turned back to me. "I 'ave to leave soon."

Etienne was a successful entrepreneur and made the sixty-mile trip back and forth across the Canadian border frequently to transact business of various kinds. He well deserved the nickname my friend Lily had given him: the Millionaire from Montreal.

Though he was clearly pressed for time, he paused long enough to explain, "Amelia, *à l'arrière, c'est superb, mais . . .* " he trailed off as he gestured towards the front door.

"Yes, the back garden is gorgeous; you did a fabulous job on it. But—"

"We 'ave 'ad two summer weddings booked there already," he pointed out, giving his index finger to Janet, who grabbed it eagerly and tried without success to pull it to her mouth. "But as I said, the front, when you compare—" He clicked his tongue and shook his head.

"But why tear up the front yard right now?"

Etienne smiled as he continued the playful tug-of-war with the baby. "*Printemps*, Amelia. Spring! The temperature is warm, the sun shines—*c'est parfait!*" The charm offensive worked. Once again, he was the suave, handsome Frenchman who so reminded me of the late actor Louis Jourdan of *Gigi* fame. "Besides, the work will be finished in just a few days, and it will be beautiful."

"Okay, you've convinced me." In my slightly stern teacher voice I added, "But please remember that we're equal partners. In the future I'd like to be consulted on such things."

"Of course! *Bien sur!*" Backing away in the direction of the office, he glanced at his watch. "*Pardon,* I must go. I am sorry for the mess, but Manuel 'ad an opening today—"

I laughed. "I know, I know, he's Stradivarius of the tiller." As he disappeared into the B&B office that had been my father's study, I murmured to myself, "Okay, Stradivarius is famous more for making violins rather than playing them. Have to work on that metaphor." Such self-editing was an English teacher's occupational hazard.

I carried Janet into the B&B's kitchen, where housekeeper Hester Swanson was pouring coffee for Etienne's wife, Marie. They were engaged in an animated discussion.

"They found her body in a big trunk in his apartment," Hester said with a disapproving shake of the head. "That poor girl—I remember her name was Tracey, Tracey Parish—had been all folded up in there for a year at least, wrapped up in a quilt, they said on that show. He'd stabbed her with a Bowie knife over a dozen times! It was the smell give it away, they said." Her shudder seemed to shake her entire buxom frame.

Marie stirred sugar into her coffee. "Didn't you also hear them say that he disappeared after he jumped bail? That was years and years ago, and they never found him. The guy's probably dead by now." She took a sip. "Sick guy like that, he could of committed suicide or something."

She adjusted one of her earrings. Since coming to work at Chez Prentice, petite, dark-haired Marie had gone from wearing jeans and sweatshirts to attractive business suits and elegant costume jewelry.

I hesitated in the doorway with my daughter in my arms. "What on earth are you two talking about?"

Hester brought her own coffee mug over to the big round kitchen table and took a seat. She pushed back a few stray gray strands that had escaped her casual bun.

"A TV show last night: *BOLO: Be On The Lookout.* It's where they show the crimes using actors and give you a phone number to call if you know anything. They had a story about this guy, the Ras . . . ras . . . something Killer. Rats something." She held up the paper and pointed to a fuzzily reproduced black-and-white police photo of a gaunt young man with long hair and a thick beard of an indeterminate shade. "Now today they got an article about it in the paper. That's him."

*That's he*, I thought. *Nobody says it right any more.*

"Rasputin Killer," Marie corrected. "He was called that, supposably after that Russian guy in history. And because his name sounds like it: Rasmussen."

I cringed inwardly a second time. Not *supposably*, but *supposedly*. I kept my own counsel, however. Correcting someone's speech outside the classroom was a good way to lose a friend.

Instead, I said, "Not a very flattering nickname. Rasputin was reputed to be a very evil man."

Marie took a sip of her coffee. "Says in the paper that the California news people started to call him that when he first got famous, because he could get the politicians to do just about anything he wanted. Like the guy did with the Russian king."

"The czar," I put in.

Hester took up the thread. "And when he killed his girl-friend, like I said, stabbed her a bunch of times—this guy in this article, not the Russian—and when they caught him, he had lots of those important bigwig friends to stand up for him and the judge let him out on bail before the trial, and he just disappeared!" She waved theatrically. "They tried him in absentee—I think that's the word."

"In absentia," I blurted in spite of myself. *Why on earth is Gil putting all this disgusting stuff in the paper?*

"Anyways, they found him guilty. The paper says one time they thought they'd found him in Mexico, but by the time they got down there, he was gone, maybe back to the States."

"But get this, Amelia," Marie said, eagerly leaning forward, "It also says that they now—" She squinted down at the newspaper, tracing the words with a forefinger as she read aloud, " '—have evidence that leads them to conclude that Rasmussen may have traveled to either Northern Europe or to *the Adirondack region of New York State!*' "

Hester shuddered once more and glanced over her shoulder. "Just think: he could be around here somewhere! Maybe somebody you see on the street or something. I tell you, it gives me the creeps!"

I shook my head. "I wouldn't worry about it too much. They also mentioned Europe. Don't you think it's more likely he'd want to get out of the country?"

Marie's dark brows came together in a worried frown. "Yeah, maybe, but it says there that they had a couple murders up in Quebec province that kind of had the same M.O. They think it might be him."

"M.O?" I asked with a smile. "Are we using police jargon now?"

Marie shrugged with a faint smile. "You know, it's in the news and TV and stuff. *Law and Order, CSI*, stuff like that."

An inadvertent chill ran across my own shoulders. I glanced down and noticed that Janet was giving our conversation her wide-eyed attention.

"Hey," I said quietly, nodding at the child in my arms, "why don't we change the subject? All right?"

Marie reached out and Janet willingly went to her. "Oh, she don't know what we're saying, do you, *ma petite?*"

Janet rewarded Marie's cooing tone with a glowing smile.

"That's our beautiful girl. She's so sweet," Hester said. "How old is she now, eight, nine months?"

"Ten last Tuesday," I answered promptly.

"She's real bright, too, I can tell." Marie stroked the baby's cheek. "When Marguerite was this age, she was, she was—" She stopped talking abruptly, closed her eyes and took a deep breath. "I'm sorry," she said, blinking rapidly.

She kissed the top of Janet's head and handed her over to Hester. "I'm sorry," she said again, "I haven't got time to sit around talking anyway. Got to get back to the bills." She picked up her coffee mug and left.

Marie was the general manager of Chez Prentice. She and Etienne lived in the ground-floor suite of the B&B and her office was in my father's old study.

"This kind of thing happens every so often." Hester bounced the baby on her knee. "She's still hurting, y'see, after that terrible thing happened to her girl."

"It's to be expected," I agreed. The LeBows' young adult daughter Marguerite had died only a year and a half ago.

"Marie's hanging in there, though, considering. This sort of thing can be awful hard on a family. You know, they said on that *BOLO* TV show that after the girl out in California got murdered, her dad committed suicide, the brother went into the Army and got killed overseas, and the mother died of cancer."

Janet grabbed Hester's index knuckle and began vigorously sucking on it.

"She's real hungry, Amelia," Hester said. "Ouch!" She pulled her hand away. "I didn't think those little gums could hurt you like that!"

It put an end to our gloomy conversation and I, for one, was glad.

"My apologies. I should have warned you. She's been doing that off and on. She already has two teeth in her bottom gums. I'll get her a bottle. That sometimes helps." I retrieved the jug of milk from the refrigerator and groped around in the diaper bag for a clean bottle.

"Amelia!" Marie appeared at the kitchen door. I could tell by her expression that the sad mood had lifted. "Why didn't you tell me?"

"Tell you what?" both Hester and I said at the same time.

Marie clutched a clipboard to her chest. "That your nephew Vern is getting married!"

Hester grinned and glanced at me. "No kidding!"

"He told us about it last night. Rather, they did, both he and Melody. I meant to tell you, but forgot."

Marie tapped a pen against her tightly-clutched clipboard. "And guess where they're having the reception?"

"No kidding!" said Hester again. "Here?"

"Yes, and it's to be pretty soon." I carefully poured the milk into the bottle and screwed on the cap. Hester handed Janet over to me. "I expect Melody's family will be coming to town to make arrangements shortly."

Marie glanced at her watch. "I can't stand around here talking. Work to do." She was gone.

As Janet earnestly pawed me to get at the bottle, I took a seat at the kitchen table and settled the eager baby on my lap.

Hester pointed. "You don't need to heat that?"

"No, she likes it cold now. Isn't it wonderful?" Little milestones like these were surprisingly important, not only in marking Janet's development, but also in aiding my sanity.

"This is a real good place for wedding receptions. I remember yours." Hester sat down at the table across from me and fanned herself with her apron. "But I guess this means we'll have to get that Valerie woman back across the lake to do her thing again," she said resignedly.

Valerie was Marie LeBow's sister, a dour Vermonter, who regularly made baked goods for the B&B.

Hester gestured at the ceiling. "And she'll bring that dark cloud with her. She always does. I gotta admit, though, the wedding cake she made for you guys was just about the prettiest thing I ever did see, with all the flowers and stuff." She leaned back in her chair. "Y'know, I can bake a cake that'll make the angels sing, all right, but I never could do much with frosting, what with all those tube things and all that squeezing. My frosting always looks kind of like Bert spackled it on." Bert was Hester's handyman husband.

She shook her head, grinning. "You know that tip thing that's supposed to make it look like a rose when you squirt it out?" She pulled a washcloth from an overloaded laundry basket sitting at her feet and began folding.

I nodded.

"Well, once when we was first married, I made Bert's mother a birthday cake." She placed the folded cloth on the kitchen table and retrieved another one, neatly arranging it on top of the first. "Went out and bought all that stuff to decorate with and squirted flower things all over the cake just like the directions said. I thought I did a pretty good job, but when she saw it, Bert's mother said it looked like little pink and green cow patties. I can tell you, I cried myself to sleep that night." She bent down for another piece of laundry.

"Hester, that was terrible! What a cruel woman!"

She popped up, shaking her head. "Nah, she wasn't so bad. We made friends and laughed about it later. When that woman died, I cried a lot more. But the thing was, Amelia, I learned early on that being a good cook and decoratin' cakes is two completely different things. So we're gonna need Valerie, dadblast it!"

"She is a little gloomy, I suppose."

"She's a mama dog, is what she is." Hester slapped a folded hand towel on the table.

"Hester!"

She held her hands up defensively. "Hey, I didn't say it. You heard what I said."

I tried not to smile as I put Janet on my shoulder to burp her. "Even if you did use a euphemism, Hester, it amounts to the same thing."

Hester bent down again. I heard her mumble, "Well, whatever it was I used, it's still true!"

Marie reappeared in the kitchen door. "Hey you guys, I just got a call from a woman downstate named Callie Huff, from something called *Mariage du Reve*." Marie pronounced the words in a perfect French accent. "And she's coming here today!"

"Dream wedding?" I translated.

"Sort of." Marie frowned and squinted at her clipboard. "I had her spell that name for me. It really should be *de Rêve*, with a circumflex over the e, but it's probably already on her stationery and business cards and online and stuff, so I didn't bother to correct it." She shrugged.

Hester said, "One of those wedding planner people, I betcha."

Marie stuck her ballpoint behind one ear and consulted the clipboard. "Right, and she's talking about the Branch wedding—I don't know who that is—and she's coming here today, bringing the bride's mother too. On their way right now, in fact."

I jumped up, startling the drowsy baby. "Branch? That's Vern! I mean, that's his fiancée, Melody Branch! Wow, they're not wasting any time."

After burping Janet firmly, I found a pacifier in my diaper bag and gave it to her. She was adept at plugging it into her own mouth.

"Marie, do you think they'll understand about the mess in the front yard?"

Marie nodded. "Oh, sure. Anyway, Etienne says that Manuel guy's gonna be finished in a day or so."

"Can I help you get ready for them around here?" I asked Hester.

She pulled herself up to her full height and frowned. "Get ready? Don't you think I keep this place ready any day of the week, any time of day?" She gestured with her hand. "Let 'em come. We're ready right this minute."

As if on cue, the seldom-used doorbell rang.

Marie jumped. "There they are! Clear that mess away!" She began pushing the laundry items off the table and into the basket.

"Okay, okay, don't get 'em in a wad!" Hester muttered. She hefted the basket and stashed it in the laundry room. "I'll hafta fold all these later on." She glanced over her shoulder.

Marie had already left.

I looked at Janet on my lap, who was vigorously sucking on her "passy." When I first became pregnant, I resolved to never use cutesy baby talk, but after the baby arrived that resolution quickly flew out the window. I couldn't have explained why; probably a hormonal thing. I'd learned a lot about hormones over the past year or so.

There were voices coming from the foyer. The tone was friendly but formal.

"Let's just stay in here," I whispered.

Janet stared up at me, sucking away madly. Her eyes were no longer the vague gray-blue they were when she was born, but had turned into the same rich amber as her daddy's. Her soft hair was a light brown, like mine. I wondered to myself whether it would stay that way or darken to the shade Gil's used to be before he went totally gray.

We had just begun a game of "How Big Is the Baby?" when I heard a pleasant and familiar voice say, "Is Amelia here? Where is she? I want you to meet her!"

It was clearly no use keeping a low profile. I rose from my seat at the table in time to see Melody burst breathlessly through the kitchen door, followed by three women who were considerably less ebullient.

"There you are! And the baby too!" She kissed my cheek and stroked Janet's head. The bride-to-be was in high gear.

*Perhaps she overindulged in coffee this morning, I thought.*

She was looking lovely in a pale aqua silk blouse with pearl buttons over an oatmeal linen skirt. Instead of her customary nurse's clogs, she wore a pair of low-heeled beige Italian pumps bearing signature wide bows and gold button insignia.

Melody's manners were impeccable. "Mama, Harmony, Ms. Huff, I'd like you to meet my friend Amelia Dickensen and her daughter, Janet. Amelia, this is my mother, Greta Branch."

Mrs. Branch fluttered heavily mascaraed eyelashes and corrected her daughter, using the lilting Italian pronunciation, "Allegretta."

She was several inches taller than Melody, but had the same pale skin and brown eyes. Her dark hair was pulled up into a large chignon and she wore dangling loop earrings a full three inches in diameter.

I extended my hand, received a half-hearted handshake, and turned to the sister.

Melody's sister Harmony had obviously learned her handshaking skills from her mother, whom she resembled only in height and distant attitude. Her own hair was dyed a harsh black with bright blue highlights and her rail-thin body slouched in an overlong black sweater topping tight designer jeans with high-heeled leather boots. Her pale face had what fashion magazines call good cheekbones.

Next to Melody, the wedding planner was by far the most outgoing. Short and stout like the proverbial teapot and dressed in a bright green ensemble, she wore her impossibly orange hair in a pageboy style that just brushed the gold-toned pashmina stole draping her shoulders. This lady was definitely an Autumn.

She stepped forward. "Callie Huff, of Mariage du Reve. My card." She gave us a wide orange-lipstick smile and handed over a stiff gray rectangle bearing the name of her firm in silver letters.

I smiled back and tucked the card in my pocket. Now it was my turn to make an introduction. I gestured toward the figure emerging from the laundry room. "And this is Hester Swanson, our CDA," I added, trying to keep a straight face.

Melody's sister lifted indifferent eyebrows. "CDA? What does that stand for?"

Hester laughed good-naturedly. "Chairman of Domestic Affairs! Can you beat that? That's all Etienne LeBow's idea. It's just a stuck-up name for housekeeper, which is what I am." She chuckled, inviting others to join her, but only Melody and I did.

Marie took over the conversation. "Well, everyone, if you like, we'll get started with the tour of Chez Prentice. As you can see, this is the kitchen," she began with a wave of her hand. "It's been remodeled with all the latest conveniences, but special effort was taken to retain the vintage feel of the Prentice home." She indicated the newly-installed farmhouse sink.

Callie Huff walked over and peered into it.

Hester looked at me. Her expression silently said, *It's just a sink. What's she looking for?*

I shrugged.

"This is where our guests like to gather for breakfast in the mornings." Marie was quoting our brochure now. "In the afternoon, English-style tea is served in the front parlor, which you just saw. If you'll follow me, I'll show you the upstairs suites and the back garden."

As everyone moved into into the foyer, Melody's mother lifted an expensively manicured hand. "I have a question: What's wrong with the front lawn?" She jerked her hairdo in the direction of the front door.

Marie was ready for this. "I'm glad you asked. We're having brand-new sod put in, to match the beautiful landscaping in the back. We've been assured that the work will be finished in a day or two."

"I would hope so!" Alegretta Branch responded. "It's awful out there. Look, Harmony got dirt on her boots!" She pointed to her daughter, who had gripped a newel post for support and was busily scraping the detritus from her footwear onto the oriental carpet.

"Yes, well, I can promise it won't be that way much longer," Marie continued as she mounted the stairs. "If you'll follow me, I'll show you the bedrooms, which have been decorated in the authentic style of the early 1900s, when this house was built. Claw-foot tubs, handmade heirloom quilts—"

"Jacuzzis?" Harmony interrupted. "Don't you have any Jacuzzis?"

"Not in a little backwater town like this, Harmony."

Though she was whispering, Allegretta's strong voice floated down the stairs. "I already told you. The cultural standards here aren't what we're accustomed to, dear."

"Mother, please," Melody said.

Now I understood the bride's nervousness. Her mother drove her crazy.

Hester and I were standing at the kitchen door, watching their ascent.

I bounced Janet on my hip. "Poor Melody," I murmured.

"And poor Chez Prentice," Hester said, heading for the broom closet. "But I think that mud will come up if I get at it right away."

# Chapter | Three

"**H**ow did it go?" I asked Marie a half hour later, after I heard the big front door close with a jingle.

"Pretty good. They've reserved the entire place for one week in August." Marie lifted the top page on the clipboard she carried. "It's going to really help put us in the black before the end of the year."

"That's great!"

"Sort of," Marie agreed, "but in the negotiations, they got a few little things out of me." She hesitated before adding reluctantly, "Well, maybe a lot of 'em."

I frowned. "What little things?"

Marie walked slowly through the entryway toward the dining room. "Well, for one, they want some pretty fancy food served at the reception, and they—the mother, really—insisted on having a wedding cake tasting session just to make sure Valerie's work is up to their standards." She shrugged. "Hey, if Val is willing do it, I want to be there!"

*So do I!* I thought. *Those two strong-willed women would be just about evenly matched. As Etienne would say, formidable!*

"And I agreed to let that Huff woman stay here a few times before the wedding." Marie stuck her ballpoint behind her ear. "On us, all meals included. She's gonna need to do a lot of the wedding stuff locally, you see, so she stays here whenever she's in town."

I deposited Janet in a playpen we kept in a corner of the dining room and handed her a musical toy that she favored. "And here I'd been thinking we should give them a discount because it's Vern's wedding. Are they willing to pay for all these extras?"

Marie frowned. "It's kind of part of the contract we agreed to. I'm giving them the off-season rate. But take a look at this." She handed me the clipboard. "It's a tentative agreement that we all signed. That's a check for ten percent stapled on top, there."

"How much are we talking about?" I mentally multiplied the check's amount by ten. "Oh, wow!"

"Yeah, right. Pretty good, huh? I made a list of everything they wanted. If it's not written down there, they don't get it. Besides, we can put the Huff woman in A, the room with the small bathroom and just the one little window."

"Good work, Marie. Well done."

She actually blushed. We smiled at each other. It hadn't been that long ago when Marie earned her living at odd jobs, wherever she could get them. The position of B&B manager had brought out talents heretofore undiscovered.

"I dunno about that, but I wasn't gonna let that Alleygretta person come in here all snooty without paying their way." She wrinkled her nose and held a droopy hand up in imitation.

"Well, at least the bride is a kindred spirit. That's all that counts."

Marie's face brightened. "I know what we'll do to get revenge. We'll have Hester decorate the wedding cake. Did she tell you the story about the cow patties?"

I nodded and laughed. So did Janet, who had pulled herself to a standing position along the side of the playpen. She bounced up and down, wanting in on the joke.

"Just look at that, will you? She's growing so fast!" Marie knelt and clapped her hands for the baby. "That's right! We're happy!" She looked up at me. "I'm sorry about the way I acted in the kitchen earlier, running off like that."

"I understood, Marie."

She watched, smiling, as Janet let herself down to a sitting position with a thump and put the ear of a terrycloth bear in her mouth. "The thing about losing Marguerite, it comes back on me every once in a while. But I'm getting better. So is Etienne. Still, you don't exactly ever get over it, y'know?" She looked at me with moist eyes.

I nodded, unable to find my voice. Now that I had a child, the idea of losing my daughter as Marie had hers was unthinkable.

She rose and took a deep breath. "But after a while, you get so you can do stuff again. You gotta keep going." She thrust the clipboard under her arm and straightened her shoulders. "That's how I do it: I keep busy. I'm gonna go call Etienne and tell him about the deal. He doesn't think I'm much of a horse trader, but this'll show him!" She smiled.

"Oh, hello, Alec," she said to the burly gentleman who had just entered the front door. "Excuse me. I've got work to do. See ya."

"You're looking well." I said, smiling at Alec.

The barrel-chested, hirsute college professor was groomed to a fare-thee-well. His salt-and-pepper hair and beard had been neatly trimmed, and he was sporting a sleek, expensive-looking business suit, complete with vest.

Due to a recent inheritance, Dr. Alexander A. Alexander now had the funds to finance his lifelong dream: a comprehensive and scientific search for the fabled Lake Champlain monster, a.k.a. "Champ," the subject of song, story, and tourism in the manner of the Loch Ness Monster. He had founded an organization called The Champlain Institute of Cryptozoology, but it hadn't gotten much further than the planning stages.

He patted his ample middle. "Oh, aye, thanks. 'Tis this fancy rig. Miss Lily picked it out."

"Her taste is impeccable," I admitted. "By the way, how are your plans coming?"

He frowned and his newly-clipped shaggy eyebrows came together. "Weel, it's an issue of location, y'see. The section of land my house occupies next to the lake would be an ideal spot to put the museum building, but t'would necessitate the tearin' of my own place down and erectin' the research center there. Furthermore, the depth of the water along the shore is inadequate to dock the larger boat that—"

I interrupted him, "Alec, that's not what I meant, and you know it." He had been dating my long-time friend and neighbor, Lily Burns, for the past year and had expressed to me his intention of proposing, which was no small ambition. Lily was lovely to look at, but she wielded a sharp tongue and belonged to a gossip network that spanned three counties.

Alec had made a number of stabs at popping the question, even going so far as to buy a ring, only to lose his nerve at the last minute.

He had the grace to look embarrassed at my admonishment. "She's meetin' me here for coffee this morning," he said. "But noo, the subject hasn't resurfaced lately." When he was distressed, Alec's Scottish accent seemed to deepen, with more rolling r's and a lilting tone.

"Don't you think it's finally time you took the bull by the horns, Alec?" I said sternly.

"Are we planning a rodeo?" said a sultry female voice.

Lily Burns walked in from the kitchen, trailing the exquisite scent of *Toujours Moi* after her. Her blonde hair was perfectly styled and her pale pink cotton sweater and gray slacks fit her petite figure exactly. No matter where she bought a clothing item, she always had it tailored for her by a local seamstress. I didn't fully understand the necessity of such added expense, but had to admit that the ultimate effect was very flattering.

"Where are your new shoes, the ones with the red soles?" I asked. She had bragged recently about getting the extremely expensive, high fashion pumps on sale.

Lily wrinkled her nose. "They don't go with this outfit, Amelia. These do." She waved a small foot in a low-heeled gray shoe that sported the flat bow of a different expensive designer.

"They're a perfect match, m'dear," Alec said.

She looked him up and down. "Is this the suit we picked out?"

Alec nodded and stood stoically as she circled him, peering intently at each detail.

"That tailor told me it was a bad idea, but I was right! Putting a gusset there has done wonders for the fit of the jacket." She paused, looking towards the floor. "But they could have taken the trouser hem up about another eighth of an inch, in my opinion. Well, never mind. You look very nice, though I do say so myself." She patted him on the back.

Alec gently shepherded Lily toward the kitchen door. "Join us for coffee, Amelia?"

"No, thanks. I have a tutoring session in about five minutes. I need to get ready."

"Maybe Janet can join us for a little bit," Lily said, picking up the baby, who seemed delighted at the suggestion.

All at once, my friend thrust the baby at arm's length and turned her face to one side. "Whoo! Excuse us, please, Alec. This little lady needs to freshen up!"

"The diaper bag's upstairs," I told her.

Janet clung cheerfully to her Aunt Lily without a backward glance in my direction. Since both Gil's and my parents were dead, I was glad our little girl had so many doting friends willing to do grandparent duty.

"So, Alec, tell me," I began, just as his phone rang.

He raised a cautioning hand and moved into the kitchen, taking a seat at the big round table. I left him to his conversation.

My own cell phone rang as I was arranging books and papers in the dining room. "I can't come today, Miss Prentice," Serendipity Shea said in an uncharacteristically subdued voice.

*She must be upset. She never uses my maiden name any more.*

"Dad and me—I—are going to see my, um, mom today. Sorry about telling you so late."

Serry's mother was serving a short prison sentence after pleading guilty as an accessory to a serious crime. Though Brigid's lawyer had been able to plea bargain her punishment down to a relatively brief incarceration, the situation was especially hard on Serry, who was finishing up her junior year in high school.

"It's all right, Serry. Tell your mother I said hello," I instructed.

We'd had our differences, Brigid Shea and I, but ultimately we'd found common ground. I'd testified at her sentencing hearing, asking leniency for Serry's sake. While forgetting what we'd been through was impossible, forgiving was definitely in my plan.

I gathered up the teaching materials and stowed them in the file cabinet drawer in Marie's office. She was sitting behind my father's old mahogany desk. She looked over the top of her iPad.

"Finished teaching so soon?"

"There was a cancellation."

"Tell me about it." Marie chuckled. "I've had my share of those lately. Listen, Amelia, could you hold down the office this afternoon? There's a couple guys supposed to be checking in today. I gotta go sign some insurance papers downtown, and somebody should be here to meet them."

"Sure. Do you need me to do anything in particular?"

She retrieved her car keys and purse from a desk drawer. "Nope. Just the usual. You know the drill."

I followed her to the door. "What time do you expect them?"

"Who knows?" She shrugged and was gone.

Shortly thereafter, Lily descended the stairs and put the whining baby in my arms. "All changed and fresh, but she wants Mama today," Lily said. "Is he in there?" She went into the kitchen.

I overheard Alec say, "M'dear, I must talk with you about something . . . "

*Could this at last be the moment he proposes?* I wondered.

"Let's give them some privacy," I whispered to Janet. We repaired to the front porch swing.

The temperature was pleasant, in the mid 60's, sweater weather, almost balmy for the North Country.

"Daisy, Daisy," I sang to the rhythm of the swing, "give me your answer do . . . "

Janet loved to hear me sing. At least, her body language indicated that she did. She bounced in my lap and pounded my arm with her tiny open hand.

"And you'd look sweet, upon the seat—"

A fine baritone voice finished the phrase for me: "—of a bicycle built for two."

It was followed by laughter. A tall, lean man came striding across the muddy yard and up onto the porch where he came to an abrupt halt and stood looking down at me.

"Might you be Mrs. LeBow?" He wiped his muddy, disreputable leather flip-flops on the doormat.

I tried not to stare. Though clearly middle-aged, he was at the height of trendy teenage fashion, wearing a small, narrow-brimmed version of a fedora. There was a silly little tuft under his bottom lip, sideburns that pointed inward towards his chin and a creased forehead over rust-colored eyebrows.

His wavy hair was an indeterminate brown-gray color, longish but not too much so, and his eyes were a warm brown, very pleasant to look at. From a distance, I would have guessed his age to be in the mid-thirties, but closer up, the creases around his eyes and mouth pushed the number a good deal higher.

His luggage consisted of a large, overstuffed fabric suitcase and a much smaller, narrower rectangular case.

"No, Marie is away at the moment." I rose with Janet in my arms and extended my hand. "But I might be able to help you. Amelia Pr—Dickensen." I still stumbled occasionally when stating my married name.

He shoved the small case in his right hand under his left arm, wiped his hand on his untucked plaid shirt and gave me a firm but gentle handshake. "Ev Holland. I'm here for a room. Good to meet you, Mrs. Perdickensen." He repeated my name exactly as he had heard it.

"Just Dickensen," I corrected. "Amelia."

"And who is this?"

We both looked down at the baby in my arms as she stared upward, sucking vigorously on her chubby fist. "Janet," I said.

He nodded politely. "Janet. Charming."

I bade him follow me into the office, where I found the appropriate papers, and he filled them out. He planned to stay for six days. I noticed that his full name was "Evelyn R. Holland." *No wonder he calls himself Ev.*

He'd put down a New York City address. "What brings you to the North Country, Mr. Holland? Visiting family?"

He was still writing. "What? Oh, no. I'm a member of the Tribeca symphony. I'm here for the charity concert. I play the flute."

So that's what the smaller case contained. "Oh, well, perhaps you could answer a burning question for me: Is it flutist or flautist?"

He finished writing and handed me the paper and pen. "I've always like what James Galway says on the subject: 'I am a flute player, not a flautist. I don't have a flaut, and I've never flauted."

We laughed. Janet giggled and clapped her hands.

"You'll be in Room B, at the top of the staircase. Breakfast is served to order between the hours of eight and ten, but if you need it earlier, just let us know. Would you like help with your luggage?"

He declined, as I hoped he would, and departed up the stairs. He'd never removed his hat.

Lily and Alec emerged from the kitchen, arguing in low tones. They stopped when they saw me.

Alec glanced up at the departing Ev Holland. "Who's the hippie?" he asked in a stage whisper.

"Shh, he's a guest," I whispered back, "a musician here for the charity concert."

"Whatever. I'm leaving."

Lily threw a withering glance over her shoulder at Alec as she flounced out the back door. Her back yard bordered on ours and it was the quickest way home.

Alec didn't seem to notice, or at least pretended not to. He snorted. "Musician? That figures. Wearing sandals and cutoffs in a fine establishment like this. Probably some New York City type who supposes oopstate is populated by hicks!"

I didn't bother to confirm his partially correct assumption. I pointed in the direction of Lily's departure and frowned at him.

"What's the matter, Alec? You seem annoyed."

"Not at you, m'dear," he said, patting my shoulder. "Never at you."

# Chapter | Four

I followed Alec to the front door, refusing to let the subject drop. "What was wrong with Lily?" I asked him baldly.

He turned and chucked Janet under the chin. "Much as I love both ye lassies, a mon has a right to keep mum on occasion."

It was said with a light tone, but there was a sad look in his eye and his accent had deepened. All was not well with my friend. I remembered something else. He always seemed to have a sacred song for every occasion.

"Alec, it occurs to me that I haven't heard a hymn out of you in quite a while. What are you humming today? Or whistling?"

He shook his head and shouldered past me. "Sorry, m'dear. No time for that; indeed, no time to talk either. Things to do, y'see. A problem has come up." He left, shutting the front door decisively, only to return within sixty seconds.

"Right this way," he said over his shoulder, and then to me, "Amelia, this lady wants to register, I think."

Callie Huff, of *Mariage Du Reve*, stood in the doorway. "Well, here I am!" She pushed a large designer suitcase forward with her designer high-heeled shoe and lowered several smaller designer bags to the floor. "Would you get someone to take this to my room, please? There are more in my car."

Alec complied, returning with three more designer cases of various sizes. By my count, there were seven.

Before she could issue another order, Alec sidled surreptitiously out the front door.

"So. Where's my room?" she asked me cheerfully.

I hefted the baby on one hip. "Upstairs, room A, I think. I—I'll see you have some help with your bags in a minute; if you'll just come into the office to register."

She waved her hand and her shawl slipped off one shoulder. "Oh, Marie already took care of that." She brushed a lock of carroty hair off her forehead and looked around. "I'm exhausted. Where can a girl get some coffee around here?"

Finding myself a bit annoyed that she hadn't said a thing about the presence of my beautiful child, I led her to the kitchen. "This is Ms. Huff, Hester. Can you rustle her up some refreshment?"

She bustled past me and took a seat at the big table. Pulling a compact from her copious handbag, she began primping.

"Coffee. White, real cream, no sugar," she ordered as she smoothed an eyebrow.

Hester's own eyebrows lifted and her eyes slid over at me. "Right." She wiped her hands on her apron and got to work.

"Where's Bert?" I asked. Hester's husband did just about everything around the B&B.

Hester's back was to me as she poured a cup from the coffeemaker. She jerked her head to her left.

"Out back, talking to Chuck Nathan about the spring plantings."

"Oh, is that the florist I've heard so much about? I'll need to talk to him. Send him in when they're through out there," Callie directed me.

Hester put a cup and saucer on the table and poured coffee. "Yeah, Amelia, you go tell Chuck Nathan to get a move on." She gave me a wry nod and a subtle wink.

Everyone knew from sad experience that the high-strung florist required careful handling to avoid triggering his short temper.

I stepped into the spacious, newly-remodeled pantry and beckoned Hester to follow. "Do you know what's going on between Alec and Lily?" I whispered.

Hester shook her head as she reached for a jar of honey. "Beats me; but the Professor got a phone call on his cell while he was sitting at the table there and it didn't seem like good news." She frowned. "When Mrs. Burns came back in, he started talking to her real low. She didn't like what he had to say at all, by the look of things."

We both sighed, and I slipped out the back door, carrying Janet.

In the garden, the two men were laughing. Chuck gave Bert's back a vigorous slap, which indicated to me that they'd probably just shared a risqué joke.

I waited until there was a lull in the conversation and stated my business. Bert readily volunteered to do bellhop duty and headed inside.

I turned to Chuck, who looked down at me from a height of six feet, four inches. "Yeah?"

It was rumored that the man had the first nickel he'd ever earned. The evidence offered by his detractors was the fact that both his dark sunglasses and his pony tail were held in place by florist's tape. Today he was wearing a faded Grateful Dead T-shirt (is there any other kind?), ragged jeans and heavy work boots, belying his reputation as the town's most successful and talented flower designer. I wondered what Callie would make of this Steven Tyler lookalike, once they met in person.

I decided to insert some etiquette into the situation. "Chuck, our wedding planner guest extends her compliments and would appreciate it if you'd join her in the kitchen to talk about an upcoming order."

"Cool, no problem." He nodded and began to follow Bert inside.

"By the way, her name is Callie Huff, and her firm is called *Mariage du Reve*," I called after him.

He stopped and turned back. "Who?"

I told him again.

Nodding, he repeated, "Callie Huff, *Mariage du Reve*. Right."

All at once, he stopped walking, reached in his pocket and pulled out a cell phone, one I knew to be about five years out of date. He snapped it open and consulted the tiny screen. Throwing us a two finger salute, he turned and began to jog around the house.

"Wait! Aren't you going to go talk to Ms. Huff?"

He held up his phone. "Just got a text! Rush job! She can call me later, no problem."

I contemplated hurrying back inside to tell Callie Huff, but changed my mind. The woman annoyed me a little. Besides, I'd never enjoyed the role of go-between.

*There's no need to rush. I'll give her the message in my own time.*

With Janet in my arms, I strolled down the recently laid garden path and took a seat on the stone bench that encircled the huge, ancient maple tree that dominated the yard. I savored the warmth, unusual for this time of year in the Adirondacks. We'd had a long, cold winter, and it was a treat to need nothing more than a light sweater against the breezes.

Janet made it clear that she wanted to practice her cruising-while-holding-on-to-something technique, so I eased her to her feet in the soft new grass. I was glad she was wearing her little pink socks with the non-skid soles.

I scanned our surroundings. It was a lovely spot for a small and intimate wedding, this garden. With Chuck's help, Etienne had drawn the layout and I'd helped select the flowers and shrubs. We'd gone to extra trouble (and indulged in some extra expense) with the selection of the white-painted wrought-iron gazebo in the back corner that made the perfect place for a bridal couple to exchange vows.

Birds were beginning to return to the North Country. As Janet watched, entranced, a sleek blue-black grackle alighted on the bird feeder hanging from the largest of the low-hanging maple tree limbs, pecked, and sailed off with a graceful dip in our direction.

"Boo!" said Janet, reaching with tiny fingers, "Daboo!"

"That's right, darling, bird!" I said, perhaps a little optimistically.

But why shouldn't our daughter talk early? Both her father and I dealt in words.

A cool breeze meandered through the yard and caused the early violets to bob their heads.

Spring, or *printemps*, as Etienne called it, was definitely here. We'd heard on the radio that the county's plowing equipment was finally decommissioned for the season. I thought sympathetically of the people in the Midwest who were still battling monster blizzards.

We frequently endured some bitter winter weather here at the northern border of New York State, but there were compensations. Our summers were beautiful, sunny, and, best of all, mild. The days were warm and the evenings, while cool, seldom required a coat.

I looked up into branches of the big tree. The tips of the pale green new leaves were just becoming visible. In a week or two this would be a delightful glade. Looking around, I pictured half-a-dozen small linen-topped tables dotting the scene, while chattering ladies sipped from teacups and nibbled cucumber sandwiches.

*I'll suggest that to Marie*, I thought. *I'll bet Lily's bridge club would love it.*

My glance fell to the ground where my daughter, now seated, was attempting to snack on an uprooted handful of grass. "No! No! Bad cat!" I said impulsively as I picked her up and began digging in her mouth with my index finger. "I mean—"

"Is the child's name Catherine?" someone asked, "Is that why you call her Cat?"

I ignored the voice, intent as I was on rescuing my child from lawn poisoning or something.

Once her small face was relatively free of foreign substances and had been wiped as clean as possible, I fished in my pocket for the pacifier case I was never without. "Here, put this in your mouth instead." As she manipulated it to a comfortable place between her lips, I looked over and saw the flutist, Ev Holland, leaning against a tree trunk with his arms folded.

In these surroundings and with his piquant expression, he resembled an oversized leprechaun. The image was enhanced significantly when he raised a small tin whistle to his lips and began playing a thin, enchanting tune.

"That was lovely," I said when the notes faded into the air.

He accepted the compliment with a smiling nod.

"And, no, her name's Janet, not Catherine, as you may remember. But I used to have a cat and, well—" I shrugged.

He chuckled and readjusted his hat on his head. "I'm not a cat man, myself. Not much for pets at all, really."

"What will you be playing at the concert?"

"Excerpts from Handel's *Water Music Suite*, then a couple of crowd-pleasers at the end, stuff from *Nutcracker*." He waved the whistle in the air and put it in his shirt pocket.

"I like the *Nutcracker*," I admitted.

"Nothing wrong with that; most people do."

A pleasant fragrance floated past to remind me of something. "There are coffee and cookies in the kitchen right now," I told him, "Shall we return?"

He turned and headed for the house. I scooped up my wiggly companion and followed.

Rather than taking a place at the big round table, Ev explored the spacious old-fashioned room, opening cabinets and peering into the pantry.

Callie Huff didn't spare the musician a glance. She was busy perusing her iPad.

"Where's the florist?" she asked without sparing me one either.

"He couldn't stay." I gave her the edited version. "He requested that you call him later."

She frowned, still staring at the screen. "Hmm. Perhaps he doesn't need my business. Surely there's another florist in this town."

Hester plopped the folded newspaper on the table. "Chuck is the best, but there's lots of ads for flower shops in the paper. Why don't you take a look?"

Callie reached across the table, slid the copy of *The Press-Advertiser* closer and began to read. She flipped the paper to the lower section that featured the article about the Rasputin Killer and suddenly sat bolt upright.

"O-M-G," she said, slowly, "O-M-G!"

I frowned, disapproving of the abbreviated oath. I never allowed it in my classroom.

"What is it, Ms. Huff?" I asked sharply.

"O-M-G," she said again more slowly, in a softer voice. She traced around the picture on the page with her index finger. "It's him! It's really him." She put a hand to her chest. "I've met this guy!" She tapped the article beneath the fold. "I knew him. I really did!"

Three of us—four, if you included the baby—peered over her shoulder and for now, at least, I was glad Janet couldn't read.

The headline read: "KILLER BELIEVED TO BE IN THE NORTH COUNTRY: Could he be among us?"

*Gil, you're doing it again*, I thought, and sighed.

Ev, standing across the room, wrinkled his nose, shrugged, and murmured, "Tabloid stuff." He held up his coffee mug and asked Hester, "Can I take this upstairs?"

Hester nodded.

I watched him go. The familiar classroom retort floated to the surface in my mind, *I know you "can." The question is, "May I?"*

I'd also cringed a little at Ev's characterization of Gil's paper as a tabloid. It was a bone of contention between my husband and me. It was true that newspapers had to scrounge for every penny these days, but Gil's rather desperate method of increasing sales was to print ever more sensationally-worded stories.

To my discomfort, Callie read aloud, " 'Gregory Rasmussen's career as a speaker and advocate for radical causes was well-known in both his native Seattle and in Los Angeles, where he made the biggest splash, especially among artists, actors, and other members of the entertainment industry intelligentsia.' "

She looked up at us. "That's right, you know. I lived in California back then, trying to get a singing career started, and I met him in Santa Monica at a fundraiser when Zack Benson was running for Congress." She blushed and fanned her face. "I gotta tell you girls, that Rasmussen? He was definitely *hot!*"

She had Hester's attention. The housekeeper wiped her hands on her apron and took a seat at the table. "Hot? What do you mean, Ms. Huff?" she asked, grinning. "That guy looks more like a mountain man than a movie star, with that beard and all."

Callie chuckled. "Oh, Greg was no outdoorsman, let me tell you. Some of the kids I knew back then loved to go camping, but not him! He liked his indoor plumbing, and, well, indoor everything." She stirred her coffee thoughtfully. "And as for him being hot—oh, I don't know how to explain it. He wasn't exactly handsome, but he was—" she groped for a word. "—charming, you might say and . . . just magnetic.

Whatever he had, it was so attractive! Everybody was crazy about him."

I couldn't help myself. I joined them at the table with Janet in my lap.

"And you met him at this political event?"

She nodded. "I did. Back then I was all about the causes. Didn't matter which cause it was, really, it was just where all the really sexy guys were. And let's face it, I was kind of hot myself in those days." She sighed and glanced down at her pudgy figure. "Well, I used to be. And I'll admit I was a little wild back then too." She tossed her hair and took on a smug expression. "And Greg Rasmussen was the hottest guy around. I mean, those eyes! I got really well acquainted with him once or twice, if you know what I mean."

Her eyes danced at the memory, but suddenly, she frowned and shook her head. "You know, everybody knew he had a bad temper, but we had no idea how bad! He was some good actor, that guy. The whole time he was partying with us, his girlfriend's body was stuffed in a trunk up in his apartment!"

She tapped the newspaper and shuddered. "And he got away with it! Listen: 'Due to the efforts of Senator Benson and a host of other local luminaries, all of whom testified to Rasmussen's good character, Rasmussen's attorney was able to obtain his pre-trial release on bond. When the accused murderer jumped bail and disappeared shortly before the trial was to take place, he was tried in absentia, found guilty, and sentenced to life in prison. Despite the efforts of law enforcement nationwide and even overseas, the convicted murder has been able to elude capture for almost two decades.' "

Hester snorted. "Weren't we telling you about him, Amelia? Horrible! Somebody like that should be put *under* the jail, that's what I say. How a person could act normal with a body like that going bad right inside your closet!"

A wave of nausea such as I hadn't felt since my pregnancy began at the back of my throat. I hefted the baby to my shoulder. "Excuse me." I could scarcely bear to stay in the room.

"It says here they think that he's changed his appearance, but I'd know him anywhere, you know," Callie was saying to Hester as I left, "I'm sure I would."

"Really? How would you know him?"

"Well, for one thing, he had this lovely singing voice," she said.

# Chapter | Five

"Alec's gone, Amelia," Lily said to me on the phone that evening, "and I couldn't talk him out of it!"

"What? Gone where?

"Scotland."

"Where? Why on earth, when everything's going so well for him? What did you say to him, Lily? What did you do?"

"Hey, don't blame me! I told him the exact same thing you just said, but he insisted that he was desperately needed at Loch Ness."

"Seriously, Loch Ness in Scotland? *The* Loch Ness?"

"You got it: kilts, bagpipes, haggis, the whole nine yards. Apparently that stupid monster hasn't been spotted by anybody in almost two years, and they're calling in every expert they can find."

I sighed and tried to put a good face on things. "Well, I suppose it's a feather in his professional cap and good publicity for the new foundation and all. Besides," I added, "surely it'll only be for a short time, not for good, right? And then maybe things'll get back to normal."

"Will they?" she said slowly. Her tone became icy. "We'll have to see about that."

"Oh, Lily, please cut the poor man some slack!"

"That's just it—I have, over and over. You think I didn't notice how he's skulked around trying to get up the courage to pop the question?"

I should have known my friend was supremely capable of reading the signs.

"But he chickened out every time. Don't tell me you didn't know."

"Well, I—"

"Amelia, he's just blown his last chance. When he comes back, he better not expect me to be waiting for him."

"But—"

"It's no use. I've made up my mind. Goodbye."

# Chapter | Six

The next day was Sunday, and after church Gil, Janet, and I dropped by Chez Prentice. Etienne was on the front porch swing, frowning at an iPad as the three of us came up the walk.

Gil said, "Amelia and I are going to Danny's Diner in a few minutes. Want to join us?"

"Some other time," Etienne replied. "Hester made her mother's Beef Stew Aristocrat yesterday and left it in the refrigerator. It 'eats up nicely in the microwave." He smiled, adding, "There might be enough for you too."

"That's all right," I said. Hester's homely, delicious stew was a special favorite of Etienne's, and I knew his offer was well-meaning but insincere. "I've been craving one of Danny's BLTs all day." I handed the baby to Gil. "We'll be heading out as soon as I talk with Marie about something."

"I checked Mr. Holland in," I told Marie in the office. "And I waited around for the other guest as long as I could, but he never arrived."

She was behind Papa's huge old desk, looking over the registration information. "That's okay. He finally checked in about eleven last night. We were in bed when he rang the bell. Etienne wasn't too happy about it."

"Is he with the symphony orchestra too?"

She nodded and held up a card. "Herbert Edmonds, tall, kind of fat middle-aged guy, not very friendly. He's a per-per-cussionist, he says. Plays the drums and stuff. I asked him if he plays that big kettle drum like you see on TV, and I said to warn us if he'd be doing any practicing here, kind of a joke, you see, but he took me serious and said no, he'll do that in rehearsal at the auditorium." She shook her head. "No sense of humor. He told me that he sleeps late, so don't expect him for breakfast. Paid cash and didn't even bat his eyes when I asked for a big security deposit."

"So three guests total: Mr. Holland, Mr. Edmonds, and Callie Huff. That leaves two more rooms vacant. Is there any chance of a full house?"

"Maybe. That benefit concert should bring a few more people to town. The charity director has our address and phone number so they can recommend us to the musicians."

"That's a good idea." I rose and headed for the door. "Oh, by the way, did you ever get that recipe from Hester for her mother's beef stew?"

She chuckled. "Not yet. Hester says her mother made it so much she stopped using a recipe. She says I'll have to look over her shoulder next time she makes it."

"Well, when you do, take notes, would you, please? After all the raving Etienne has done, Gil's determined that I make it for him." I sighed. "I'm trying to learn to cook, honestly, but it's not really my forte."

"I hate to say it, but you're right." Marie closed her laptop. "Remember the brownies you made for our grand opening? Crystal and Courtney still talk about 'em." The teenaged Gervais twins frequently served as part-time maids and/or babysitters at Chez Prentice.

"I don't believe for a minute that Courtney cracked a tooth on my brownies," I said defensively. "Her sister told me that she has a habit of chewing on ice." The high school gossip network was every bit as efficient as Lily Burns's.

Marie said, "That's probably why she didn't sue, but cheer up. Hester's beef stew is pretty soft. Of course, I used to think the same thing about brownies!" She giggled.

I couldn't be irritated at her. Everything she said was true. Besides, it was a pleasure to see Marie making a joke.

"Very funny. Just get that recipe for me, if you don't mind."

She patted my back as we moved into the foyer. Gil was standing near the front door with the baby in one arm and a cell phone, held firmly against his ear, in the other.

The look on his face alarmed me. "Honey? What is it? Is everything all right?"

He frowned and shook his head slightly, continuing his conversation and turning so I could retrieve the baby from his left arm. "Yes. I'm heading out now." He concluded his call by tapping the screen and pocketing the phone. "Amelia, I've got to go." He pulled car keys from his pocket and looked around. "You two get some lunch and then, um, you . . . "

Marie stepped forward. "Don't worry. If you gotta go, Etienne 'n me'll take her home after we eat. We got plenty of stew." She glanced at Etienne. "Really."

"Gil, please, what is it?" His grave expression was scaring me.

He kissed me on the cheek and Janet on the head. "It's okay, just a breaking story. I can't afford to miss a chance like this. I've got to go out to Bluff's Head for a bit, and then maybe stop back at the paper. I'll call you at home later and let you know."

With a wave, he was out the door.

"What's at Bluff's Head?" I asked Marie. "All I know is that there's a beautiful view from up there. It's featured in magazines all the time."

She shrugged.

"There's that retirement 'ome, Sunset Bluffs, remember?" Etienne offered, strolling to the door and watching Gil back out of the driveway.

"Oh, yes. It's very expensive, I understand." I wondered what kind of urgent news story could possibly come from there.

Etienne pulled his own cell phone from his pocket. It was similar to Gil's, a small rectangle, resembling a tiny television screen. He tapped it.

"I 'ave the app for the police radio." He headed into the office. "I'll listen. Maybe I 'ear something."

In the kitchen, Marie retrieved the large container of stew from the B&B's huge refrigerator and began reheating it in

the microwave oven. I dragged the high chair from a corner
of the pantry, placed Janet in it and started setting the big
round table for lunch.

"Where are the napkins?"

"Fourth shelf down, in the pantry," Marie answered. "Get
the paper ones. Here you are, *ma petite*." She handed the fret-
ful Janet a spoon, which the child proceeded to use to beat a
steady rhythm on the tray before her as she sang a baby song.

I located the napkins and a basket for bread. There were
always delicious baked goods on hand at Chez Prentice,
thanks to the skills of Marie's sourpuss sister Valerie (of wedding cake fame).

Etienne walked slowly through the kitchen door, shaking
his head gravely. "Murder," he mumbled, "it's a murder at the
'ome." He took a seat at the table. "Don't worry, Amelia. The
police are there now. Gil will be fine."

"What do you think?" Marie said, ladling stew into a
white china tureen. "Maybe one old man killed another old
man?"

"What's this?" Ev Holland appeared at the door of the
kitchen. "Somebody kill somebody?"

It didn't feel right, speculating on such tragic news. "Just
some kind of emergency by the lake. My husband's checking
on it."

Ev nodded.

Marie fetched the butter dish from the refrigerator while I
poured water into the glasses. "Do you have everything you
need, Mr. Holland?" she asked our guest.

Ev was once again wearing the small fedora and the leather flip-flops and now sported a fisherman's vest over a faded plaid shirt and ragged jeans. He looked longingly over at the lunch table.

"I see you're having your family meal. Could you direct me to a good restaurant?"

I was relieved that he'd read our brochure. Chez Prentice offered a sumptuous breakfast and snacks in the dining room throughout the day, but Marie was strict about other meals. For lunch and dinner, the guests were strictly on their own.

"I'd recommend Danny's Diner," I said, pulling a bib from the diaper bag. I tied it around the baby's neck and handed her a teething biscuit. "Turn left and go three blocks down, just beyond the Court Library. It's one of those old-fashioned silver diners. It's really good."

He smiled. "Sounds colorful. Thanks." We heard the front door close as we sat down together and said grace.

"Oh, something smells marvelous!" Callie Huff stood at the door, her eyes alight.

Hester frowned.

With a gesture, Marie directed her to a place at the table. She looked at me as she fetched another table setting. Her expression said, *This is part of the contract, remember?*

"By the way," Callie began conversationally as she opened the paper napkin in her lap, "you know, it's very fortunate that you have enough time before the Branch wedding to have some painting done."

"Painting?" Etienne, Marie, and Hester said all at once.

"What painting?" Etienne asked slowly, his eyes narrowing.

Callie waved her hand around. "Well, I mean, that shade of yellow out there just screams farm house, doesn't it? I was thinking something along the lines of the painted ladies out in San Francisco: lavender with white gingerbread—you'll need to add a bit of gingerbread—and some quaint maroon and green accents." She held her hands up to make a frame for her imaginary image, then clasped them together. "Oh, it would make this place a standout!"

There was an extended silence, while baby Janet, wide-eyed, looked from face to face with concern, all the while sucking her cookie.

Marie broke the ice. She stroked the baby's head, turned to Callie and said, "We'll think about it." I could tell by her tone that she really meant, *We'll do no such thing!*

Callie nodded. "Good. And we're going to want to change out those quilts too. They're so—I don't know—kind of homemade-looking. You're going to want some satin ones."

*Hester made every one of those quilts*, I thought. I saw her open her mouth to speak, but Etienne jumped into the exchange before anyone could form an outraged retort.

"*Bon appétit*, everyone!" He began to serve the soup bowls, giving Hester and Marie warning glances. "Amelia and Gil are crazy about this stew."

"Hold off on mine, please, until I finish feeding Janet. I'm fixing her some rice cereal and some of this strained lamb." I pulled a box from the diaper bag, poured a little bit of the powder in a plastic cup and dampened it with tepid water from the tap. "She doesn't like it much, but if I hide the meat stuff under the cereal, I can sometimes sneak it into her."

Marie looked at the rice mixture over my shoulder. "Yuk! That looks like glue. Wait a minute." She went to the stove, pulled out a sliver of carrot and a chunk of potato from the stew and mashed them together in a small bowl. "Here."

"But it's carrots—and potato."

"Yes, it is. She'll love it. It's got to taste better than— that." She grimaced as she pointed to the cereal. "My mother started all her kids out on mashed carrots and potatoes. They loved it. I did it with Marguerite too. Go on," she urged. "Let it cool down first, though."

I had an impulse to respond as some of my students did to an obvious instruction by striking an impertinent pose and saying, "Duh," but I restrained myself and handed the baby another biscuit.

"Mm, this stew's not bad, despite having such a silly name," Callie admitted, spearing a green bean. "Could use a touch of wine, though."

Hester's sidelong look was not appreciative. "This is my mother's recipe. No wine."

The stew was delicious, with a thin, flavorful broth, vegetables, and tender chunks of beef. After having consumed half the contents of my bowl, I offered Janet a taste of the cooled mixture on the tip of a tiny spoon.

She opened her mouth obediently, but the texture of the food surprised her. She waved her tongue around and wrinkled up her face as if in pain.

"Oh, dear," I began, but Marie put her hand on my arm and said, "Shh! Wait a second."

Janet's demeanor changed almost immediately as she swallowed the tiny morsel. She looked at me expectantly and opened her mouth to receive more.

"See? She likes it!" Marie crowed and everyone laughed.

Janet pounded the high chair tray in excitement and eagerly consumed all of the new treat—that is, all that didn't end up on her bib. In the time-honored tradition of mothers, I gently scraped the oozing goo from her chin with the little spoon and replaced it in her mouth. She happily consumed every smidgeon.

Etienne smiled and leaned back in his chair. "Did I not tell you it was delicious, Amelia? Everybody likes this stew. And we have ice cream for dessert."

As the meal wound down, Etienne and Marie cleared the table.

Callie stood. "Well, this was very nice and, um, homey," she said with a definite note of condescension.

"I am very glad you like it. We eat a lot of this stuff around 'ere." I spotted a twinkle in Etienne's eye.

"Yes, well, I'm afraid I won't be able to join you for dinner tonight, so don't wait for me." She left the room with a swirl of her Paisley shawl, fortunately missing Marie's muttered, "Don't worry, we won't."

Hester added, "What's wrong with a farmhouse, can you tell me that? Painted lady, my big toe! There's only one painted lady around this place and we all know who that is."

I kept silent, though I shared the sentiment. My grandparents had selected the lovely pale yellow and for almost a century, through countless coats of paint, it had always been the same color.

The baby, who had been enthusiastically drinking milk, lowered her sippy cup. Her eyelids drooped and her head did a few bobs. "She'll be out like a light in a minute," I said. "Do you mind if I stick around here for a while before going home?" I was anxious about that murder and I wanted to hear from Gil.

A few minutes later in the dining room, Janet dozed peacefully in the little travel crib that we kept at Chez Prentice for just such occasions, while I sorted through the various pieces of paperwork required to help high school students make it to graduation.

Serendipity Shea was doing better in her essays. I looked over her piece entitled "How to Change a Tire." It was no surprise that she'd chosen this subject, since only last year she'd received a car as a birthday present from her indulgent father. Clearly she had been coached by her boyfriend, Jason, in this skill, but it was a vast improvement over the depressed-sounding subjects she chose when her mother was first incarcerated.

Mrs. Richards, the teacher who replaced me at the high school, had given her a solid C. "Not bad, Serry," I murmured, scanning the page. "Let's take a look at where your mistakes are. But what's this? Green pencil?"

Instead of the traditional red pencil that I always used, Mrs. Richards had made corrective notations in green. *That's strange*, I thought, *she used red on the earlier papers. In honor of St. Patrick's Day, perhaps?* I looked at the date on the paper. *Or maybe she just ran out of red ones. Odd.*

Chez Prentice had celebrated the holiday weeks ago by putting a huge green wreath on the door and serving some of Valerie's delicious soda bread at breakfast and teatime.

I was interrupted by the sound of the big front door opening.

"Marie?" Gil called. "Did you guys take my family home already?"

The familiar voice woke up our little girl and she started to cry. I pulled her into my arms and emerged into the foyer.

"We're here, Gil." I jiggled the baby on my hip, but she continued to wail.

"Give her to me," my husband said.

He held Janet close and made soothing noises, but without success. She'd been startled and wanted to express her outrage.

"What happened at Sunset Bluffs?" I told him what Etienne had gleaned from the police radio. "It sounded bad."

As he patted the baby on the back, he frowned and shook his head. "It was bad. A man was murdered, a resident, retired attorney with dementia." He gently shifted his squalling burden to the other side and starting jiggling her again. "The place is made up of two main buildings: a large old mansion with the dining room and activity rooms and, behind it, the separate residential part that's all on one floor. They think somebody might have sneaked in through a window and stabbed the man while he slept. That's better, sweetie," he said to Janet, who had quieted down and was now hiccupping.

He pulled a handkerchief from his pocket and wiped her damp face. The three of us walked into the kitchen.

"It sounds so terrible! Don't they have a security system?"

Gil shrugged. "I don't know. Maybe not. Or maybe they do and it wasn't turned on. The facility is very well maintained, though. Sunset Bluff's a really nice place, but the police told me it was an awful mess in the victim's room."

"Oh dear." I felt shaky.

"I talked to an attendant who said he thought the victim was originally from here. I'll need to fire up the computer, do some research about the man's hometown, his career, things like that, for the article I'm writing. The police asked me to hold off publishing his name for now."

We sat at the table and Gil bounced Janet on his knee. "How long has she been trying to swallow her fist like that?"

I sighed. "I told you about it, remember? She's teething, poor thing. There's not much to do for it, the book says, just give her something to gnaw on. Here, Janet, try this." I pulled a teething biscuit from the diaper bag.

The baby accepted it eagerly.

Gil looked over at me thoughtfully. "Look, Sunset Bluffs isn't that far from our house along the lakeshore. I think I want you two to stay here for a few days, at least until they find out who did this."

"I don't know, Gil. There's that symphony orchestra in town for the charity concert. Marie hoped she could fill up the other two rooms with paying guests."

He handed the baby to me. "This is important. I'll go talk to her. We'll pay, if necessary."

He headed out of the kitchen and across the foyer to the B&B office, which had formerly been my father's book-lined study. Many of Papa's books still filled the shelves.

I sighed. It wouldn't be all that inconvenient; that wasn't the issue. We had some clothes and supplies squirreled away here, but I didn't want to take undue advantage of my position as partner in this business venture. Etienne and Marie had worked so hard to make a go of it. Granting use of the house and grounds was more or less the extent of my contribution.

On the other hand, I would feel uneasy, alone at the lake house. Though our place was not all that accessible from town, we were also located right on the shore of Lake Champlain, a quick and easy boat ride from Sunset Bluffs, and our home was complete with a handy short pier.

Marie and Gil entered the kitchen together. "Of course you'll stay here," she said firmly.

"What is that baby chewing on?"

I looked over at Janet, who had managed to reduce the biscuit to a kind of muddy goo, which she'd spread on her face like war paint. "She's teething." I dampened a paper towel and repaired the damage.

"Wait a minute." Marie opened the door of the big new restaurant freezer Etienne had installed and pulled out a zip-lock plastic bag containing a white washcloth.

"I always keep a few of these around in case a guest has a headache or something; I bet it will help." She pulled the washcloth from the bag and handed it to Janet. "It's okay," she assured me, "it's clean and everything."

After a moment's hesitation, Janet began vigorously sucking on the icy washcloth.

"It's the cold, you see. It helps the gums or something." Wrinkling her nose, Marie took a paper towel and wiped up the damp remains of the biscuit from the floor where the baby had dropped it and tossed it in the trash.

"Show me which room is available for these two." Gil began folding up the travel crib. "I'll carry this upstairs."

"D, the Ausable Suite, between the two musicians." Marie moved toward the door. "I'll be in the office if you need anything."

I was in the foyer, watching Gil begin to lug our baby equipment up the stairs when the front door opened and Ev Holland strolled in with a pleasant smile on his face. As before, he didn't bother to doff his hat, even indoors.

I smiled in greeting and turned back to watch Gil. I felt a tap on my shoulder.

"Could I ask you a question?" Ev asked.

"Of course."

"I need a general idea of how to get to 621 Brinker Street. I've been told it's an easy walk. I'm supposed to be there by seven this evening."

I tried to keep the surprise out of my voice. "It's the house behind this one. You can walk around the block or go through the back garden; there's a gate, but that would take you to the back door. I imagine you'd want to go to the front door."

"That I would!" he said brightly, "Thanks." He took the stairs two at a time and made it to the top at the same time that Gil did.

I stared unseeing up the stairs for a full minute, thinking. Six hundred twenty-one Brinker Street was Lily Burns's house. What was going on?

# Chapter | Seven

Once Janet and I had settled into our designated room at Chez Prentice, I made a call on my cell phone. "Lily, what's going on?"

Her voice was silky; not a good sign. "What do you mean 'going on?'"

"You know very well what I mean. Why should a flutist want directions to your house?"

Bell-like laughter erupted. "Oh, you mean Ev! What a charming man, so erudite, so well read. We met at the diner and struck up a conversation. He bought me lunch."

"He's hardly the type of man I pictured you with. I mean, the flip-flops, the little hat, the—" *And he doesn't like cats*, I remembered, but didn't mention. Lily adored cats.

"Are you saying I should stick to corpulent men obsessed with reptiles?"

I was surprised to hear her use the euphemism. She usually said fat.

I sighed. "Lily—"

She headed me off at the pass. "Don't start, Amelia."

"But—"

"You heard me. I've made up my mind. That relationship is over, *fini*, kaput."

"Have you heard from him?"

"He put a letter on my door when he left, but I haven't opened it. I'll probably throw it away."

I gasped. "Lily! How could you?"

"How could I? How could *he?* Look, Amelia, you've watched the little do-si-do dance number Alec's been doing. Just when I think he's going to propose, the cookies burn in the oven or some other lame, stupid thing happens and everything's off again!"

I'd been wasting my time, keeping Alec's plans a secret.

She continued her rant, "We both know that some slimy sea monster will always rate higher on his list than me!"

"Than *I*."

"Oh, you and your miserable grammar fetish! I never told you this before, but it's extremely unattractive. Cut it out. As for your friend the Professor, I'm thoroughly sick of waiting around for him to fish or cut bait. I quit. I've got a date with this Holland guy tonight and I intend to enjoy it."

"Where are you going to go?"

"Who knows?" I could picture her waving her hand airily. "I told him I'd show him the high spots in town. We'll probably go out to dinner, then maybe a movie or LaPlante's Road House."

"But—"

LaPlante's had a pretty rough reputation. Make that a very rough reputation. She'd obviously thrown in that detail to needle me.

"Where I go and who I see my business, Amelia."

*Whom,* I thought. Putting the grammar aside, it was almost the same phrase she'd used the last time she dated someone other than Alec. It hadn't ended well.

"But don't you owe the man the courtesy of letting him know you've broken up with him?"

"What do you suggest I do?" She mocked Alec's accent. "The cell service is terrr-ible oot there in the hee-lands!"

"You could call his hotel. What hotel is he staying at?"

"How should I know? And while we're on the subject of grammar, didn't you just end a sentence with a preposition there?"

I indulged in a deep sigh and admitted, "Yes, I did."

"Gotcha!" She laughed.

"Look, Lily—"

"No, you look, Amelia. Please don't think I don't appreciate how much you care—I do—but you can't always have stuff turn out the way you want. You need to stop doing that. You can't arrange things and people the way you used to do with your Barbie dolls. I remember you even used to make sure they were wearing their underwear before you put them away!"

"Come on! I can't see how that's relevant."

"It's very relevant. I'm no Barbie doll, and I think we can all agree that Alec is no Ken."

"Lily—"

"It feels so good to be admired again, Amelia."

"But Alec admires—"

"Maybe he does; I don't know any more. I do love Alec in my own way—not that it's any of your business—but it's been a kind of emotional roller coaster with him, you know?"

She had a point. I remained silent, remembering.

"Is that all you wanted to talk about?"

"I guess so."

"All right, then." She hung up.

I flopped back on the big bed and stared at the ceiling. *There's nothing I can do about this*, I thought.

*Except pray.* It was an unbidden thought from an inner voice I'd learned to pay attention to.

"Yes, pray," I murmured.

*Please be in the situation between my friends, Lord. Only You know what is needed.*

I heard a door slam. It seemed to be coming from the room next to ours.

I slid off the bed, crept quickly to my own door and looked out. The guest, whom I presumed to be the drummer Herbert Edmonds, was locking his door and strangely, pleasantly humming a tune. I recognized "Coming through the Rye."

The percussionist was a far cry from his fellow musician, Ev Holland. In his apparel, for instance: Edmonds was wearing a dark suit and tie and even at a distance, I could see that his haircut was what the military people call high and tight.

Before I could step back and close my own door, he pocketed his key, turned rapidly, and began walking briskly toward the stairs. When he realized he was being observed, he stopped humming in mid phrase. As he passed, he assumed a hostile, squinting stare that seemed to drill right into my head.

I blinked hard and shrank back.

The aggressive, pounding sound of his tread on the staircase perfectly matched his unpleasant expression.

"Was it something I said?" I asked the empty hallway.

# Chapter | Eight

I filled Gil in about the Alec-Lily-Ev situation when he came back to the B&B that night.

"So Alec has a rival, huh?" he said, chuckling.

He put his attaché case on the dresser and took his place next to me on the loveseat. Across the room, Janet slept peacefully.

"You're not taking this very seriously," I said with a slight pout.

"Don't worry, honey." He threw one arm along the sofa's back. "All Alec'll have to do is bring Lily another cat and she'll melt into his arms."

I had to smile. "I must admit, it did work, didn't it?"

He loosened his tie. "And you told Alec not to do it, as I recall."

"Well, all the books said—"

He rubbed his eyes with his thumb and forefinger and sighed. "Honey, let's think about this: In all the years you've known Lily, exactly how many times did your interference—"

"Caring!"

"Okay, your caring. How many times did it alter the ulti-mate outcome?"

I tried to recall. There was an extended silence.

Gil laughed. "Admit it. You got nothing."

"The proper phrase is I have nothing, but yes, Mr. Know-it-All, you're right. Lily will do what Lily will do, and the best thing I can do is pray for her."

He kissed my forehead and scrambled to his feet. "That's the ticket. Now, what's—oops! I was about to ask you what's for dinner. Forgot where we were."

Still trying to remember at least one single time I'd influenced Lily, I answered absent-mindedly, "There should be plenty of Hester's stew left over from lunch. It's really good. Even Janet liked it. We could heat that up."

He brightened. "There's another advantage in staying here besides the relative safety: Hester's cooking."

"Very funny." I was painfully aware that I didn't cook very well and didn't enjoy being reminded of the fact. "Gil, while it's quiet, I thought we could talk. Sit back down, please." I took one of the plush Victorian chairs and patted the seat of the other one.

"Talk about what?"

"You're worried about something, I can tell. Stressed."

He didn't sit, but stood a few yards away, jingling change in his pocket. "Oh, you know, the usual."

"No, it's not. It's—"

He rubbed his forehead. "Amelia, if you don't mind, I don't feel like talking about work." He handed me the baby monitor. "Here. Plug this in, and let's go downstairs and raid the refrigerator."

I decided to let things rest—for the time being.

There was plenty of leftover stew. We used the new microwave to heat it up.

"This is like the dashboard of a jet," Gil complained as he surveyed buttons on the front of the big oven. "Does it do the laundry too?"

"I sure wish it did," Marie responded from the doorway. She nodded to the old pantry that had been converted to a laundry room. "Hester says that washer and dryer are running all day long when there's people staying here. I had no idea there'd be so much to wash in this business. But you gotta do it." She poured herself a glass of milk and took a seat at the table. "I'm glad to see you're having more of the stew. Hester made enough for an army."

"Join us?"

"No thanks, Gil. I had a snack earlier. This glass of milk's plenty for me."

"You said you'd get me the recipe for the stew," I reminded her, trying to ignore Gil as he rolled his eyes. I knew what he was thinking: *No way you could cook this.*

We set our bowls down, placed the baby monitor in the center of the table, and said a short blessing.

As we ate, Marie asked, "Is that snoring I hear?"

Gil speared a cube of beef and popped it in his mouth. "Mm-hm."

"I asked the doctor about it. He says it's nothing to worry about," I reassured her.

"It's kind of cute—tiny like." Marie sipped her milk.

We ate quietly for a time.

Finally, Gil sat back and said, "Amelia was right. This is delicious. Can I have some more?" He glanced at me. "*May* I have some more?"

Marie smiled sleepily. " 'Course. Help yourself." She looked into her glass. "It's odd. I got used to living by myself all those years, but these days, when Etienne's out of town, I have trouble getting to sleep. I thought this might help." She drained the glass and rose to rinse it in the sink. "Gil, what happened over to the Bluffs? When you left, it sounded pretty serious. Who was it got killed?"

Gil dipped out more stew into his bowl and headed to the microwave. "One of the attendants told me that he was a retired lawyer named Conner Channing, age fifty-eight. Not quite as old as some of the other folks out there—folks who are pretty terrified, by the way," he added.

"They would be," Marie said, "I would be."

"Just in the brief time I was there, six families came to check their parents out of the place." The oven dinged and he opened the door. "The sad part is, this Channing guy—the victim—was diagnosed with Alzheimer's a few months ago. Once the symptoms started to really show themselves, he moved to the Bluffs. He wanted to be near his father, who lives there too." He carried his bowl to the table. "The old man, Hugh Channing, is in his nineties, but he's sharp as a tack."

"So they already told him what happened to his son?" Marie asked.

Gil shook his head. "Worse than that. He's the one who found him."

I gasped. "Oh, that poor man!"

Marie went pale.

"Yeah. And it was pretty gross, they tell me." Gil poked at the last of his stew with his spoon and sighed. "I guess I've had enough dinner. It was really good, though."

"I'll tell Hester you said so." Marie headed for the door. "I think I'll go check all the locks before I turn in."

"Is everyone tucked in for the night?" I asked as I put our bowls in the huge, professional-sized dishwasher.

"Not everybody. Mr. Edmonds, that drummer, is out again. He told me he'd be late, come in after midnight sometime, so I give him a key." She shivered. "Wish I didn't, now."

"Does something in particular about the guy make you nervous, Marie?" Gil asked.

I nodded, remembering the look the man had given me, but Marie said, "Not really. I just feel kind of weird that there's a murderer still out there somewhere. Etienne told me not to watch that movie last night."

"What movie?" I used a wet paper towel to wipe off the table.

She shrugged. "Oh, just some old black-and-white thing about a woman who rents a room to a guy that turns out to be Jack the Ripper. I wish I hadn't of watched it, but I had to find out what happened." She hugged herself and frowned. "Won't do that again."

"*The Lodger?* Was that the name?" Gil asked.

"Yeah, that's it."

He chuckled. "No wonder you're uneasy. That was a creepy film, all right. I reviewed it a couple of years ago for a column. George Sanders, Merle Oberon and . . . I forget who played the bad guy."

"Well, whatever his name is, he was big and scary looking. He kind of reminded me of Mr. Edmonds."

I laughed. "Marie, you're letting your imagination run away with you."

"Probably. I'm gonna say a prayer about it. That always helps."

Gil patted Marie on the shoulder. "I wouldn't worry about it, you know. The police are going over Sunset Bluffs with a fine-toothed comb. They'll catch the perp, you'll see."

*Everybody uses TV jargon now,* I thought. I had to ask, "Perp? Is that what they really call them?"

"Yes, I actually heard them say it." In spite of the grim subject at hand, Gil smiled ruefully. "But it wasn't like *CSI* or *NCIS* out there today. It was like pulling teeth. I was lucky to get any information at all. Between the police protecting the crime scene and the director being afraid of a lawsuit, I was more or less given the cold shoulder. All the news people were frustrated. The only person I could get to talk to me was that orderly. He seemed pretty shaken up, but he did tell me that old Mr. Channing—the victim's father—is kind of a favorite of the staff."

"Poor man."

I picked up the baby monitor and followed Gil and Marie into the foyer, where they took turns checking the lock.

"See? You're all set," Gil said.

"Maybe we ought to of got one of those security systems with the cameras and everything," Marie mused. "I'll talk to Etienne when he gets back tomorrow. Good night." She headed down the hall toward the first floor suite.

"I admire your tact," Gil commented as we trudged up the stairs.

"Shh! The guests. We need to whisper. What tact?"

"We ought to *have*, not ought to *of*," he said. "You didn't even flinch. As the Ozzies say, Good on ye!"

"I would have preferred that she said it differently, but I'm not expecting miracles. She's my business partner and deserves respect, grammar notwithstanding."

We reached the landing. Gil put his arm around me, still whispering, "Honey, I can tell you're exhausted when you start sounding like a textbook. C'mon, let's get our jammies on and read each other a bedtime story."

A familiar cry emanated from the monitor in my hand.

"Uh, oh. Sounds like somebody needs a diaper change. Your turn." Gil turned the doorknob of our room.

I stepped back. "What do you mean, my turn? You never change diapers."

He cocked his head to one side. "How do you think I manage when I take care of her, then?"

"I've figured it out. Whenever you do take care of her, you make sure you're here instead of at the lake house, and you get Hester or Marie to do the dirty work."

He raised his palms in surrender. "You found me out. *Mea culpa*." He pulled a coin from his pocket. "Look, I'll flip you for it. Heads or tails?"

"Forget it. You don't know my method, and I'm too tired to teach you anyway. Coming, Sweetie," I called out—quietly—to our daughter.

# Chapter | Nine

T he next morning, we awoke to the sound of men's voices in the front yard.

Gil pulled back a curtain and peered out. "It's Etienne with some workmen. He must have left Montreal at dawn to be here now. They've got a truckload of sod down there. I guess the new lawn is about to be put in. Dibs on the shower." He headed for the bathroom.

Etienne and Marie had finished breakfast by the time we came downstairs. Across the kitchen, Hester, already wearing a fine coating of flour on her arms and apron, was busy pouring batter into a waffle iron.

"Sit down," she ordered over her shoulder. "They'll be ready in a minute."

We obeyed. I put Janet in the high chair and fetched the economy-sized box of Cheerios from the pantry.

"Honey, I need to get some things from the house," I told Gil as he brought mugs of coffee to the table. "When can we go back?"

He poured orange juice for the two of us. "Soon, I think, but not yet. I want to see how the investigation is going. I'll ask O'Brien about it."

Our good friend, Police Sergeant Dennis O'Brien was Gil's contact in the local police department.

"I understand, but I only have one spare outfit here. I at least need to get some more clothes, and there was a book I was reading on the bedside table. How about letting me take the car for a quick trip?"

"By yourself?"

"Of course not. Janet will be with me, won't you, sweetheart?" I said to our daughter as she delicately picked up the cereal from the bowl, Cheerio by Cheerio, and conveyed each one slowly to her mouth.

*Her hand-eye coordination is coming right along,* I thought, pleased.

He shook his head. "That won't work. Look, I need to go out to the Bluffs again this morning. I can stop by the house afterward. How about making me a list of what you need?"

"That wouldn't work, either. You wouldn't know where to find anything."

Hester set a plate of waffles in the center of the table. "I got an idea. You go with him and leave the little princess here with me. Sorta take a break. She can help me with the laundry, can't you, bunny rabbit?" She chucked the baby under the chin.

Janet responded by looking up and giving her a festive smile as she tossed a handful of cereal into the air. "Eee!" she squealed, and then leaned over to look at the mess on the floor with an expression that seemed to say, *Did I do that?*

Hester laughed, wiped her hands on her apron, and fetched a bottle of syrup and a butter dish, which she plunked on the table. "See? She likes the idea. We'll be fine. You two go on."

An hour later, after stopping at our house to pick up the things I needed, Gil and I turned at a sign that read: Sunset Bluffs, Independent and Assisted Living. The facility was at the end of a long drive through dense woodlands. As we crested a hill at the end of the drive, the vista opened up and revealed a wide, well-groomed lawn topped by a large four-story white wedding cake of a house, dripping with architectural detail. Beyond this sprawled a huge, curiously flat and incongruously modern, one-story brick building that rather resembled a motel, and beyond that, a breathtaking view of Lake Champlain sparkling in the spring sunshine.

"It's so nice," I said.

"You sound surprised," Gil replied. "What did you expect, a prison?"

"I don't know. Sometimes these places can be depressing, but this is lovely."

"Costs a pretty penny too. I did some research. It's as much as six grand a month, depending on the size of the room. But it's the best place of its kind in the North Country."

I had a strange fluttering in my chest as we drew nearer. It wasn't the acrobat I sometimes fancied occupying my stomach when I was self-conscious, but something quite different. The word *foreboding* might describe it.

*It's because I know the terrible thing that happened here.*

"Where are we going?" I asked, eyeing the white mansion. Each porch step held a terra-cotta pot containing a bright red geranium, and white-painted wicker rocking chairs with chintz cushions lined the porch. "That looks like the front."

"It is, but we're headed to the residential annex."

The driveway circled around the house and created a barrier between it and the low brick building. The sprawling one-story, utilitarian-looking annex facility was fairly pleasant upon close inspection, though at one end we could see the flutter of yellow police tape. A white police van stood guard in the parking slot nearby. Another van with the call letters of the local television station stood next to it.

Little patios graced the doors to the individual apartments, and there was a short walkway leading to the front entrance, flanked on either side by a well-tended rock garden. I noticed a number of the little green cabbage-like plants my grandmother used to call hens and chicks.

On the right a small fountain splashed cheerfully, and on the left was something I hadn't seen in years: a blue-tinted gazing ball on a white column pedestal. The round surface of the ball reflected us grotesquely in miniature as we passed. Just as we were about to go through the automatic doors, we heard a sound.

"Psst! Psst! Over here!"

We followed the voice around the rock garden on the left past a large louvered white wooden screen, beyond which was a wide sunny patio with wrought-iron chairs and a beautiful view of the lake in the distance.

A number of residents were enjoying the unusually warm midmorning sunshine, some in conversational groups, with four at a matching wrought iron table, playing cards. They were all quite well dressed. The men—there were only three of them—wore well-pressed Docker-style trousers, golf sweaters, and deck shoes. The women—I counted nine—were in a variety of outfits, including one sweet-looking little lady in a lavender wool pantsuit holding an open lace-trimmed parasol in the exact same shade.

Two of the men were bald, and the other one had an abundance of faded rust-colored hair. Surprisingly only two of the women were gray haired. The others had clearly chosen to assist nature with varying hues of red, blonde, and jet black.

When we appeared, laughter and low conversation stopped, and every eye turned our way. There was fear in nearly every face, and anger in a few.

A woman stood and demanded in a shaky voice, "Who're you? Who're you looking for?"

Gil and I stood next to the screen, uncertain. Gil opened his mouth to speak.

From nearby, a man in a set of green cotton scrubs with "Jess" embroidered on the breast pocket stepped forward. "It's okay, Sadie," he called out to the woman, giving her a casual wave. "They're just here for the tour. Right this way, folks," he said smoothly, adding in a half-shout, "I think your mother'll love this place." He waved indulgently at the group as we moved away. "They're just a little edgy after having the police here and everything," he said to us.

We followed him through a side door of the brick building into a laundry room that boasted two coin-operated washers and two extra-large dryers. There was a center counter for folding and a horizontal pole along the opposite wall for hanging clothes. The cloying, pseudo-perfume of laundry detergent saturated the air, and a man's pajama top on a hanger added a jaunty note of orange to the drab surroundings.

The man took my hand in both of his. "Who's this?" He gave me an oily smile.

"My wife," Gil said in a low voice. "Amelia, this is Jess Renaud." He pronounced it in the French way, "*Ray*-noh."

Renaud looked at me appraisingly, up and down. "It's a real pleasure. But I'm sorry, Mr. Dickensen," he added, turning to Gil, "this transaction was supposed to be strictly between us two."

The man was half a head taller than Gil and at least thirty pounds heavier. His arrestingly blue eyes were set off by long, almost feminine eyelashes. In contrast, he had that five-o'clock-shadow, not-quite-shaved look that some of the high school boys were sporting now, though there was a rule against it. I was not fond of it.

Gil smiled. "It's okay. We work together. Honey, give me something to write with." He held out his hand.

I shot him a quizzical look, but fortunately had a small pen in the pocket of my slacks. "Here." I slapped it into his palm like an operating room nurse.

Gil pulled his perennial notebook from his pocket and asked, "What's been happening since yesterday?" He held the pen at the ready.

Renaud scratched his elbow and kept glancing at the door leading to the hallway. "Well, the police are still all over the place talking to everybody, asking the same questions, over and over. And people keep leaving. We're only eighty percent full now, and those that are left, they're scared sh—silly," he amended, looking at me. "Excuse me."

I nodded in recognition of his apology. "How is Mr. Channing's father doing?" I asked.

Gil bumped me slightly on the side with his leg. The laundry's big folding table masked the action. He wanted me to keep quiet.

Renaud kept looking from Gil to me and back again. "The old dude's kind of confused. He feels like he could of stopped it, but that's impossible."

"Why?" I asked, moving a step to one side to avoid another of Gil's bumps.

The man shrugged. "Because he went to breakfast that morning by himself. Didn't even go into his son's room. He didn't know what happened until he went back to the suite afterwards. He couldn't of done any good. His son was already dead for hours."

*Couldn't have,* I thought. *It's an epidemic!*

Gil asked, "What kind of security does this place have, anyway?"

Renaud sounded defensive. "We've got security. There are deadbolts on the outside doors, and there's a buzzer that goes off if somebody goes out when they're not supposed to."

"It must not have occurred to them that there'd be a problem with somebody coming in," Gil said, shaking his head.

"Yeah, well." Renaud shrugged. "I mean, it's not like we've got a nest of gangsters here or anything. They're all nice, quiet, regular types, church people. They got a priest or minister doing services here every Sunday afternoon and most of our residents go. Sometimes the rabbi from Temple Beth El comes. We have a guy on the staff who plays the organ keyboard and there's a standing order for flowers, all the trimmings, you know. The old people like that," he added with a touch of condescension.

I said, "I understand Conner Channing was a lawyer. What kind of law did he practice?"

"How should I know? The man wasn't here long enough to tell me his life story." Renaud turned and reached across the top of a dryer. "Excuse me a second. I think I know who this belongs to."

He pulled the orange pajama shirt off the hangar. After checking a nametag inside the collar, he folded it and tucked it under his arm.

"Most of them do, you know—tell me things, I mean. They tell me all about what they did for a living and where they lived and their children and everything." He put his hand to his chest. "I'm polite, of course. I nod and act like I'm listening, but most of them tell me the same stuff over and over." He twirled his finger around his ear in the time-honored hand signal for crazy. "Their short-term memory isn't so good at this age."

I glanced at Gil, then back at Renaud. "I understand they think the attacker came through the window. Aren't they kept locked?" I could feel, rather than see, Gil frowning at me.

The man shrugged again. "It's been nice and warm out lately. Some of the folks like to open the windows to let the breeze in. There's screens, but—"

Someone abruptly opened the door of the laundry room and stuck her head in. It was a stern-looking woman wearing a white coat over her dress.

"Jess, have you done today's blood pressures?"

Renaud glanced at his wristwatch. "Is it that time already? I'm sorry, Mrs. Blair." He gestured to us and said in a saccharine tone, "I was just giving these folks a tour. But I'll get right on it. Mrs. Blair is the head nurse around here and keeps everybody healthy. Everyone loves her!"

Even at a distance we could see that the compliment went down well. All her sternness seemed to vanish at the compliment. She lowered her gaze and smiled.

"We do our best. Please forgive the confusion around here," she added. "We're almost back to normal now." She pointed her pencil at Renaud. "Remember, Jess, I'm going to need those vitals by four o'clock sharp."

He gave a mock salute. "Consider it done."

The door closed.

Renaud pulled a set of keys out of his pocket and looked over his shoulder. "Look, I have to go do this, but if you wait here, I think I can get in the office and take a look around. Maybe even get some pictures of Channing's file." He held up an iPhone.

"Look, honey, I want you to wait in the car." Gil reached into his pocket and pulled out his wallet.

"But—"

"Please, Amelia, do what I say. Go. The car's unlocked. Wait for me there." His tone, through gritted teeth, brooked no argument.

I went to the outside door, paused, and turned back.

Gil and Renaud were talking in sharp whispers. I heard numbers mentioned.

As I emerged into the pleasant spring sunshine, I was worried. *Is that man really going to photograph a file? Is Gil really going to let him?*

I circled the entranceway and gazed out into the parking lot. There was the car, sitting in the sunshine. It would be hot inside and boring. I was too restless to just sit there worrying.

I surveyed my surroundings. This place was exquisitely landscaped and had a beautiful view. Why wait in the car?

I turned back, circumnavigating the clutch of lounging seniors on the large patio, and headed across the wide lawn to the bluff overlooking the lake behind the brick annex.

No expense had been spared on the decorative trees, carefully-manicured shrubs, and lawn furniture here. But apparently the cool breezes blowing directly off the lake on this side

of the building were too much for the delicate internal ther-
mostats of most of the residents. There was only one elderly
man bundled up in an overcoat and muffler sitting on a park
bench, gazing toward the lake. I began to button my sweater
and turned to leave.

"Here, please, have a seat," a deep, melodious voice suggested.

I looked back and saw the man patting the bench beside
him. "I don't want to disturb you."

He shook his white head. "You won't. If anything, you'll
provide me with a windbreak. How about it?" He didn't smile,
but had a pleasant, slightly sad expression. "Please?" he said
again.

I sat and held out my hand. "Amelia Dickensen."

His hand, though ropy with prominent veins, was surprisingly strong. "Hugh Channing."

"Channing?" I said, "You're—"

"Yes." He withdrew his hand and turned to gaze out at the
lake again.

"I'm so sorry." I began to stand.

He turned back. "Don't go. I'd be glad for your company.
They treat me like Typhoid Mary around here right now,
though I imagine you're too young to know who that was."

"Of course I know." I sat back down. "I'm older than you
might think. And I read a lot."

He actually chuckled, low and under his breath. "I like
bright young people. I liked teaching them."

"You're a teacher too?" I tapped myself. "High school English." The wind whipped my hair into my eyes and I brushed it back.

He tapped his own chest. "Torts and criminal law."

"You taught in law school?"

"Yes, quite some time ago." He leaned back and folded his arms. "I miss it."

I glanced over at his profile and tried to imagine this handsome old man in the front of a classroom. Somehow I knew he'd be good at it.

He tilted his head toward me. "So where do you teach?"

I leaned forward and pulled my sweater tighter around me. The wind was getting brisk.

"Well, I'm on hiatus right now, for a little while. We have a baby girl, and though I know it's not politically correct these days, I want to spend time with—"

He interrupted me, "Say no more. I concur completely. One's children should always come first." He squinted up at a fat cloud. "I have quite a few regrets in that department myself."

I didn't know what to say.

*Lord, comfort this poor man. Give me the right words, or show me when to keep quiet.*

I kept quiet.

He sighed. A tear ran down one of the deep wrinkles in his cheek.

"It's all right. I'll be with him before very long. I believe that and take comfort in it, I truly do." He looked over at me.

"Do you believe that?" He pulled a monogrammed cotton handkerchief from his coat pocket and blew his nose.

I answered carefully. "Yes, I do. I mean, not that you're going to, um—"

"Die. You can say it: Die. It doesn't frighten me. Don't say pass. I hate weasel words. I've heard my share. Lawyers use far too many of them."

"All right, die. But it may not be soon. And I agree with you about what the Bible teaches. You will see him again."

"That's it, you know." He wiped his nose one more time and replaced the folded handkerchief in his pocket. "The Bible is the ultimate law book. Everything stems from it, or should."

I nodded. Once again I felt the need to be silent.

He let out another sigh, a long and slow one. "The body is only a receptacle of the spirit. It wears out in time. You may find this hard to believe, but I used to play football, you know, in college. I was quite good at it."

He picked up a cane that had been leaning on the arm of the bench. "These days, I need this to walk, need these to read." He reached in another pocket and pulled out a glasses case. "They insist we drink some kind of obnoxious milkshake in a little bottle to keep our strength up, and they bring in crowds of gangly adolescents to sing things at us, usually off key."

Abruptly, he turned his face toward me. His thick white eyebrows were knotted in concern. "I mean no offense to your students, my dear."

"None taken. It's true that not all my students can carry a tune."

We sat in companionable silence for a while longer.

I prayed.

Finally, he said, "I found him, you know. My son. I hadn't wanted to disturb him that morning, because he often liked to sleep later than I. We share—shared—a two-bedroom suite, you see. I waited for him at breakfast, but he never came. His dementia had been intermittent so far, but it was getting worse by the day. I thought he might have become confused, lost his way to the dining room, so I went to check."

He cleared his throat. "When I looked into his room, it was . . . " he drew a deep, shuddering breath " . . . sheer chaos, the mattress pulled off the bed, the sheets everywhere, and blood . . . " He stopped and closed his eyes, overcome by the memory.

"Oh, my. I'm so sorry."

He patted my hand and continued, his eyes closed, "I just stood there in the middle of the room, staring, for the longest time. I don't know why I decided to look in the closet, but he was lying on the floor—on top of his shoes—wrapped in the quilt my wife made for him . . . when . . . when he went off to college. It had little houses on it, but you couldn't tell that for all the—" He gestured with his hand, which trembled. "You know, I was in the Navy in the Korean War and saw every kind of horror, but finding . . . "

I patted his back. "Mr. Channing, you don't have to talk about this anymore."

He looked at me as though suddenly remembering I was there. "Oh, I'm sorry, my dear. This is disturbing you. It's just that you have such a . . . sympathetic presence. You know, the police kept saying 'the victim' when they questioned me. Finally I said, 'I'm not speaking another word if you continue to call him that. He was my boy, my Conner.' We were going to grow old together, here."

Apparently realizing the irony of his words, he smiled slightly. "Well, he was going to catch up with me, so to speak."

"Mr. Channing, do you feel safe here now?" I asked.

I didn't know what I could do about it if he didn't, but I had to ask. The murderer was still out there.

"My dear young woman, weren't you listening to what I said earlier? Perhaps I didn't make myself clear." The stern voice made me feel as if I was one of his students. "As St. Paul said, 'To live is Christ and to die is gain.' That's me! I win, either way, you see?"

"Oh, but—"

He held up a restraining hand. "St. Paul also said not to become involved in foolish, useless arguments. That's my own translation, of course."

"I understand."

He reached for his cane and leaned on it heavily to rise to his feet. "It's beautiful out here, but I feel the need of a nap coming on. Will you walk inside with me?"

"Of course."

He took my arm when I offered it. As we walked he pointed out the various flowers and shrubs; clearly trying to change the subject.

"That bush there will be blooming soon. They're my favorite," he said pointing as we reached the back entrance. "Gardenias."

"Because of the fragrance?" The doors opened for us automatically.

He nodded. "And they were my wife's favorite."

Through the second automatic door, we entered a wide hallway bustling with staff, people using walkers, and one tall man, apparently making a delivery, his face concealed behind a large, beautiful floral arrangement. When he stepped to the nearby desk and set down the flowers, I recognized him.

Florist Chuck Nathan waited with his huge burden, while the woman behind the counter signed something on his clipboard. The man really was a historically accurate throwback to the days of Woodstock.

"Why, hello, there."

He glanced up and did a subtle double take at me over the tops of his dark glasses, which were still affixed in the middle with green tape. Retrieving the paperwork, he pushed the glasses up his nose and turned to me.

"Miss Prentice, what are you doing here?"

I didn't bother to correct him. I had been single so long in this town that people still called me by my maiden name.

I nodded at my companion. "Just visiting."

Chuck followed us as we moved down the hall. "Did you hear about what happened—the murder right down the hall from here?" he asked eagerly.

He might have been shocked by the crime, but it was hard to tell. The impenetrable lenses of his sunglasses gave him a blank, dead expression.

"They said maybe a break-in," he went on, "The guy must have interrupted a burglar or something. Makes you wonder."

"It does, indeed," agreed Mr. Channing sadly. He stopped walking. "Here's where they've put me for the present. My own suite is still festooned in yellow police tape, with the constabulary doing what they usually do in these situations." He glanced at his watch. "Ah, there's just time for a power nap before lunch." He patted my arm. "You know, it has helped me to talk about this . . . thing. You've been good for me, Amelia Dickensen. Please come again."

"I will." I couldn't stop tears filling my eyes.

"It will also give me a certain cachet to have such an attractive younger woman visit me," he added with just a trace of a twinkle before he closed the door of his room.

"You know who that was?" I turned around and found myself standing alone.

Chuck Nathan had clearly lost interest in the conversation and had gone on ahead. The man was socially awkward, to say the least. *One thing is true, though,* I thought as I passed the stunning arrangement standing proudly on a table near the desk. *Chuck knows his flowers.*

I walked through the automatic doors and found myself standing on the walkway next to the little rock garden in the front of the building, thoughtfully gazing—appropriately enough—at the blue gazing ball. I could see the leaves of the nearby shrubs reflected in the shiny surface and I stepped forward to see the distorted image of myself. Another form suddenly appeared beside mine, and I jumped.

"Oh! You scared me!'

Gil looked grim. "Sorry about that, but *scary* is the word, all right. This is a terrible business. Hey, I thought you were going to wait in the car. After what all happened out here, I was a little worried."

"I'm sorry. I just got bored."

He took my arm and headed for the parking lot. "Come on. Let's get going. I need to stop at the bank."

"For?"

"For . . . some cash."

"For?"

He had the grace to look a bit sheepish as we approached the car. "For Renaud."

"Why are you paying him?"

"He's doing something for me," my husband mumbled.

"He's looking in those files, isn't he?"

He didn't answer.

"Gil, if those are confidential files, you could be getting him in trouble and yourself as well." I climbed in the passenger seat. "Is it even legal?"

He started up the engine. "There are differing schools of thought on that, Amelia, since the man is dead. Besides, I'd be foolish to neglect this opportunity. A big story like this has the potential to put the paper back in the black. There's lots of interest right now, so I need to keep on it. This thing could go international! One of the local TV stations is already here. And, hey, to prove my point here come more of the ravening hordes!"

Turning into the parking lot of Sunset Bluffs was a large colorful van with the call letters of a well-known network and the face of a famous TV news personality on the side. They passed us at a rapid speed.

Gil turned the car onto the highway. "If I can get this exclusive, honey, it'll make a big difference. It'll help stop the hemorrhaging at the paper."

"Hemorrhaging! Are things really that bad? I had no idea." There was a hollow feeling in my stomach that had nothing to do with the fact that it was almost lunchtime.

He reached over and took my hand. "Yes. They're bad. But don't worry. I have plenty of possible avenues to keep the ship from sinking."

"You're mixing your metaphors," I pointed out absently as I watched the beautiful, pale green, early spring scenery fly by. Though it was beautiful, it did nothing to relieve my nagging fear.

We drove in silence for a while. I prayed.

An idea struck me. "I could go back to full-time teaching. I miss it."

He smiled a little. "That's one of my possible avenues, but it would be a bit further on down the road. Hey, how's that metaphor?"

"Not too bad."

He looked over at me. "You hungry? I'm hungry. Let's stop at Fritzi's. Would a Michigan and a chocolate shake cheer you up? Or does the idea still sound nauseating?"

"Oh, Gil, I'm not pregnant any more. It sounds wonderful."

The North Country's particular delicacy—a hot dog with a delicious, spicy sauce—would definitely go a long way toward lifting my spirits.

Gil signaled for the turn heading toward town. He glanced my way and said sternly, "I'm not sharing my fries, though. You always steal my fries. You get your own order."

# Chapter | Ten

After we gorged ourselves at Fritzi's, Gil dropped me off at Chez Prentice. I entered the big old familiar front door to find Etienne pacing back and forth in the entry way, talking on his cellphone. From his tone, I could tell he was not enjoying himself.

"When? But you told me tomorrow! All is in readiness! It must be done by tomorrow, or it will—" He paused, listening and wiping perspiration from his brow with the back of his hand. "Yes, yes, I know what the contract says, but you said it would probably be early. Yes, I know what *probably* means. I speak English. But now you say—" He paused in mid sentence. His expression brightened as he said, "But perhaps you would make the extra effort for the extra fee, *hein?*"

He listened for a time, nodding, "*Oui, je sais.* Yes, all right. If you bring the grass by tomorrow morning, I will add, oh, say, four percent." He frowned. "*Non!* Four! *D'accord.* Yes, I will be waiting. Remember, the deadline for this bonus is noon tomorrow." He tapped the screen of his telephone and muttered an oath in French.

"Problem, Etienne?" I set down the bulging bag I'd brought from the house.

He shrugged. "Not if you pay extra." He rubbed his finger-tips together in the universal gesture meaning money.

"I heard you say grass. Does that mean the lawn? I don't like the way it looks right now, but surely we could wait a couple of days. Why are you really willing to pay extra for them to bring it early?"

He blinked. "Did you not 'ear? Did Marie not tell you? Ah, yes, you were gone this morning with your 'usband."

"Tell me what?"

He ran a well-manicured hand over his handsome features and sighed. "This wedding woman, this 'Uff person, she invited some people from 'er *société* of planners of weddings to tour Chez Prentice. It is a great opportunity, but they are coming tomorrow afternoon. Hester and Marie, they are next to each other with—"

"Do you mean beside themselves?"

"*Oui*, that is it. They are very busy, making everything ready." He waved his arms vaguely as he headed for the B&B office.

A thought struck me. "But where's Janet?"

He frowned. "I don't know. I—"

I didn't wait for any more. I ran into the kitchen, where Hester was running an iron over a pillowcase.

"Where's the baby?"

Calmly, she propped the iron on its end and laid the pillowcase on top of a stack of freshly-ironed ones. "Don't worry, Marie has her out in the yard. They're picking flowers or something." She jerked her head in the direction of the back door.

Before I left the room, I stopped and said, "Since when do we iron our pillowcases?"

Hester pulled another one out of the laundry basket. "Since we got all the wedding people coming. Thank goodness I don't have to do the sheets too. They don't show when the bed's made up."

Though I had always made beds by pulling the bedspread over the pillows, Marie and Etienne had introduced a more trendy method with the pillows on top. I had to admit, it did look like a magazine illustration.

I smiled. "I thought you said the place was ready for anybody, any time."

She unplugged the iron and wound up the cord. "Etienne said they might wear white gloves to go over the furniture for dust. Can you figure that?" She folded up the ironing board and hung it on hooks in the laundry room that had once been a pantry.

"No, I can't." *No wonder Etienne was so nervous.*

I opened the back door and paused for a moment, dazzled again by the sight. Spring had made progress here in the past few days: Flowers lined the flagstone path, and the large planters standing guard on either side of the gazebo in the back corner contained miniature crabapple trees which would soon be bursting with glorious scarlet blossoms. There were lilies of the valley and tiny violets just beginning to peek from under the lacy white wrought iron bench that circled the huge maple, but no human forms could be seen.

"Marie? Janet? Where are you?"

All at once, I heard a cry I instantly recognized: that of my offspring in a state of anger or frustration. "Come on, baby," Marie said, coming around from behind the gazebo with said child in her arms, kicking and flailing.

Quickly, Marie walked along the path and thrust the child into my embrace. It didn't help matters very much. Janet was clearly furious. It was then I noticed that both of them wore dirty smudges all over.

"What were you doing back there?" I asked, using my sleeve in an attempt to wipe dirt off the baby's tear-dampened face. She continued to wail.

Marie wore an apron and gardening gloves. She put her hands on her hips and looked back over her shoulder. "Well, I was planting some flowers, and this one—" she nodded toward Janet with a fond expression "—was making mud pies."

Janet hiccoughed and stopped crying. She laid her head on my shoulder and sighed.

"Making a mess, you mean. Marie, what were you thinking, letting her play in the dirt like that? I've already had to stop her from eating it."

Marie pulled off her gloves. "Don't worry, Amelia, she was having a great time. Besides, my maman always said you had to eat a peck of dirt before you grew up. Didn't anybody tell you that? That's why she's so mad, you see. She didn't want to stop playing."

I looked at the child in my arms. She had calmed down and was already twisting her body and leaning away, hinting that she wanted me to put her down. "I can't say that I agree with your grandmother, Marie, but she doesn't seem any worse for the experience."

In fact, Janet was clearly eager to return to gardening, but I had other plans. I brushed off her head. "Look, it even got in her hair. Time for a bath."

The word *bath* sent the baby into a frenzy of joy. "Baf!" She clapped her hands in delight. She did love her bath.

Marie picked up the empty plastic pots that had contained the flowers and headed for the back steps. "I need a bath, too, but I'll have to hurry because I promised to help make crumpets for our company tomorrow. I made some lemon curd this morning. We're going to offer them an afternoon cream tea," she announced proudly.

"Sounds delicious."

Our grimy little group proceeded up the back steps, across the screened porch and into the kitchen, where Hester chuckled at our appearance while polishing a cut-glass tumbler.

The countertops were filled with all the B&B's best glassware, inverted on dishtowels.

I paused in the middle of the room. "Aren't you both going to a lot of trouble for these people?"

Hester finished with one glass and reached for another. "Are you kidding? If they like us, Etienne says we'll get twice the business we do now. They might even put us in a magazine article or something." She looked over at me and the wriggling baby. "You look kinda down. Say, did you and Gil go to that murder place? That would bring anybody down."

She reached into a large jar on the counter and handed Janet a graham cracker. "Here, pumpkin."

"We did, and I met the victim's father, poor man."

"No wonder you look so sad. How was he? He's pretty old, isn't he?" She gestured toward the cookie jar. "Want one?"

I shook my head. "He's in his nineties, I believe; delicate physically, but very sharp mentally."

Hester nibbled the corner of her own cracker. "Well, I'd be going bat crazy, wondering if the murderer was still hanging around and stuff! Hey, isn't it odd: Marie and me were just saying there could be that—what's his name?—murderer guy might be in the North Country, remember?"

I shuddered. "I remember."

She reached over and brushed a few crumbs of soil from the baby's hair. "Well, what d'ya think? Was it him?"

"I don't know, Hester. Probably not." I hefted the baby on my hip and headed for the door. "Time for your bath, sweetie."

Janet wiggled happily and dropped what remained of her soggy cracker on the floor.

Stooping to pick it up, Hester said, "Well, it gives me the creeps. I think we all oughta be real careful."

"Good advice."

Though it's a fruitless exercise, over and over I've wondered if there was anything we could have done to prevent the tragedy that lay ahead.

Probably not.

## Chapter | Eleven

Shortly after lunch the next day, I made a phone call. "Hugh Channing's room, please," I said to the person who answered the phone at Sunset Bluffs.

"He's in the library right now," the woman told me. "You want me to ring the phone in there?" She didn't wait for an answer.

"Library." I knew right away it was Mr. Channing. His voice, deep and clear, belied his age.

"It's Amelia Prentice. Do you remember me? We met out on the back lawn yesterday?"

"Don't worry, my dear, my memory is as good as ever. Of course I remember you. How may I be of service?"

He'd been in my thoughts ever since we met. I'd liked him right away, yet he made me feel strangely uneasy. Perhaps it was that he was so sanguine about the possibility of his own death. More likely it was because he reminded me of my late father.

"I wanted to invite you out to lunch tomorrow," I blurted without preamble. "I'm not sure what kind of food you like. Danny's Diner is fun for nostalgia and home cooking. Ernie's is great if you like Italian food, or the Lion's Roar is—"

He interrupted my babbling. "Here's an alternate idea: You dine here. Our meals are quite good and served restaurant style, and it would please me no end if you would be my guest."

"Having lunch with you there sounds very nice. Would you mind if I brought my daughter?"

"What a charming idea! Everyone here loves having small children visit. Oh, I'm so pleased."

"Until tomorrow, then," I said.

"Noon sharp. I'll meet you in the lobby of the Bluffs House."

"The big white house in the front?"

"That's the one. The annex in back is only residential suites. Bluffs House contains our amenities on the lower two floors: the dining room, the library, the exercise room and everything else," he explained.

"We'll be there."

The shrill, grating shriek of the seldom-used doorbell shattered the calm of the afternoon. Mother had always planned to have that doorbell replaced with something more genteel even after my father died, but its importance faded with the rapid progression of her terminal cancer.

Janet, jarred out of her mid-afternoon nap, echoed with her own expression of disapproval.

I picked her up. "Sorry, honey. It's just Uncle Etienne and Aunt Marie doing their thing."

Baby in arms, I strolled out of our room and stood on the broad second floor landing, looking over the railing at the activity below.

"They're here!" Marie stage-whispered to Hester. As she hurried back into the kitchen, I heard her say, "Etienne, they're here! Thank goodness the grass got put in!"

Etienne emerged, pulling on his suit jacket. "Quick! Get rid of that dust mop! I don't care where you put it, just hide it!"

"Keep your hair on," Hester snapped. "I'll take care of it."

"Wait in the office," he instructed his wife.

Brushing off the sleeve of his jacket, he straightened his shoulders and walked slowly across the foyer to the front door. Though the action was now out of my line of sight, I heard the familiar jingle of the doorknob and the squeak of the hinges as the big old wooden portal swung open.

"*Bienvenue!* Welcome to Chez Prentice!"

A familiar voice answered. It was Callie Huff, easily recognizable by her pronounced downstate accent. "Thank you, thank you! Come on in, everyone."

I heard the pleased murmur and footfalls of a herd of half-a-dozen people.

There was a pause while each member of the society was introduced. Not including Callie, there were two wedding planners from Lake Placid, three from Vermont and one from Montreal, five women and one man. The names came and went in my memory.

From my vantage point, I could only see the tops of the visitors' heads as they followed Etienne, single-file, across the foyer and into the office, murmuring among themselves.

A small frisson of anxiety ran down my spine. *Will they like us?*

In response, Janet squirmed to be let down. I bounced her on my hip. "Not out here, sweetie." Ever since the baby had become ambulatory, the steep old-fashioned staircase appeared more threatening than elegant in my eyes.

We retired to our room, where I had moved all the B&B's decorative knick-knacks to the top shelf of the antique wardrobe. It was impossible to totally baby-proof the place, however. Even after my many precautions, there were still the sharp corners of the side table next to the velvet-upholstered Victorian chairs. And those two low, wine-colored chairs, with their bandy legs and claw feet, were adorned with a gold-colored braid trim that must have looked appetizing to a teething child, because I'd found several damp patches of spit on it.

Immediately upon being released, the baby headed for one of the chairs, pulled herself to a standing position and fastened her drooling mouth not on the trim this time, but on the rounded end of the armrest.

With a sigh, I scooped her up and set her down in the travel playpen in the corner.

She protested slightly, but decided to make the best of things, rummaging around until she found her favorite chew toy, the stuffed rabbit she called Dab.

I busied myself sorting out the clothes that Hester had kindly run through the laundry for me, folding socks and underwear and placing them in the dresser drawers.

Our brief quietude was interrupted by voices in the hall and a rap on the door. "Amelia? Can we come in?" Etienne asked.

The knock had startled Janet, who began to wail in protest. "Just a second!" I called.

Surprised and slightly frantic, I hastily slid the loaded laundry basket into the bathroom and noticed the unpleasant odor emanating from the diaper disposal system. Making a swipe with the large can of air freshener, I sprayed the room and managed to drop the can, which rolled out of the bathroom and underneath the bed.

*Leave it, Amelia.*

The baby was still expressing her unhappiness.

I hurried to the door, but not before inhaling a lungful of the lingering air freshener. Coughing, I opened it to Etienne, standing with a crowd of couture-dressed women and one elegantly turned-out man. I hurried over and extracted Janet from her prison. This pleased her and she stopped bawling.

"Amelia, I'd like to show them your room, *s'il vous plait.*"

I nodded.

Etienne turned back to the group. "Come right in. This is the Ausable Suite, not so large as the Grand Isle Suite down the 'all, but with the same amenities."

The wedding planners filed in slowly, sweeping the room with their eyes, their faces blank.

Etienne nodded my way. "Allow me to introduce our partner in business, Amelia Prentice-Dickensen," he said, unnecessarily hyphenating my name.

He went on, "Chez Prentice has been the 'istoric 'ome of her family for a century."

I had a strange urge to curtsey, but restrained myself.

"And this is baby Janet."

My child stared wide-eyed at the strange people. One of the visitors waved wiggly fingers at her, but she maintained her deadpan expression.

Etienne began to move towards the bathroom.

Hastily, I hurried to close the door. I was too late. "You'll notice that every suite 'as its own private bath," he said, stepping in the tiny room, then turning around quickly when he caught a whiff of *eau de diaper*. "Ah, well, the bathrooms, they're all the same," he said quickly and closed the door.

He gestured to the ceiling. "You'll notice the original crown molding as well as the period wallpaper and furnishings," he continued. Clearly, Marie wasn't the only one who had committed the promotional brochure to memory.

"May I?" the lone male in the group requested, not waiting for an answer. He hoisted himself up onto the high, old-fashioned canopy bed and sat.

I was so grateful that I had thought to make up that bed—only a few minutes before.

"That quilt was made by a local woman," I pointed out as he bounced a little. "You see the small applique picture of Ausable Chasm there in the center?" I leaned around the man and pointed. "By this time next year, we'll have a theme quilt for every room," I added, picturing Hester as I first met her, with a huge quilting hoop in her lap, surrounded by stacks of brightly colored fabric squares. "They'll all be hand-pieced and hand-stitched. Works of art, really."

This sent a please ripple of approval through the ladies. The man hopped down.

"*Et maintenant*, you must see the garden," Etienne said and shepherded the group out the door. "*Merci*, Amelia," he said, darting his eyes toward the bathroom and frowning at me.

I smiled and held out a double thumbs-up.

He arched his eyebrows and closed the door.

"How did it go?" I asked Etienne and Marie that evening at dinner.

They both spoke at once.

"Wonderful!" said Etienne.

"We don't know," said Marie, adding, "They'll let us know if they're going to put us in their directory."

"*Que Dieu t'entende*," Etienne said. "God willing."

# Chapter | Twelve

J anet was sleeping in her convertible car seat as I pulled Etienne's borrowed station wagon into the parking lot at Sunset Bluffs for our lunch date with Hugh Channing. A large police van was parked there, but I didn't see any of the yellow tape that had been there before. Perhaps they had finished their investigation. I was even more pleased to notice that all signs of the news media had disappeared.

"You two moving in?" a smiling senior with violet-blue hair asked me as we passed each other on the walkway to the Bluffs House.

I smiled back at her. The jest was apt. On one shoulder, I carried a designated tote equipped with a week's worth of disposable diapers, two clean baby bottles, a bottle of spring water, three jars of baby food, a miniature spoon, a bib, wipes, and, just in case, a complete change of clothing for Janet.

On the other shoulder was my equally copious purse with the myriad things I always carried, wallet, comb, cosmetics case, tissues, breath mints, mirror, nail file, and now, in light of my motherhood, a compact brag book full of photos of my offspring—and a stain stick. Also, just in case.

Furthermore, I pushed a huge convertible baby stroller,

complete with a small collapsible awning, in which was slumbering said baby.

Not for the first time, I mentally blessed whoever had arranged for wheelchair ramps. Those who couldn't manage the steps weren't the only ones who appreciated the smooth, gentle slope up to the front porch.

Inside, the lobby was every bit as elegant as I'd imagined. A chandelier graced the ceiling. There were rich Victorian-patterned wallpaper and various furniture pieces, which appeared to be valuable antiques. Only a large modern bulletin board on one wall, covered with announcements, and a reception desk indicated that this wasn't a wealthy family's mansion.

"Ah, here you are!" Hugh Channing advanced slowly to meet us, making full use of his cane.

He waited as I signed in. A cheerful woman in a smock gave me a visitor's nametag that I stuck to my blouse lapel, then Hugh beckoned me to follow. The hall near the wide, double-door entrance to the dining room resembled a parking lot, with more than a dozen rolling walker contraptions waiting patiently for their owners to finish their meal.

I gestured toward them. "This stroller. Should I leave it outside?"

"Certainly not. Come along, Amelia."

He took the lead and walked slowly but confidently into the room as I rolled along behind. Heads turned. Our progress was intently watched. I smiled at random to show the natives that I came in peace.

The dining room was beautifully appointed, with a white linen tablecloth, napkins, and a small vase of flowers on each table. Tall maroon drapes framed a row of old-fashioned ceiling-high windows along one wall, where diners could enjoy a view of the lake in all its moods. Today, the waves sparkled in the sunshine.

Carefully navigating between the tables, I followed Mr. Channing to a choice spot by one window.

"Here you go, Sport," a short and pretty pink-uniformed waitress with a ponytail pouf of unruly brown waves approached us and pulled out a chair for the old man. "Push that wagon around here, ma'am," she said to me, pointing at the stroller. "And park yourself over there."

I complied.

As he settled in his seat, Mr. Channing said, "Amelia Dickensen, I'd like you to meet Bing Bailey."

"Hi-yah." Bing nodded and narrowed her large green eyes. "Before you say anything, my real name is Beryl, but I hate it, so I'm Bing—no relation to Crosby." Her gesture indicated her name tag. Abruptly, she pulled a small pad and pencil from her pocket and turned to Mr. Channing. "So what'll it be, Bud? The usual fruit plate?"

"Yes, the smaller luncheon size, but," Mr. Channing frowned and reached for a printed card propped against the salt and pepper shakers, "perhaps Mrs. Dickensen would like a few moments to consult the menu."

"The fruit plate will be fine," I said.

"And iced tea to drink," he added with a glance at my nod.

Bing-not-Beryl saluted with the pencil and turned on her sneakered heel.

Mr. Channing chuckled noiselessly. "She's quite something, isn't she? Like a character straight out of a Damon Runyon story."

I watched the little woman charge across the dining room and burst through the swinging doors of the kitchen at the far end. "I like her."

"So do I," he whispered as he followed my gaze. "It might not surprise you to learn that she's quite the *femme fatale* around here, at least among the staff." He leaned forward and peered down at Janet in her stroller. "About the infant: Doesn't she need to eat something?"

"She had a big meal right before we left. I think we'll let her sleep some more." I looked carefully at the old man's face. "Mr. Channing, how are you doing?"

"Oh, call me Hugh, please."

"Uh—Hugh," I said, hesitating.

He leaned back. "And as to your question, I am doing fairly well, considering that I spent the past two days on the library computer, planning my son's funeral. I even picked out a casket online. Amazing what one can do on a computer."

"Oh, my. When is it to be?"

He sighed. "The police haven't released him to the funeral home yet, but they assure me it will be soon. Sergeant O'Brien tells me it might be tomorrow or the next day."

"This all must be so difficult for you."

He nodded. "Yes. But let us move on to more cheerful subjects: What is your little girl's name?"

I lifted the edge of the stroller canopy and smiled fondly at her. "Janet Lillian Dickensen, after my mother and my good friend."

"I always think it's a good idea to name a child for someone. Some even believe a name imbues the child with the characteristics of the person for whom she is named."

He hadn't ended the sentence with a preposition, as most would. Here, indeed, was a kindred spirit.

I smiled. "In that case, she'll be one confused little girl. If there were ever two people more polar opposites than Lily Burns and my mother, I wouldn't know them."

"How so?" He opened his napkin and laid it in his lap.

I did too. "Well, my mother was a quiet person, quite down to earth. She was tenderhearted, too, but painfully honest, sometimes."

"And your friend Lily was not?"

"Lily's still very much alive. No, I don't mean she's not kind. Lily can be very tenderhearted," I said, remembering the loving care she lavished on her new kitten and the way she doted on Janet. "And when it comes to being painfully honest, I think Lily McKendrick Burns probably wrote the book."

He smiled gently. "So are you truly sure they're not alike?"

"Now that I think about it, perhaps they are." I looked over at him. "Why, I do believe you used the Socratic method on me, sir, asking questions like that."

"So I did. Sorry, my dear. Force of habit, I suppose. Ah, here we are."

Bing appeared at the table carrying a platter of food in each hand. "Eat hearty, folks," she said, gently setting down our orders before us.

"So this is the smaller luncheon size?" I asked.

Hugh murmured, "Probably not, if experience is any teacher."

They were large dinner plates, and virtually every inch was covered with artfully arranged fruit and cheese, including strawberries, blueberries, sliced peaches, sliced pears, and apples on a bed of fresh lettuce. As I eyed my huge meal with bewilderment, Bing promptly returned bearing a small pitcher and a basket.

"Your salad dressing and your bread. Butter's in the basket." She pointed at my new friend. "I want you to clean your plate, young man."

"Don't patronize me, young woman!"

Unfazed, she walked away, saying over her shoulder. "You heard me, kiddo. That's an order!"

He sighed. "I'm sorry I reacted so sharply. The girl means well. She's been worried about my appetite. It has not been very good lately. Will you say grace, Amelia?"

I did, and we concentrated on our meal for a few minutes while the sound of clinking silverware, liquid pouring, and murmured conversation drowned out the piped-in music.

Presently, Bing appeared at Hugh's elbow and pointed at the half-full plate. "Look here, Doc, you need to at least eat your cheese. It's good for your bones." He looked up at her frostily and she shrugged. "Okay. Hey, Jack," she said over her shoulder. "Pick up the plates here, okay?"

A tall man, all in white, covered by an ankle-length apron and pushing a rolling tray, hastened to collect our used dishes. This unflattering getup—which included a hairnet—didn't disguise his broad shoulders and friendly gray eyes. He winked at Bing.

She pretended not to notice and tilted her head. "Okay, dessert. Folks, I got apple pie, butterscotch pudding, or sugar-free Jello. Take your choice."

"The pie, of course, for both of us. And coffee too. Is that all right, Amelia?"

I nodded agreement, but my attention was on Jack the busboy, who appeared to be waiting for Bing to head back to the kitchen. When she did, he fell into step beside her and bent down to say something in her ear.

She shook her head, but we heard her giggle as she pushed her way through the kitchen's swinging doors. Jack shrugged, turned back, and resumed his clearing duties at some empty tables.

Hugh watched them too. "As I said, she is quite the *femme fatale*. And that new fellow Jack has set a few hearts a-flutter too. You should have seen the reaction at karaoke night—you know, with the microphone and the lyrics on the screen?— when he sang a song about exes in Texas. Quite a good imitation of the original singer, they tell me." He leaned over toward the stroller. "How is your little one doing?"

I pulled back the folding canopy. "She's still wiped out. I wish she'd sleep like this at night."

Hugh smiled. "Very much like my son at this age. It was admittedly a long time ago, but I can remember that at first my poor wife was exhausted all the time. Our boy turned out well, though." A proud smile faded into a faraway melancholy expression. "He really did, you know, though heaven knows we had our differences. Oh, thank you." He leaned back to allow Bing to place his pie and coffee cup before him.

"This time, finish every bite, you understand?" she said as she placed a carafe of coffee in the middle of the table and set down my slice of pie.

"Begone, impudent child!" the old man grumbled.

Bing patted the top of his head and flounced away.

Hugh sighed again, rolled his eyes and stirred cream into his coffee.

I picked up the thread of the conversation. "You said you had differences, but apparently, they were resolved when he came to live here." I reached for the cream.

"In a manner of speaking, they were. That is, when we knew he was getting sick, of course, any rifts were forgiven and forgotten." Hugh put down his spoon and slowly shook his large white head. "Well, perhaps not totally forgotten. I truly regret the harsh words between us in the past, but I felt so strongly about it at the time."

I kept my own counsel and sipped my coffee. Lily Burns would have boldly asked what the disagreement was.

He continued, even without my prompting. "I suppose if we hadn't been in the same profession, it wouldn't have mattered so much. At first, I was extremely pleased that he wanted to follow in my footsteps. He made excellent grades in law school and graduated near the top of his class. I nursed hopes of his becoming a district attorney in our home county downstate, but apparently he felt differently called."

"What did he do instead, corporate law?"

Hugh's shaggy brows lifted. "Oh, no. Would that he had, my dear. No, he became a defense attorney." He cut off a bite of pie with his fork.

"Isn't that a good thing?"

I followed suit. It really was excellent pie, not too sweet. I hated it when apple pie was too sweet.

Hugh chewed and swallowed. "Certainly. It's how our system works, but as time went by, I became more and more dismayed at the clients he took on: corrupt politicians, embezzling businessmen, even an alleged drug dealer—a wealthy one, of course. I know what you're going to say," he said, raising his hand defensively. "'Everyone is innocent until proven guilty and entitled to a vigorous defense.'"

That hadn't occurred to me, but I nodded and let him continue.

"But over time, you see, he seemed to change, become more and more enamored of the money and power and less of true justice. My wife and I talked about it frequently, and she begged me to say nothing for the sake of family harmony. I forbore to speak of it until after she died, but as time went by,

Conner seemed to become even worse, and I eventually felt I must say something. As you might expect, it did not go well. Finally one day we had a huge, rancorous argument and he left, saying he was going to move as far away from me as he could." He sighed and put down his fork. "He did. California, of all places."

"I've heard it's a beautiful state, with the climate and everything." My effort at lightening the mood sounded banal, even to me.

"So rumor has it. I didn't find it so. Not long after arriving, Conner became engaged to a socialite, and out of regard for my wife's longing for family unity, I flew out to attend the wedding. It proved to be a mistake. I didn't take to his friends—or his new wife—at all. And clearly, they didn't take to me. I left immediately after the ceremony, and we never spoke until recently, when I realized what was happening to him." He finished the last bite of pie and hid his growing emotion behind his coffee cup. "His wife was long gone, of course. Divorce."

"I'm so sorry, Hugh."

"We had become resigned, the two of us, to the future and the prospect of Conner's slow decline, but then, this . . . horror." He shook his head and stared off into space.

We were both silent; both poised as if waiting for the other to speak. As before, I prayed.

Finally Hugh pulled the usual huge white handkerchief from his jacket pocket and dabbed his eyes. "No, don't be sorry. I'm sorry. Here I am in such delightful company and I become maudlin." He blew his nose and straightened his shoulders. "I admit, it has been hard, but one must keep going."

I was reminded of Marie LeBow's brave way of coping with her grief. "That's true." In an effort to change the subject, I indicated his handkerchief. "What an elegant monogram."

He smiled. "It is rather nice, isn't it?" He folded it carefully before replacing it in his pocket. "This is a little luxury I've permitted myself over the years. I generally have half-a-dozen on my person at any given time." He patted the pocket and stood. "Now, might I tempt you to take a walk with me around the grounds? The gardening staff has just planted some new flowering plants—I saw that florist friend of yours deliver them. I could give you a tour."

"It sounds lovely, but I need to be going. I promised I'd help out at the B&B this afternoon." I began gathering up my purse and diaper bag.

"Oh, yes, I've heard about your enterprise and admire it so much."

"If you like, I could bring you over for a visit one day—for brunch, perhaps?"

"Oh, yes, please. When?" he asked eagerly.

I had only just thought of it, so it took me a few seconds to process. "The day after tomorrow? I could pick you up around ten."

"Excellent!"

He accompanied me to the door and as I drove out of the parking lot, I saw him walking around the back of the building, limping a little, but making good use of his cane.

# Chapter | Thirteen

On the appointed morning of the visit, the telephone rang just as I was about to leave the B&B.

"Amelia?" Hugh's voice was strong and assertive. "I wanted to catch you before you left. There's no need to come out here to pick me up. I have arranged for transport for myself and should arrive there within the hour. Goodbye."

"But how, and—" I began, but too late.

As I hung my coat back up, I decided that it was a relief. I wasn't eager to go out and about today. The delightful spring weather of a few days ago had given way to heavy, threatening clouds. I wondered just what arrangements Hugh had made.

My answer arrived about forty minutes later in the form of a small white transit bus pulling up in front of Chez Prentice. On the side in colorful but tasteful lettering were the words "Sunset Bluffs." From the front porch, I could see several passengers through the windows. The door opened and a familiar figure bounded down the steps.

A chill, driving rain had begun minutes before. As I hurried down the walk with an unfurled umbrella, I recognized Gil's secret source, Jess Renaud, standing stoically at the bus entrance. He glanced my way, gave a tiny shake of his head and frowned. The shake was fraught with meaning.

His expression said, *You don't recognize me.*

My answering shrug replied, *Oh, whatever. That's between you and my husband.*

Pulling my cardigan tighter against the surprisingly cold wind, I asked him in a bland tone, "Is Mr. Channing in there?" He nodded and reached out a hand to the white-haired gentleman descending the steps.

"Have a good 'un, Mr. Channing," a clear tenor voice called from within the bus. It was Jack, the tall lothario from the Sunset Bluffs dining room, sitting in the driver's seat.

Once Hugh's feet were firmly on the ground, Renaud hopped back aboard and the door folded closed. The bus began to pull away from the curb.

"Nice young fellows," Hugh remarked, gesturing toward the departing vehicle. "They were happy to give me a lift. They're taking the others to the mall."

"Welcome to Chez Prentice," I said, and gave him my arm.

"What on earth?" Hugh said, craning his head.

I followed his gaze. The bus had stopped abruptly and backed up a few feet.

The door unfolded itself again and Jess Renaud emerged once more, Hugh's cane in hand. "You forgot this." He loped over to us and handed it over, then returned to the bus.

Before the doors could close once more, Ev Holland, hunched a bit under a tiny umbrella with instrument case under his arm, walked briskly down the porch steps, along the front walk, and up to the white bus. As Hugh and I watched, he leaned in the open door and seemed to ask a question. Apparently, the response was not to his liking because he frowned, turned on his heel and began taking long strides down the sidewalk.

"A young man in a hurry," Hugh remarked as we reached the front porch.

"It's not feeling very spring-like out there today," I informed Hester, Marie, and Etienne after the proper introductions were made in the kitchen. I put my dripping umbrella on the back porch. "That rain is cold!"

"*Oui*, I know," my partner said, "I just 'ope we don't 'ave any more frost tomorrow morning. *Ma pauvre pelouse.*"

Hugh apparently understood French. "This weather could indeed be hard on your lawn. I heard a prediction on the radio before I left. They said we could be in for a bit of a cold snap."

Etienne sighed and turned to leave. "*Plus ça change, plus la meme chose,*" was his exit line, accompanied by one of those charming Gallic shrugs.

Hester crossed her arms and rolled her eyes. "What's he sayin' now?"

"The more things change, the more they stay the same," Hugh translated.

# Chapter | Fourteen

"Uh, oh, I think we're losin' your friend," Hester said as she refreshed everyone's coffee.

All eyes turned to the end of the dining table. Indeed, Hugh had sunk down in his chair and was leaning against the left arm. His chin was on his chest, and we heard a soft, ruffling snore.

"Worn out, bless him," Marie said.

Janet chose that moment to chirp out a baby song of her own composing, accompanying herself by pounding the tray of the high chair with a spoon.

The old gentleman stirred. "Oh, dear. Was I dozing? I am so sorry. It has become a habit of mine to drop off after a meal. Most embarrassing. Please forgive me."

Hester smiled. "Forget it. Y'know, there's a little spare bedroom at the back of the office. Bert uses it sometimes. You could finish your nap there."

"Yes, of course," I concurred.

I hadn't paid much attention when Etienne had first suggested putting a cot in the large closet that once served as a butler's pantry. "You never know," he'd said sagely, "when it might come in 'andy."

Hugh pushed back his chair and stood, reaching for his cane. "Well, if you don't mind, I accept. I'll be fine if I can just have a few more winks."

I escorted him gently into the office and the small chamber beyond, flicking on the light switch. The room contained a small cot and a little table with a lamp. It was made up with a pillow and sheets and there was a blanket neatly folded at the foot.

"Well, isn't this nice?" Hugh sat on the cot. "Thank you so much, my dear. I can take it from here." He rotated and placed his head on the pillow. "Turn out the light, will you?"

"Sweet dreams, Hugh," I whispered, and closed the door, feeling very motherly.

The rest of the household had gone about their business. In the kitchen, Etienne was at the table, bouncing Janet on his knee and singing something in French, while Ev looked on, smiling. Hester was clearing the table, while Marie followed her with a clipboard clutched to her chest, asking about needed B&B supplies.

From the top of the stairs, an unmistakable voice trilled, "Helloo! Oh, am I too late for brunch? I must have overslept."

We heard the clunk of heels on each step as she descended.

She appeared at the kitchen door and paused. It was Callie Huff, in full diva regalia: a much-layered pale pink tulle peignoir and dainty kitten-heeled mules with the requisite pink pom-poms.

Ev moved quickly away, across the hall and into the front parlor.

Callie swept into the kitchen, saying, "What a night. I couldn't sleep a wink, because somebody's baby would keep crying." She smiled and tilted her head accusingly at me. "I simply must have some coffee. Hester, dear, will you please?"

Hester leaned over and whispered to me. "Will you get a load of Her Highness? She hasn't been up before noon since she got here. She claims she couldn't sleep? It must've been the pea I put under her mattress."

I couldn't help myself. I snickered.

"What's more, she eats whenever she feels like it."

"It's part of the contract, but I wonder how often she's supposed to stay?" I whispered back.

"Who knows? Ask Marie."

"I must look a mess!" Callie declared, taking a seat at the table. She didn't mean it, of course. Her orange-red silken pageboy was perfectly smooth and her makeup flawless.

"Not at all," said Etienne gallantly.

None too gently, Hester plopped a mug down on the table and began pouring. "You gonna want some brunch?"

Callie waved her hand and fluttered her eyelashes. "Oh, no, I don't think I could eat a single bite." She took a delicate sip of coffee, pinkie extended.

Hester shrugged and continued bringing in the used brunch plates and platters from the dining room.

Callie said, "On second thought, is that bacon there? I

adore bacon. Maybe just a short rasher . . . and some toast and some of your lovely apple butter."

Hester set to work. I could read the set of her shoulders. She was not pleased.

"By the way," the wedding planner asked, "When I woke up earlier, I heard talking and looked out my window. Why was there a little bus out front?"

"The white one?" I asked, and responded to her nod while I put away the baby's high chair in the pantry. "It was the shuttle from Sunset Bluffs. They brought Hugh—Mr. Channing—here and were taking some other residents to the mall. Why do you ask?"

She waved her hand. "Oh, no reason, really. I thought I knew someone, but obviously I was wrong. It would have been the weirdest coincidence . . . " She took a sip of coffee.

Hester set down a plate with toast and bacon before Callie, accompanied by a jar of apple butter.

Callie frowned. "Oh, dear, this toast is cold. Would you fix me another piece?"

"Allll rightie," Hester said.

Shortly, a fresh slice of hot toast was placed before our guest.

"D'you think he's gonna want to finish this?" Hester asked, indicating the full coffee cup still sitting at Ev's place at the table.

Etienne leaned out the kitchen door. "That guy left a while ago. Just ran out of 'ere *sans parapluie*. He's going to get very wet, I think."

"I believe he had a final orchestra rehearsal," I commented. "The concert's tonight."

"I gotta get home," Hester announced to me as she removed her apron and hung it in the pantry. "Bert's gonna want his lunch, and with the cold front coming through this afternoon, I wanna remind him to bring in some firewood."

"Oh, I doubt you'll need much firewood," I said. "This is just one of those spring cool snaps."

Hester pulled on her raincoat and reached for her purse. "Maybe, but you know Bert. It's because of him being a Boy Scout when he was a kid. He's always prepared. Have a nice time with our guests," she added in a low voice, giving me a wink. She opened the back door and was gone.

I watched her open her umbrella and pick her way around the puddles to the driveway. "You were right, Etienne; it's really coming down out there. Isn't all this rain beneficial for our new front lawn?"

"So long as it doesn't freeze. The sod squares will put down roots more quickly. I will be saved much trouble."

I hefted Janet on my hip and proceeded to mount the staircase. She needed a diaper change, the perpetual chore of early motherhood.

I heard Callie's high-heeled mules clacking quickly after me.

"Oh, Mrs., um, Amelia," she called. "Just a second." She began walking up the stairs beside us. "You were out there at that Bluffs place the other day, weren't you?"

"Yes, having lunch with Mr. Channing."

"Did you happen to see that florist guy that was here the other day, what's-his-name?"

"Chuck Nathan? No, I didn't, not that second visit. He may have been there, but I didn't see him. Why?"

She frowned. "I was out there yesterday and they said I just missed him." We reached the top of the stairs. Callie Huff put her hand to her forehead. "I've been all over the place, trying to catch up with that character."

"I thought you said you were going to try other florists."

"Yeah, but I took a look at their stuff and it, well, it just wasn't up to my standards. Everybody says that Chuck Nathan's the best for flowers in this town."

"He is very talented."

"I stopped by his shop yesterday—by the way, what's with that gift shop, with all that lumpy souvenir pottery and those ugly knotty-pine tchotchkes? Do people really buy that stuff? I must admit, though, he's a DaVinci compared to the other florists around here." She sighed. "I guess I'll just have to work out a contract with his assistant if I can't catch up with the owner. It's just that I'm accustomed to dealing with top management, you know?"

I nodded. "I see." I just wanted to end this conversation before the baby's soggy diaper started irritating her bottom. Or leaking.

"By the way, do you have an umbrella I could use?" She paused and looked around. "Listen." The sound of a heavy rainstorm was all around us, beating on the windows, the roof, and the outside walls in a dull roar.

"I know Marie keeps a few in her office for guests to borrow." Etienne had only recently ordered the umbrellas, emblazoned with "Chez Prentice." I thought it an unnecessary expense at the time, but as usual, the Frenchman's business instincts were correct.

"That's good. I'll check there later." She glanced at her wristwatch. "Well, I'd better get dressed and head out." She disturbed her makeup enough to give me a quick, social smile. "I'm glad we had this little talk." She opened the door of her room and slipped inside.

I changed the baby and zipped her in a cozy footie suit. "It's rather cool in here," I explained to her and closed the drapes to the image of cold, driving rain.

Once she was fresh and clean, Janet's eyes began to droop, and she rolled over gratefully in her little travel bed when I laid her down.

Her drowsiness was contagious. I'd donned a sweater to keep the chill off. Fully dressed, I kicked off my shoes, climbed into the big bed and snuggled under the covers.

The sound of the rain slowed and faded and a kind of peaceful silence descended. I'd meant to read a few chapters of my current novel, but the letters blurred before my eyes, and I drifted off, cozy under the beautiful hand-made quilt.

# Chapter | Fifteen

A brisk knocking on the door woke us both. "Amelia! Amelia! Can I come in?"

I slid out of bed and opened the door. It was Marie, wearing a thick college sweatshirt over her nice dress.

All at once, I noticed something. "Marie, it's like a refrigerator in this room."

I picked up the drowsy baby and held her close. Even in the terrycloth footie, she was shivering. I pulled a baby blanket from the crib and wrapped it and my arms around her.

"What's happened?"

"Here's what—look!" Marie's eyes were wide. She walked over to the window and pulled back the drapes. "Snow!"

The dim room was suddenly bright. It was snowing, all right, snowing hard. In fact, it was impossible to see into the garden below. All was whirling whiteness.

I stared out the window, hypnotized. "When did this happen? I mean how? I mean—why is it so cold in here?"

Marie closed the drape and broke the spell. "It's 'cause the furnace isn't on. You know how slow the heat was comin' on over Christmas? We promised ourselves we'd get it fixed when the weather got warm. So Etienne had the furnace repairman in, and the guy said he had to order a new part and it would take a week to get here. Etienne told me yesterday that there's pieces of furnace insides in a neat little pile down there in the basement."

She sighed and headed for the door, "Oh yeah, your friend Mr. Channing woke up from his nap a little while ago. Come on downstairs."

"Let me change her first."

As I worked, I thought of Gil who had walked to the newspaper office, only six blocks away. I pulled more clothing on the baby, including a little cotton bonnet; not all that warm, but better than nothing.

I reached in a pocket for my cell phone and pressed Gil's number. There was no answer. The little screen showed that there was plenty of power in the phone, but the little bars indicating transmission were missing. There was no signal.

"Come on, sweetie." I scooped Janet up and was soon descending to the first floor. The air was palpably warmer.

"Oh, it feels so much better in here," I said, "positively toasty. Marie, I'm going to go in the office and call Gil on the house phone."

"Sorry, the line's dead. I already tried it. Ice on the wires, I bet."

The tight, anxious feeling that had plagued me earlier returned. *Oh, please protect him!* I prayed.

Hugh was seated at the table with a mug of cocoa and a plate of cookies before him. "Hello, ladies!" He had the blanket from the cot wrapped around his shoulders. "A bit brisk in here, isn't it? Mrs. LeBow has been more than kind. Won't you join me?"

I slid the high chair out of the pantry and buckled Janet in, tucking the baby blanket around her legs.

She quietly surveyed the room until her eyes lighted on the cookies, and she began making demands, accompanied by gestures that were clear in their meaning. "Coo! Coo!"

"I believe I can actually understand her. She wants one of these," Hugh said, smiling. He picked up a cookie. "May I give her one?"

"I bought some special cookies for her just the other day," I said. I walked to the pantry and swept my gaze over the shelves. "Marie, where is that box of Zwieback?"

Marie put more mugs on the table. "Oh, come on. That stuff is like sandpaper. Hester made these. They're healthy; there's applesauce in 'em. That's fruit. Let her have a cookie."

"Well, I guess one would be all right."

I leaned in to examine the treat in Hugh's hand. No frosting. I nodded.

With a flourish, Hugh bowed in his chair and handed over the treat to Janet, who grabbed it and immediately began sucking on it. We all watched as she reduced the thing to crumbs, which she gathered in her fists and shoveled into her mouth.

"Careful there, *ma petite*," Marie warned. "Don't want to choke."

But Janet had already mastered the art and was soon leaning toward Hugh, demanding, "Coo!" all over again.

He looked at me.

I shook my head. "That's enough for now." While Janet continued her lobbying for a second cookie, I filled a sippy cup with milk, which she then eagerly accepted.

"Good idea," Hugh said cheerfully. "Cookies always require a milk chaser." He glanced at his watch. "It is getting rather late. This has been delightful, but I'm afraid I'll have to head back to the Bluffs soon."

Etienne appeared at the door. "Sorry, sir. We've got plenty of cars, but all the roads, they are out of commission."

"But what about the snowplows, the road clearing equipment?" Hugh asked. "There usually isn't a problem."

Etienne shook his head. "It was supposed to be spring right now. They put the stuff away last week. It's going to take a while to get all the plows running again." He grabbed a mug from the cupboard and poured himself a cup of coffee. "The furnace, it's the bad news too," he mumbled, taking a sip. He took a seat at the table and explained about the little pile of parts in the basement, sitting next to the gutted furnace. "The guy said he'd be back when the new part came in."

Hugh smiled sadly. "And may I surmise that because of the road conditions, that will be some time in the future?"

Etienne nodded. He looked deflated.

Marie came around and massaged his shoulders. "It's okay, *mon cher*. We'll use the fireplaces. We'll be fine."

"But that is not all." He reached up and patted one of her hands. "It is below freezing outside now. If it stays this cold—"

I finished for him, "—the new grass in the front might die."

He nodded again.

"And maybe it won't," Marie said decisively. "Don't think about that right now. We've got work to do." She picked up her clipboard from a nearby counter, sat at the table, and began making a list. "Okay, first of all, there's lots of food; that's no problem." She turned in her chair. "Mr. Channing, we can't take you home, but you can stay in that room you were in behind the office, if it's okay. You can use the bathroom in our suite here on the first floor."

Hugh nodded his white head. "I accept your invitation. It's very good of you."

She returned to her clipboard. "Since the furnace won't work, we're going to need to get the fireplaces going. I know the one in the front parlor works. Etienne, how about the dining room?"

Her husband wrung his hands and glanced in the direction of the dining room. "I didn't yet have it cleaned. I must go check." He left the room.

"I know the ones upstairs in the two big bedrooms don't work," I volunteered. "Papa had them sealed off when I was a child."

Marie sighed and tapped the clipboard with her pen. "Well, at least we have some electricity, thanks to Etienne's new generator. It won't run everything, but it'll help. The stove won't work, but maybe we can use the microwave to warm up the kitchen somehow, boil water or something."

We heard Etienne in the dining room say loudly, "The fireplace here is okay." He appeared in the door. "But we need a lot of firewood. There are some wood scraps in the garage." The ancient detached double garage served as a workshop for Bert and Etienne. "But we don't have any real wood for burning." He went to the kitchen's back door, opened it and stepped back immediately, shivering and rubbing his arms. "Woof! It is freezing out there! I almost cannot see the furniture in the garden, the snow is so deep."

Marie looked out the kitchen window. "And it's still coming down out there."

"Oh, my! Gil was going to walk home from the newspaper office," I said. "He wasn't even wearing a coat!"

Janet, sensing my unease, started to whimper.

Marie put an arm around my shoulders. "Don't worry, dear. He's a smart man, lived here almost all his life. He'll stay put."

# Chapter | Sixteen

I just couldn't get to sleep that night. We had set up Janet's travel crib downstairs in the parlor near the fireplace, and I'd brought down my pillow and several thick blankets. But outside the ten-foot radius of warmth, the house was cold and getting colder by the hour.

Add to that my concern for Gil, who was probably trapped in the newspaper office, and a feeling of uneasiness over the whereabouts of our three B&B guests, Ev Holland, Herbert Edmonds, and Callie Huff.

"They're probably fine," Marie had said as she handed around mugs of chicken soup an hour before, "Those musicians will be with the band people, and the wedding planner, well, she knows how to look after herself, I'm sure."

My thoughts flew to Lily Burns. Was she all alone in her own house, with nothing but a half-grown cat for company, only a few yards away? How I wished Alec was here! He'd make sure she was all right. I still couldn't get any signal on my cell phone to check on her.

There was no need, we all agreed, to worry about Hester. She and Bert were the most practical, resourceful people we'd ever known. They were the only ones who had actually made preparations for the upcoming cold weather and were bound to be safe in their own trim bungalow under several of Hester's handmade quilts.

"And I hope she's sitting there in front of the fire, stitching on the Fort Ticonderoga quilt," Marie had said. "We need them all finished by midsummer."

Everyone in Chez Prentice was safe and relatively warm. Marie and Etienne had gone to bed in their downstairs suite as soon as dark set in.

"We'll keep each other warm," Marie had assured me.

Hugh Channing seemed perfectly comfortable in his little garret behind the office. Bundled up in two layers of footie pajamas, under a loose blanket and wearing her cotton bonnet, Janet slept soundly, while the fire flickered and crackled.

I was too keyed up to sleep. I tried reading one of the books from the shelf in the parlor. I got through the first few pages of one of my long-ago favorites: Mary Stewart's *Madame, Will You Talk?"* but the numbness that threatened my toes mocked the book's descriptions of warm Greek sunshine.

I put it down and started to pace. And pray. I prayed for Gil, of course, and for the missing guests. I prayed for everybody snowbound this night and for anyone who might be outside in the cold: line repairmen, firefighters, police . . . maybe even Callie Huff.

*But surely she's found shelter,* I thought.

All at once, there was a hard and desperate knocking at the front door. Someone scratched at the keyhole, then began to pound loudly and franticly.

"Open up! Please, please, please, open up!"

I peered through the side window and beheld the pitiable outline of Ev Holland, in the light clothing he had been wearing when he left, hunched over and trembling. His flute case was clutched to his chest. Quickly I unlocked and opened the door.

"Come in!"

He stood for a few seconds as if not believing his eyes, then stumbled inside. I closed the door against the cold and put my arm around the shivering man, guiding him into the parlor.

"Here—sit here." I dragged a brocade wingchair up to the hearth.

He obeyed meekly. I put a blanket around his shivering shoulders and removed his hat, which was covered in snow, with several actual icicles hanging from the brim. There were icicles in his hair too. It was then that I realized why he never took off his hat. He had a small, freckled bald patch at the crown of his head.

"How long were you out there?" I asked, putting an additional blanket over his long legs.

"Hmm," he said, shaking his head, his voice hoarse. "Not yet. C-can't ta-talk."

He was still shivering uncontrollably. His lips were cracked and his ears were cherry red. He put trembling hands over them.

"I'll get you some tea."

Etienne's generator only powered certain appliances, but

the microwave heated the water quickly. In a few minutes I carried a steaming cup of heavily sweetened tea to the parlor.

Ev was leaning back in the chair, sound asleep and dripping on everything. I took the tea back to the kitchen and fetched a towel that I put on the floor under him to catch the drips. Not all that effective, but it was the best I could do.

Fortunately Janet continued to sleep.

All at once I felt terribly fatigued. Quietly I slid down under the covers on my sofa and within minutes was out like a light.

It was probably several hours later that I awoke to see Janet standing in her crib, holding onto the side, cheerfully babbling baby talk to the still-sleeping figure in the wingchair. When she saw me, she pointed at Ev and said, "Ma!"

It was dawn, and the fire had gone down considerably. I edged my way up to it and was poking the embers when a blast of cold air announced the arrival of Etienne from outdoors.

The back door in the kitchen closed with a loud slam and Ev stirred, blinking awake. In moments Etienne walked in, carrying an armload of firewood.

"Look what that 'andyman left us. *Dieu lui bénisse!*"

"Oh, my, yes! God bless Bert!" I said. "What a thoughtful thing to do."

"These were stacked in a corner of the porch. At first, I didn't see them." Etienne deposited the wood on the hearth and put a hand on Ev's shoulder. "You okay? You look, um, not good. It is so good you came back! It's very cold out there; I 'ope you still have your fingers and your toes!"

Ev was a shambles, his clothes wrinkled and damp and his hair wildly disheveled. Smiling sheepishly, he flexed his hands and reached down to his feet, still shod in the highly inadequate sandals. He wiggled his toes.

"I thought last night I might lose them. The tops of my ears still feel tingly."

"What happened to you?" I asked, picking up my daughter.

He stood, stretched his arms with a groan and reached for his damp hat, which I had placed on the mantelpiece. "It's a long story. Do you mind if I get a shower first?" He turned to Etienne. "That is, if we have hot water; do we?"

"You're okay. We're on a generator, but we still have natural gas for the water heater." Kneeling, Etienne piled the wood in the fireplace and straightened it with the poker. "It's cold in the rooms, but when you're dressed, come back down and 'ave breakfast. The kitchen is not too bad. Marie made instant coffee in the microwave and now she's cooking eggs in it." He chuckled. "I can tell you one t'ing she learned: You must poke a little 'ole in the yolk or it will explode."

"It will?" I asked.

"Marie told me to say, 'Don't ask.' " He jerked his head in the direction of the kitchen. "But she is scrubbing away egg from the inside of the oven right now."

Ev nodded and left the parlor.

By the time I changed Janet and freshened up in the

downstairs powder room, Marie had succeeded in preparing a large bowl of scrambled eggs for us. "Toast doesn't work in that thing, so we're having plain bread and apple butter," she said as she set the table. "I told Etienne not to make the kitchen all electric. If we had a gas range, I'd be able to cook everything."

"It sounds delicious anyway," said Hugh agreeably as he sauntered into the kitchen. He was still wearing the suit from yesterday, now crumpled from sleep, with one of Etienne's thick winter bathrobes draped around his shoulders.

"You get a good sleep?" Marie asked, pouring orange juice all around.

He smiled broadly. "Indeed I did. Last night reminded me of my childhood. My father would turn off the heat at night. I learned early how to enjoy sleeping in the cold, all bundled up."

"Well, not me!" Marie took her place at the table. "I like a nice warm house."

"So do I." Ev entered, wearing a similar ensemble to last night's, but the sandals had been replaced by a pair of thick socks. "My shoes are drying out. I hope you don't mind my stocking feet."

He received general permission and sat down.

"May I return thanks?" Hugh asked.

His blessing was a prayer of thanksgiving for our shelter, our food, and the congenial company. As he prayed, Janet pounded her high chair tray with her spoon and yelled encouraging "amens" in fluent baby language.

After the prayer, I offered her cooled scrambled eggs, which she devoured enthusiastically with both hands and chased with occasional sips of milk from her sippy cup.

"Tell us about last night," I asked Ev as we ate. "Why one earth did you try to walk here in all that snow?"

Ev frowned. "In retrospect, I must admit it was a stupid thing to do." He topped a corner piece of bread with apple butter and took a bite.

"You could have froze to death out there," Marie commented.

He nodded. "I know that—now. It's just that after rehearsal, we looked outside and saw all the snow, and then the electricity went out and the concert was canceled and everybody was going to stay at the theater—you know, spend the night there. And I kept thinking, why should I sleep in a hard theater seat or on the floor when I'm paying for a nice soft bed at the B&B? I'd walked to rehearsal and it hadn't seemed that far, so I headed out."

"Did you happen to see Mr. Edmonds?"

Ev nodded. "I did at rehearsal, but not after it broke up. Isn't he here?"

Marie shook her head. "No. I thought maybe you two might be friends, seeing as how you're both musicians and all."

Ev grimaced slightly. "He's not a real member of the orchestra, just a last-minute hire for this concert when our regular percussionist had to bow out for some reason." He lowered his voice slightly. "To tell you the truth, he can play, but he's not very good."

"That's too bad. He's not very friendly either."

Ev shrugged.

"Well, I still say, it was a pretty foolish thing to try, Mr. Holland, and it's a miracle you didn't get frostbite!" Marie added more sugar to her cup of tea and took a sip.

Ev turned in his chair and extended a foot. "I might have it, I don't know. What does something like that look like? My toes are kind of red, but I can still feel them. My fingers are okay. That's what counts." He struck a pose holding an imaginary flute, and wiggled his fingers. "They still work."

"When all this is over," Hugh commented, "I recommend you consult a doctor, just as a precaution."

Still looking at his foot, Ev nodded. "I probably will." He looked up. "Hey, I haven't seen that Huff wedding woman around. Isn't she still staying here?"

Marie frowned. "She was, but she went out yesterday a little before you did and didn't come back."

Ev finished the last of his orange juice. "I gotta say, she gets on my nerves, but I hope she's okay. It was pretty rugged out there last night. At one point I got kind of lost in all the white, but I couldn't give up and leave my flute out there to get ruined."

Hugh chuckled. "You, sir, are a true musician."

Etienne stood. "How deep is the snow now, I wonder?" He walked to the window and looked out. "*Mon Dieu!* It has stopped! The snow has stopped!"

Acting as if we didn't take his word for it, we all got up and joined him at the window. The sun was beginning to emerge slightly from behind the gray clouds and the deep, deep snow sparkled like diamond dust.

"So lovely and peaceful," Hugh murmured.

"So deep!" Etienne retorted. "It's buried the cars. It will do no good to shovel them out with the roads so bad. We won't be going anywhere until the snow melts, and my poor grass lawn squares, so beautiful. I know they are frozen!"

"That would be a bad break." Ev dropped his napkin on the table and headed for the door. "They said they might try to put on the concert in a few days if we ever get dug out of here, so I need to practice. Do you guys mind?"

None of us did.

# Chapter | Seventeen

Ev retired to the parlor and trilled out various flute scales and other sounds, while everyone else got to work making things more comfortable. I gathered and folded the myriad blankets we'd used and put them in a stack with the spare pillows, then helped clear the table of the breakfast dishes, which Marie washed.

Hugh offered to dry. He accomplished this by sitting on a tall stool next to the counter.

Janet occupied the travel playpen we kept in the kitchen. She enjoyed Ev's music, bouncing up and down on her plump, thickly-insulated legs, while she sang lyrics of her own composing.

It was Etienne's job to see to the two fireplaces, one in the parlor and the other in the dining room. He came into the kitchen, wiping his hands on a dishtowel.

"Okay, the fires, they're going nice now, but I know what we need to help it. I saw it in the cellar when I checked on the furnace the other day: that thing, *le soufflet*—what do you call it in English? The thing that blows air on the fire?"

"A bellows?" I offered.

"Yes, that is it. It is needed for keeping the fires strong."

He headed for the back door.

"Wait!" Marie said suddenly. "It's pretty cold out there! Are you sure you really need that thing?"

I understood the concern in her voice. Her husband had seemed to visibly age in the past few days. There were dark circles under his eyes, and the creases running along his nose and mouth were deeper, more pronounced.

Etienne turned and went over to Marie, put his arms around her, and kissed her on the forehead. "I am fine, *cherie*. Please don't worry."

I'd seen this happen with Gil. Whenever I expressed too much concern about his safety, he'd go all masculine and determined on me, his little woman. It was a primal instinct, I was sure, and since we were first married, I'd learned to dial down the anxiety in my voice a bit.

After hugging his wife, Etienne turned back toward the back door. All at once, we heard a roaring sound coming from outside the house. It grew steadily louder, and we all, including Ev, with flute in hand, hurried to the front door.

Marie flung it open. I gasped as a bitter cold gust swept into the foyer. The drifting snow had formed a four-foot high barrier in the doorway. I could hear Janet expressing her objection to be left alone in the kitchen, but I didn't want to subject her to the sharp, cold air that literally hurt to breathe in.

We could just see over the top of the snow, and what we saw was a most welcome sight. There, vibrating noisily, was a snowmobile, a kind of motorcycle on skis. And perched on it, the Stradivarius of the sod, the Tchaikovsky of the Tiller, the gardener extraordinaire, Manuel Esperanza, and sitting behind him, my long-lost husband, wearing a trash bag around his shoulders and looking red-faced and uncomfortable.

"*Ola*, people!" Manuel shouted over the sound of the engine. "Are you all right?"

We all laughed and assured him of our safety at the top of our lungs. I stepped forward to go to Gil, but Etienne grabbed my arm and pulled me back.

"You will freeze!" he scolded.

"Look what I have brought to you!" Manuel indicated Gil.

"Come in, come in! *Vite!*" Etienne began digging in the snow to make an opening on the porch.

The two men struggled through the hip-deep powder snow, emerging into the warmth of the house and leaving the noisy, vibrating machine still running.

With tears in my eyes, I threw my arms around Gil and laid my head on his chest. "I missed you," I whispered.

I looked up at him. Even his breath was cold, but there was warmth in the look he gave me.

Marie slammed the door with a grateful sigh and said to Manuel, "Can't you turn that thing off?"

The gardener pulled off a stocking cap coated with ice and laughed loudly as he shook it. "I do not dare! It is an old one, a Polaris, and it took me thirty minutes to get it started already." He looked around at the assembly. "Do you want to buy it later? I will sell for five hundred."

We all declined as we led the travelers into the kitchen.

"I cannot stay long, only just to get warm." He gratefully accepted the cup of tea Marie prepared.

I offered Gil the same, but he shook his head. He had shed his makeshift raincoat—which turned out to be lined with newsprint—but was still trembling. "Just let me sit here for a while."

I fetched Janet from her playpen and sat next to my husband at the table. Janet kept reaching her arms out to be lifted, but when that didn't happen, she began patting his arm and smiling at him.

"I have a CB radio at my house and the police asked anybody with a snowmobile to help our neighbors," Manuel explained.

Gil answered my puzzled look. "Manuel's mother lives in an apartment next to the newspaper office. She very kindly made me some soup and told Manuel about me when he came to check on her."

"Is she there all alone?" I asked, worried.

"Don't worry. She's okay. They got their electricity back first before anybody. She's nice and warm there," Manuel said in answer to my other question. He pointed at Gil and smiled. "It was nice and warm at the newspaper office, too, but this gentleman wanted bad to get back here."

"*Gracias,*" I murmured, my hand to my heart.

Manuel smiled and sipped his tea.

"Mr. Esperanza—" I began.

"Manuel, *por favor.*"

"Manuel, did you see many people out on the street? I mean, in the snow? We haven't heard from two of our guests, Ms. Huff—Callie Huff—and Mr. Herbert Edmonds."

He nodded. "I know this lady," he waved his hand around his head, "with the red hair, but I did not see her."

I sighed.

"I have a question, too," Etienne began, "about my grass—"

"Ah, do not worry. *Si*, it's freezing out, but the brown grass, she is only sleeping!" He waved his hand. "She will wake up again soon."

"But brown—"

"Look," Manuel drained his cup and stood. "If the grass is truly dead, we can fix it. Do not worry!" He clapped Etienne on the back and looked around. "My cap?"

I held out his stocking cap. "I wrung it out with a towel. Got it a little bit dryer."

"*Gracias.* I have to go now. My snowmobile is still running, but the gas is going fast. It is good you are home," he said to Gil. "*Adios!*" He waved his hand again and followed Etienne to the front door.

When the Frenchman returned from seeing Manuel off, he was yawning. "Marie, I am going to sleep for a little. Tell me if the fire goes down too low. I never did get that—" He fumbled wearily for the word, but gave up, "—*quelque chose* in the basement."

She nodded. "It's okay. You go rest."

After the initial surprise had faded, I found that being snowed in was boring. There was little to do in the chilly house but try to keep warm. I thought about a nap under a half-dozen quilts, as Etienne was doing, but I was too restless. Reading was out of the question, for the same reason. Eventually Gil went upstairs, and Marie, Hugh, Ev, and I ended up huddled around the fire in the parlor, talking as we sipped warm beverages.

Janet was sitting in her playpen near the fire, drowsily sucking on the ear of a stuffed toy.

"It's funny, but I feel safer with all this snow everywhere," Marie declared in a soft voice.

Ev cocked his head. "Safer than what? What do you mean?"

She carefully set her cup in its saucer on the nearby side table. "Oh, people can't get around much in all this snow. You know—after the murder out there at the Bluffs." She looked over at Hugh, remembered who he was and stopped. "Oh, golly, I'm sorry."

He shook his head. "No, it's all right. I agree with you. I haven't felt really safe since, well, you know. And spending time here enjoying your kind hospitality, despite all this unforeseen inconvenience, is the most relaxed I've been in quite some time."

"I'm glad to hear that, Hugh," I said. "I've been worried about you."

He gave a half-smile. "And that's why you've been hovering?"

"You noticed? Guilty as charged."

"Guilty of what?" Gil walked into the room, rubbing his head with a towel. He'd showered and changed into dry clothes. He threw the towel over his shoulder and took a chair by the fire. "Who's guilty?"

"I'm guilty of being worried about Hugh's safety, especially after what happened."

Marie hopped up. "Just a minute." She returned with a newspaper. "This is from the other day, but here's who's guilty. He did it. I just know it!"

Ev sat back and groaned. "Not that again."

"Yes! It has to be! I mean, look at this: The paper says there might be a murderer in the North Country, and what do you know? There's a murder!"

"Pure coincidence," Ev said with a snort. He stood and headed into the chilly hallway. "I'm going to make some more tea."

Hugh leaned forward. "What did you mean?"

Marie folded the paper to the article in question and handed it over. "Here it is, in black and white."

Hugh pulled reading glasses from his jacket pocket. "I'm afraid I'm quite a bit behind on my newspaper reading," he said as he scrutinized the article.

Marie tapped the paper. "See? There. That Rats—um—Rasputin guy's supposed to be somewhere around here."

I looked over at Gil, editor of said newspaper, who shrugged. "I must admit I was speculating a little bit when I wrote that one, Marie."

Hugh looked up sharply from the paper he held and jerked his glasses from his face. He glared at Marie.

"Whom did you say? Rasputin? Are you referring to Gregory Rasmussen?"

"Yeah, that's what the article says his name is."

"Oh, dear." Hugh put his glasses back on and sighed deeply as he turned his attention back to the newspaper.

We all sat silently staring as the old man read. Presently, he looked up, tucked his glasses in his pocket and handed the newspaper back to Marie.

"Ms. LeBow, I believe I agree with your theory."

"See, everybody? He agrees with me! I'm right!" Marie pulled her shawl tighter around her shoulders and crossed her arms.

Gil leaned forward. "Look, this is getting out of hand. I admit, the story makes it look like he's here, but it's highly unlikely. Stuff like that sells newspapers."

Hugh rose with difficulty, walked over to the fireplace and warmed his hands. "I'm afraid," he said over his shoulder, "I must beg to differ with you, sir."

Marie nodded decisively. She had an ally in this argument.

Hugh turned and looked around the room at all of us. "You see, my son was Greg Rasmussen's defense attorney."

# Chapter | Eighteen

"**I** never met Rasmussen," Hugh explained, "but this case in particular drove a wedge between my son and me that we both came to deeply regret in later years." He returned to his chair and settled in. "It was a terrible crime, the brutal murder of that young woman, and there was absolutely no doubt in the minds of the police that Rasmussen was guilty. It was an airtight case, as they say."

"Then how did they let him get away?" Marie's eyes were wide.

"I believe some of the circumstances are explained in this article." He pointed to the now-discarded newspaper. "Inasmuch as a family member was involved in the case, I took it on myself to learn all I could. I had connections with the police here on the East Coast who put me in touch with two of the detectives working in California."

"You got the inside story," Marie said breathlessly.

"Right. They told me that this Greg Rasmussen was a well-known and popular figure locally. He had a rather magnetic personality and had espoused some popular causes. He'd used his influence to help several important officials get elected, and he charmed the social elites of the community into paying my son's rather considerable legal fees for him." Hugh's eyebrows lifted almost to his hairline.

Marie was triumphant. "That's what it says in the article!"

"The article is right. The police were furious when bail was set at a surprisingly low amount—somebody else paid for that, too, of course—and he disappeared the day before the trial was to begin."

"Yeah, I read about that."

"He was tried and convicted—"

Marie interrupted. "I know: in absentia!"

Hugh's teacherly instincts had kicked in. He nodded.

"You are correct. He was found guilty and sentenced to life in prison. And there remains a warrant out for his arrest to this day."

I had a question. "But why would he want to harm your son? He was the man's defense attorney—on his side, I would imagine."

"Well, I'm afraid that in recent years, Conner became rather careless in his statements about that case. A little over a year ago, he gave a television interview and declared that he knew where the authorities could probably find Rasmussen and that he was, in Connor's own words, 'guilty as sin.' "

"But that's not—"

Hugh completed my thought. "Yes, you're right, it's completely unethical. An attorney is never supposed to comment on his client's guilt or innocence, even after the fact. I'll admit I was shocked. Even with our differences, I'd always thought that Conner adhered to the rules of professional conduct."

The room had gradually become colder, and Marie got up to poke the embers of the fire. "Well, didn't he get in trouble?"

"Not professionally. I think most of his colleagues had already realized that he was—well, not himself anymore. Apparently his practice had dwindled to almost nothing. It had been ten years since we spoke, but I called him up to ask about it, and he didn't even remember giving the interview. That's when I realized the truth."

"That he had dementia."

"Yes, Gil. I flew out there right away to make sure he had a proper medical workup. After his official diagnosis, I arranged for him to come live here, share a suite at the Bluffs with me. It was strange, but rather comforting as well."

Hugh's pale eyes filled with tears. He pulled the inevitable monogrammed handkerchief from his jacket pocket and blew his nose.

"You see, I was a father again, taking care of my son. I thought we would be together all the way through his illness. I could be with him to the . . . end." Hugh hung his head and pleated and re-folded his handkerchief. "But as you all know . . . it didn't . . . work out that way." He gave way to a muffled sob. "I'm sorry. I'm sorry, I'm just—"

Marie moved forward and embraced the old man. "Don't talk any more. It's all right. It's all right. I'll get you some more tea, okay?"

Marie well understood the grief that accompanies the sudden death of a loved one.

I stood and rubbed my arms. I called after her as she headed to the kitchen, "You know, Marie, it's really getting cold in here. Why don't you go tell Etienne we need the fire built up?"

She shook her head. "No, he's worn out. I'm not gonna wake him up. I know how to do a fire. Just let me get some more tea started."

"Where is Ev, by the way? Wasn't he going to make some more tea?"

Marie paused at the door and shrugged. "Maybe he made some and took it up to his room."

Gil stood. "Hey, what am I, chopped liver? I'm perfectly able to get this fireplace going again. I'll just get some more firewood from the back porch." He left the room.

I sat down next to Hugh. He managed a pale smile as he met my gaze. "I apologize for the emotional outburst."

I patted his hand. "We all understand. Marie and Etienne lost their daughter about a year ago under similar circumstances."

Hugh stared into the dying embers. "Oh my."

"Here y'are!" Marie placed a steaming cup of tea on the side table. "It's really hot, so be careful." She spotted Gil returning with his arms full of wood. "And we'll get this room warmed up in a jiffy, you'll see. Right now, I'm gonna go get you guys some cookies."

Shivering, I followed Marie into the kitchen. "Woof! I think I'll have a cup of tea, as well."

As I poured hot water over a teabag, Gil's voice came from the parlor. "Hey, can somebody bring me some matches? I'm having a little problem here."

Marie brought him a box of the big wooden kind from the pantry. When she returned bearing a winter coat on a hangar and carrying a pair of boots, she said, "He's still blowin' on the embers. What he needs is that blower thingy that Etienne talked about. It's in the basement, didn't he say?"

"The bellows?"

"Yeah." She pulled on the coat and boots. "I'm gonna go get it."

She tugged a stocking cap over her head and went to the back door. A knife-like draft swept in, and she pulled mittens from her coat pocket.

"Brr! It's deep out there! If I'm not back in an hour, call the Mounties." Smiling, she grabbed a broom that hung from a hook on the wall.

I wrapped my shawl tighter around my shoulders. "Let me help you."

She shook her head. "I'll just sweep the snow off one of the doors. It won't take but a minute." She patted her pocket. "I've got a flashlight, and I think I know right where it is. See ya!"

Shivering on the screened back porch, I watched her make her way through the snow with difficulty. Her breath made clouds in the air. Her boots sank deep into the snow, and by my reckoning it took her four or five minutes to reach the raised entrance to the cellar, only a few feet from the porch steps.

Immediately she began pushing the snow off one of the two doors with the broom. It was fortunate that the doors stood at a slight angle, so there was less snow on them than on the flat surfaces. At last she pulled one of the doors open. Spotting me, she dropped the broom, gave a wave, pulled a flashlight from her pocket, and descended into the basement.

While I waited I looked out over the back yard, where our carefully-selected and arranged wrought-iron furniture had disappeared under a thick white blanket that sparkled in the faint sunshine. The branches of the trees were also heavily weighed down with mounds of snow, and there were icicles hanging from the roof of the gazebo.

*So much for spring!*

I glanced at the thermometer tacked to the doorframe. "Sixteen degrees! It's warming up," I called to Marie. "A couple of hours ago it was eleven."

There was no answer from the open cellar door.

I looked around the screened back porch. Snow had floated through the mesh and made small drifts on the cartons of frozen foods that Marie and Etienne had cleared out of the now-nonfunctioning freezer.

"I'll freeze to death out here. This is ridiculous," I muttered, with my breath coming out in clouds. I turned to go inside, but stopped when I heard a strangled cry behind me.

Now unheeding the cold, I ran to the back door steps and leaned out. I could just see the entrance to the cellar.

"Marie? What is it? Are you all right?"

Her head appeared first out of the basement door's dark rectangle. Without answering, she scrambled rapidly up the few basement steps and outside. She turned and slammed the outside door shut, hard, then fell backward into a drift and righted herself. Making little high-pitched grunting sounds, she virtually swam the short snowy distance back to the porch. She was out of breath when I ushered her inside.

"Marie? What's the matter?"

She seemed not to hear me. She looked around the kitchen as if in unfamiliar surroundings. She was gasping and mumbling to herself. All at once she plopped down into a kitchen chair and began removing her mittens.

"Did you find the bellows?"

She seemed to notice me at last. "What?" She pulled off her knit cap and tossed it on the table, still trembling. Next she unwound her scarf and tossed it aside.

"The bellows? Were they there?"

"The what? Oh, that. No, I mean, yes, it was probably there, but I didn't get it," she said with a dismissive wave of her hand. She patted her pockets. "Must've dropped the flashlight down there," she said to herself.

She leaned forward in the chair, crossed herself, put her elbows on her knees and covered her face with her hands. Her lips moved and I heard her faint, muffled murmur,

"Hail, Mary, full of grace—"

I waited until her prayer subsided, then pulled up a chair in front of her. "Look, Marie, what happened out there? You must tell me."

Staring into space, she nodded slowly. "Terrible," she said, "terrible."

"What did you see in the cellar, Marie?" A scene from a British comedy flashed into my mind: an old woman, gasping, "I saw something nawsty in the woodshed."

Perhaps it wasn't so serious. "Was it a rat?" *Probably not, she's too upset for that.* "More than one rat? Or perhaps a dead one?" I added for good measure. That certainly would have given me the vapors.

"I don't know what to do," Marie said. "Maybe call—"

"The exterminator?" I finished for her. "They won't be able to come right away, you know."

She sat up and stared at me and began pulling off her coat. "What? Are you crazy? No! The police. I gotta call the police!"

# Chapter | Nineteen

I squatted beside the chair and in the same low tone she used repeated, "The police? Marie, what's going on? What did you see down there?"

She sat up and put her finger to her lips. "Shh! I gotta figure this out. Please, don't say anything yet. Please, Amelia!" She sighed, and it came out with a whimper.

Gil walked into the kitchen just then. "What's going on?" He noticed the discarded damp mittens and scarf on the table. "Marie, did you go outside?"

I stood. "She was looking for the bellows, but she didn't get them for some reason."

He shrugged and walked to the sink, where he rinsed his hands. "No problem. I got the fire going without them."

Behind his back, I signaled frantically to Marie that we should tell him.

She shook her head.

I frowned, but complied. "You're chilled. Let me get you some cocoa."

I joined Gil at the sink and filled a mug with water, which I heated in the microwave. "I think the temperature is rising a bit. The thermometer on the porch was up five degrees.

And look at that." I pointed to the window where sunshine was at last was streaming in.

"Maybe." Gil pulled his cell phone from his pocket. "I think I have some bars here." He pressed a number and put the phone to his ear. "Oh, good, it's ringing. I'm calling the paper."

He stood waiting for a minute as the two of us watched him. At last, he shook his head.

"Nobody answering."

"Maybe we should call the police—" I began. Marie started from her seat, then backed down as I hastily added, "—to see if the roads are going to be opened anytime soon."

Gil leaned toward the window. "Doesn't look like it from here yet," he said. "We'll just have to sit tight for now." He sauntered out of the kitchen.

I brought Marie her cocoa and pulled a chair close to her. "You're going to tell me right now," I whispered firmly. "Why do you have to call the police? Why won't you tell Gil? What on earth is in the basement?"

She hid behind her cocoa mug and avoided my gaze.

"Tell me!" I whispered fiercely.

"Not now. Please, not yet. I gotta talk to Etienne about this first." She rose and stopped suddenly. "And I gotta go make sure to lock the doors to this place." She scurried out of the kitchen, still carrying her mug.

"That does it," I said to myself.

My heavy winter coat was still at our lakeside cottage, but there was no need to stand on ceremony. I went into the hallway and extracted one of Etienne's heavy coats and a pair of rubber boots from the coat closet. I returned to the kitchen, where I donned the outerwear and slowly pulled open the back door.

The sun was surprisingly bright reflected off the snow. Quietly I moved across the porch and opened the screen door. The snow-covered top step still bore the print of Marie's feet. I put my foot in it and gripped the railing. The next step took me waist-deep into the snow, which was gradually developing a firm top layer. It was rather like wading through a giant pie.

Fortunately Marie had broken up most of the crust, and I was able to get to the double doors of the basement easily, though a good deal of snow had found its way over the top of the boots, dampening my feet. I gripped the handle of the right-hand door and pulled. It wasn't too heavy, and made no sound as I pulled it open. I grimaced anyway, as though my facial expression could help matters.

It wasn't quite as cold inside. A string hung from a light bulb on the ceiling, but I knew it would be futile to pull it. The light from the open door was all I had to see by. I sat on the bottom step and waited for my eyes to readjust.

As a child, I'd been a little bit frightened of this place, of its deep shadows, of the dank smell, of the possible spiders or other interlopers. In recent years, I'd ventured down here occasionally, but had mostly ignored it. Now, however, was not the time for long-ago bugaboos. I squinted into the darkness with determination.

Gradually forms became apparent. Off to the left was the bulky form of the furnace. Closer were several unidentifiable parts that would presumably be replaced by the repairman.

I huffed on my ungloved hands, which were becoming numb, and rose to relieve my hindquarters, made equally numb by the cement step.

*Now, what could have upset Marie so?*

I continued scanning what was visible in the dim light. To the right of the furnace, two old brooms leaned against a stack of cartons and nearby, three very old plungers bedecked with thick cobwebs, stood at attention on their own.

*Why has nobody thrown those things out?*

Off to the right, I remembered, was an indented area that had originally been filled with shelves constructed to hold a colorful myriad of home-canned vegetables and preserves. There were only a few jars left, containing who knows what ancient decayed foodstuffs. Still squinting, I stepped forward, and my foot struck something metallic that rolled off into a shadow. I pursued it and discovered Marie's flashlight.

"That's better," I said, flicking it on.

Now I could investigate more thoroughly. I stepped around the corner and swept the beam over the remaining jars on the rickety shelves. I'd neglected this space in the years when my parents' health declined. Maybe with Etienne's help we could repair these shelves and put—

All at once, the light picked up a corner of something light-colored, half-wadded under the shelf. "It's a quilt," I said aloud. "What's it doing here?"

Apparently Marie had pulled it partly out. I knelt down and pulled on it some more.

It wasn't one of Hester's quilts. By the light of the flashlight, I could see the long, clumsy stitches and rusty stains. I pulled some more. Something heavy, very heavy, was weighing it down. I knelt, tugged harder, and the burden moved slightly forward.

The pointed end of an umbrella emerged. I pulled it out all the way. It was one of Etienne's new ones, purchased especially to loan to our guests.

But there was also something else back there. I shoved the umbrella behind me. "What is that?" I mumbled.

Still kneeling, I bent my head down almost to the dirt floor and aimed the flashlight underneath the lowest shelf. It spotlighted a high-heeled shoe with a red sole.

Occupied by a foot.

Connected to a leg tangled in the folds of the filthy quilt.

The beam of light followed the leg up to a skirt.

"Lily?" She had a pair of shoes just like this. "Oh, no!"

I was down on my hands and knees now, pulling with all my strength. The quilt came out from underneath the body all at once and I fell backwards.

It landed on top of me, and I fought frantically to push it away. There were dark red stains all over it.

I pushed the disgusting thing away and got back down, level with the floor. My hand was shaking as I directed the flashlight back at whatever—whoever—was back there. The beam fell on a face, blankly wide eyed and ominously still.

It was a face that I recognized.

I shook with relief. "It's not her," I said breathlessly, then corrected myself, "It's not she." My friend Lily, as far as I knew, was alive.

"Oh, but—" I made myself take one more look, just in case I could help this poor woman.

She stared back at me with the dreadful, passive patience of the dead. No one alive could have remained so still in that twisted position.

Marie had been right. This was no time to stick around. This was a job for the police. I took a deep breath, grateful for once that it was still so bitterly cold. There was no smell.

"Amelia!" a voice called from the door. It was Gil. "What are you doing down there?"

I scrambled to my feet and followed the flashlight beam back to the base of the stairs. I shielded my eyes from the out-side glare and said, "It's—it's someone . . . Oh, Gil, it's some-one . . . dead!"

I was surprised to realize that I could hardly breathe. I dropped the flashlight, turned and sat down again on the bottom step, with my head in my hands. I didn't think he could hear me, but I said it anyway: "I think I'm going to faint."

# Chapter | Twenty

I didn't faint, but I did put my head between my knees.

Gil came scrambling down the stairs, nearly knocking me to the floor in his haste. In response to my trembling, pointing finger, he retrieved the flashlight, kicked the umbrella aside, pulled back the bunched and bloody quilt, and investigated under the lowest shelf, seeing for himself what the fuss was all about.

"Come on," he said, grabbing my elbow unceremoniously. "We've got to get you out of here right away."

I eagerly complied, struck with the sudden realization that the perpetrator might still be down there somewhere. "Gil, I think I know who that is."

We were struggling through the snow. "Not now, honey. Let's get inside and call the police."

"When can they get here?" I asked Gil several minutes later.

I had been gently seated in the kitchen and given cocoa for shock by a somewhat recovered Marie. Currently Janet sat in a high chair nearby, eagerly munching handfuls of Cheerios.

Gil was on the other side of the table, talking to the police on his cell phone. "Shh!" he said sharply and put held his free hand over his ear. "That's right," he said into the phone, "No, I don't know who it is."

Etienne looked on, frowning.

I looked over at Marie. "It's Callie Huff."

"Yeah," Marie said, joining us at the table, "I think so too."

Gil scowled at us and shook his head. "Yes, we understand. We won't touch anything."

"Got that right!" Marie said with a shudder and took a swig of cocoa. Etienne patted her shoulder.

Gil ended the call, replaced the phone in his shirt pocket and ran a hand over his face. "Okay, here's the situation: It's going to be a while until this thing is worked out. Unfortunately, as you know, the highway department had already removed the snowplows from the trucks and put away the salt they use to melt the ice. The official term, if you're taking notes, is 'ending winter maintenance.' " He sighed and continued. "Of course, when they do get things going again, the interstates and highways will get priority over city streets, and . . . there's another little wrinkle."

Marie groaned, "Oh no! What?"

"Apparently, one of the police cruisers was hurrying to a call in the worst part of the storm, got disoriented in all the snow and took out two parking meters and a fire hydrant, which proceeded to spew water down Samuel Street. Fortunately nobody was hurt."

"But that's right around the corner," Etienne remarked.

Gil nodded. "Yep, right where Samuels crosses Jury, so there's a sheet of ice on our street too. People with snowmobiles like Manuel have been helping out with emergencies, but our little problem is just going to have to wait."

"Wait?" Etienne said sharply. "Wait?"

"Just a second, hear me out: In order to properly investigate, they're going to need their crime scene people and a lot of equipment, which won't all fit on a snowmobile." He arched his back and stretched.

The foreboding flutter I'd felt before returned.

Etienne paced. "This is a matter of seriousness! We cannot keep dead bodies here, even in the basement! This is a place of respectability!"

"*Cherie*," Marie said, putting a restraining hand on her husband's arm, "it is what it is. We'll just lock the door and stay away. We didn't know it—she—was there before, and we can pretend like we don't know now, okay?"

Sullenly, Etienne nodded. "There is a padlock in a little tackle box in the pantry. I will get it to keep people out." He donned the coat I had recently borrowed, fetched the lock, and proceeded outside.

Marie looked around. "Well, we're still in business—at least until people find out about this—so I better go up and do the rooms." She pulled a plastic carrier full of cleaning materials from the pantry.

"Can I help?" I asked.

She shook her head.

"My room's fine. Since Mr. Edmonds hasn't been here since yesterday, it's only Ev's that needs it."

Marie smiled wanly. "Thanks." I heard her trudging up the stairs.

Gil held out his hands to Janet, who had finished her prelunch lunch. "Come here, missy." He took her into his arms. "I missed oo when I was stuck in that bad ol' office." He looked over at me. "You too."

"Thanks," I responded dryly. "I wasn't halfway out of my mind over worry about you, really I wasn't."

He smiled. "I knew you wouldn't be." He sat Janet on his lap and helped her play pat-a-cake.

I took a deep breath. "Let's do as Marie suggested, pretend we don't know what's downstairs."

"Good idea."

"Okay, changing the subject: Tell me what it was like for you in this storm."

"Well, you hear people say this over and over, but it's true: It all happened so fast. I was sitting at my computer typing, and all of a sudden, whoomp! The lights went out, and things went straight downhill from there."

"Tell me more."

"Not without motivation. Come here, you," he ordered.

I came over to him, leaned down and gave him a big kiss, while Janet arched her head and watched, transfixed. "Ba," she commented.

"Woof! Daddy won't need a coat outside if Momma keeps

giving him kisses like that," Gil remarked to the baby as I straightened up.

"Waba," was her sage reply.

A stiff breeze from the back door announced Etienne's return. "Well, now she is all locked up."

When he said "she," I knew he was using French vernacular, but mentally, I chalked it up as a poor choice of words.

Etienne pulled off his gloves. "I don't know how long the police will be taking, but down there, it is cold, so everything is okay. *Ou est ma femme?*" he asked me briskly.

"Upstairs, doing our guest's room."

He nodded and left the kitchen. We heard him mount the stairs.

For a minute, we just sat and stared at each other until Gil broke the silence. "Well, it looks like we'll be waiting around for the constabulary for quite a—"

For the second time that day, a strangled cry rang through the house, but this time it came from upstairs. We heard footsteps coming down the stairs at a rapid rate. It was Etienne, at full speed.

"*Noo!*" he wailed, sailing across the entry hall, "*La pelouse! Noo!*"

Gil and I exchanged distressed glances. "What now?" he said.

The three of us hurried into the hall in time to see my business partner throw open the front door and, ignoring the four feet of snow piled up on the porch, plunge in. "Stop!" he called, "*Ma pelouse!*"

We ran to the front window, which was half-obscured by a snowdrift. "What was he yelling about?" Gil asked, bouncing Janet in his arms.

"The lawn. He's upset about the grass. But it doesn't make sense."

We pressed our faces against the icy glass, but couldn't really see anything.

"Stay here with Janet," I ordered, and ran to the coat closet. Etienne's coat was there—the man was probably freezing to death outside—and Marie's heavy winter coat hung beside it.

"Don't go out there!" Gil said.

"He needs something to wear." I donned Marie's coat, gloves, and boots and draped Etienne's coat over my arm.

As I headed across the entryway, Marie descended the stairs carrying the cleaning tote and wearing rubber gloves. "Where's Etienne? He was talking to me while I scrubbed the toilet and all of a sudden, he looks out the window and runs out of the room, yelling his head off." She saw what I was wearing. "Where're you going?"

I held up her husband's coat. "He went outside without this. I'm taking it to him."

I opened the front door and plunged into the snow, trying to follow the indentations made by Etienne. A few steps along I located the porch railing and, holding on to a post, climbed up high enough to see over the top of the snow.

What I saw made me laugh out loud, albeit a trifle hysterically.

# Chapter | Twenty-one

H ad Santa Claus come early? Or late?

It was yet another surreal sight in a day full of them. There, in the middle of the front yard, was a shiny black six-passenger sleigh with bright red runners and trim, hitched to two massive draft horses that stood huffing and pawing the snow, their breaths making huge clouds.

In the stillness I could hear the squawk of a police walkie-talkie.

Seated in the sleigh were three heavily bundled police officers, sharing the space with a number of large metal bins. Etienne had already climbed into the sleigh and was haranguing the policemen, using wild hand gestures and rapid French. At the same time, he was rubbing his shirt-sleeved arms in the cold. One of the officers handed him a blanket and gestured for him to put it around himself.

"Etienne!" I called, "LeBow! Your coat!"

It took several tries on my part, but at last he paused and turned his head.

One of the police officers jumped from the sleigh and made his way toward me, struggling in the thick snow. When he got close to the porch, he looked up and grinned.

"Miss Prentice! I thought that was you! How are you?"

I looked down into the eager young face topped by a fleece-lined Russian-style winter hat. "Kenny Bedard?" I said with surprise in my voice. "I haven't seen you since your graduation, what, three years ago? Is this your father's sleigh?"

The grin grew broader. "Yeah! The one he takes the tourists for rides in at Christmas." He cupped his hand confidentially. "It was my idea, 'cause they couldn't get the CSU van out of the shed. My dad brought the rig in from the farm."

"And you're a police officer now. That's wonderful."

He ducked his head modestly. *His cheeks aren't red just from the cold*, I thought.

"Yeah, I like it. Got my associate degree in criminal justice and now—" he stopped, interrupted by a shout from the sleigh. "Oh, you better give me that." I handed him Etienne's coat. "Maybe I'll see you around."

I retired to the warmth of the house and announced to Gil, Marie, Ev, Hugh, and Janet, "The police have arrived."

While everyone flocked to the windows, the front door was again flung open and Etienne stumbled inside, shivering and muttering to himself in French. Marie hastened to greet him.

"Are you okay? Let's get you some cocoa." She ushered him into the kitchen.

I was hanging up my coat when Gil approached and thrust the baby into my arms. "She's really wet now," he said accusingly.

Indeed, there was a squishy texture to the back of her little pink corduroy overalls. "I'll handle it," I assured him, mounting the stairs.

Janet waved her arms. "Da! Ba!"

"That's right," I answered her. "You need a new pair of pants, my dear."

Gil followed me. "Why was Etienne so bent out of shape?"

"You heard him, *la pelouse!*" I waved my hand in imitation of the Frenchman's expressive gestures. "It's the front lawn. Those horses will probably tear up any remaining grass underneath the snow."

Gil scratched his chin. "I don't know. It's pretty thick out there. All that snow might sort of protect it."

"Maybe, but there's something else: this murder. It could definitely hurt business at the B&B, Gil. Who's going to want to stay in a place where somebody was killed? I know that's what was worrying Marie."

"You might be surprised. Let's wait and see how it plays out, honey."

I'd told Gil about part of my fear, but there was even more: Who could have done such a terrible thing? Were they nearby? Would they return? A deep-seated, palpable sense of dread hadn't left me since that terrible moment in the basement. My hands shook as I turned the key in the lock.

I gritted my teeth. "All right," I said with determined good cheer, "let's get down to business."

One-handed, I lay a waterproof cloth on the bed and placed the baby on it. She proceeded to roll over.

I turned her back over and began to unsnap her overalls. "No, you don't, young lady! Gil, would you hand me a diaper and those wipes from over there? Thanks."

When we descended, all clean and fresh, we saw Marie hurrying to answer the door. It was a smiling Officer Kenny Bedard, accompanied by two other police officers with rolling metal containers marked, "CSU." Along with their equipment, they brought in a good deal of snow, which thoroughly soaked the thick Oriental rug under their feet.

The door opened again, and Police Sergeant Dennis O'Brien strode in, clad in all the necessary warm regalia. He pulled off a glove and shook hands with Gil. During my first year of teaching, he was a student of mine, but in recent years he had become a good family friend.

We all greeted him accordingly. "And how are Dorothy and Meaghan?" His wife and daughter were our good friends too.

"Worried about me in all this weather and sad about missing a few days of second grade, in that order," he replied offhandedly.

"She's in second grade already? I can hardly believe it."

He scratched his ear. "Yeah, me, too. Listen, Amelia, we're going to need to get started on this business." He gestured to the policemen accompanying him.

"So where is this body you reported?" one of them asked.

Etienne pulled on his coat and yanked a knit toboggan on his head, folding down the ear flaps. "Follow me. We'll have to go out the back."

The short parade headed toward the kitchen, while Marie hastened to roll up the rug and tell Hester to fetch a mop.

Dennis stayed behind. He pulled a pad and pen from his pocket and approached Gil and me.

"I'm going to need to question everyone here. How about if I use your parlor? We can close the pocket door to keep it private."

I showed him into the front room, where pillows and a stack of folded blankets filled one of the corner love seats. "It's warmer near the fireplace," I suggested.

"So how about I start with you?" He took one of the brocade chairs near the coffee table and pointed with his pen at a nearby matching chair.

"I notice this one has done a lot of growing since I saw her last." He indicated the child on my lap, who was squirming to get down.

"Waba!" Janet said, reaching out her hands to Dennis. "Ba!" She wanted to sit in his lap. I bounced her on my knee, trying to placate her.

He opened his pad. "Full name?"

I tilted my head. "Amelia Prentice Dickensen. I would have thought you knew that by now."

"I was just kidding. I already wrote it down here. But now, how about you tell me what happened?"

Janet had begun to voice her further objections to the situation.

I grimaced. "I'll be glad to if you don't mind a little background music."

He shrugged and chuckled. "Hey, been there, done that," he said over the din, "You wouldn't believe the kind of fuss Meaghan could make at that age. She sends her love to Miss Janet, by the way, and can't wait until she's old enough to babysit. Now, why don't you tell me what happened, in your own words. Start at the very beginning."

"Well, it was getting colder in here," I yelled over the baby noise. "And we thought the bellows would help . . . "

"And you didn't hear the cellar door open at any time during the snowstorm?" Dennis asked when I finished my narrative. "It didn't squeak or anything?"

Gil had heard Janet's cries and kindly rescued her from my clutches.

I shook my head. "Etienne went around a couple of weeks ago and oiled all the doors, inside and out. We didn't want a squeak to disturb the guests." I shrugged. "It seemed a good idea at the time."

Dennis nodded. "Well, maybe it was for the best. I wouldn't have wanted any of you to go outside and bump into—" he waved his pen "—well, you know."

His questions had brought back all the feelings I'd experienced in the basement: curiosity, apprehension, fear, horror, sadness. *Poor, poor Callie; I wish I'd liked her better!*

"Have you contacted her family? I believe she was from Long Island. I'm sure Marie can give you her information."

"She already did. Ms. Huff didn't have any immediate family, just some staff in her office. The police downstate broke the news."

The sadness increased. "What about, um, arrangements?"

Dennis frowned and shook his head gently. "Amelia, don't get involved. It's all being taken care of."

"But—"

"I know you have a kind heart, but this isn't your job. Your job is helping students and taking care of that baby. And Gil, too, of course."

I sighed. "I take your point, but may I make just one more observation regarding this case?"

"By all means, Miss Marple." He rolled his eyes, closed his notebook, and put it in his pocket along with his pen.

I gave him one of my stern teacher glances, but he definitely wasn't intimidated. It had been a long time since I'd stared him down in my classroom, and even then it hadn't worked.

"I think Callie knew whoever it was. Remember, I told you she thought she recognized somebody when she looked out the window that morning."

"Yeah." Dennis stood.

"You might look into her business associates. And another thing: When she first got here we were reading the newspaper, and she mentioned that she'd actually known the Rasputin killer. She said she'd recognize him anywhere. Dennis, I think that's what might have happened."

"Hmm. Not too bad a deduction—for an amateur." He patted me on the shoulder and headed for the door.

# Chapter | Twenty-two

Everything seemed to happen all at once the next morning. The sun began to shine, the electricity came back on, and the snow started melting fast.

For a time our street was a rushing stream, and by the following day the only evidences of the catastrophic storm were the occasional cool wind gusts and grimy crusts of leftover snow in shady spots along the curb. Topping it all off was the fact that the temperature was suddenly warmer than it had been all last week.

Bert had just driven Hugh back to Sunset Bluffs in his sturdy pickup truck and I had brought our packed suitcases down to the foyer when the front door opened. Lily Burns looked fresh as a daisy in a yellow polka-dot raincoat.

"I'm fine, thanks for asking," was her sarcastic greeting to me before I'd even opened my mouth. "Not a single word from you in how long? Three days?" She made a show of counting on her fingers.

I hugged her. "I'm sorry about that. It's just been so awful around here."

She hugged me back. "That's okay. I read all about it in the paper."

"Besides, I knew you were all right. I remembered that you bought a generator the same time Etienne did."

She nodded. "True. Sam Junior and I spent the whole time nestled in front of the fireplace. It was safe, but a little boring. And now I'm totally out of kitty litter."

"So you can't stay for coffee?"

"Not now, thanks. I have shopping to do."

I smiled at her. "Are you going out on another date with Mr. Holland?"

She looked at me mysteriously. "Remind me to tell you about him sometime." She was out the door before I could ask another question.

Dennis O'Brien had interviewed everyone at the B&B except the drummer, Herbert Edmonds.

Officer Kenny Bedard asked about the drummer when he returned that morning.

"No, he hasn't come back," I told him, "Did you ask the orchestra director?"

"Sure we did, and we called his landlord in the city too. Nobody's seen or heard from him since shortly before the storm hit. He had breakfast at the diner. That's all we know. You going somewhere?" he asked, pointing to the motley collection of luggage and totes I had placed by the front door.

"Back home to our lake house as soon as my daughter finishes her nap. I stayed here to get away from the Sunset Bluffs thing, but, well . . . " I paused and shrugged, trying to suppress a shudder. The oppressive sense of dread had not left me.

He nodded and held up the yellow bundle he'd collected. "Yeah. Well, I just came by to take down the crime scene tape and ask you to let us know if you think of anything else that could help us."

"I'll pass the word on. Right now our general manager is out buying office supplies, and you probably saw my partner, Mr. LeBow, outside, watching the workers try to repair the front lawn."

The young officer chuckled. "He's doing more than watching. He's supervising. He looks pretty worried."

"I'm afraid your father's horses were a little hard on the new sod. Between their hooves and all that melting snow, it's in pretty bad shape."

"Sorry about that, but at the time it was—" he was interrupted the abrupt opening of the big front door.

It was Etienne, once again looking wild-eyed and disheveled. "*Mon Dieu*, Amelia!" he cried. "*Quelle horreur!*" He spotted Kenny and grabbed his elbow. "*Venez voir ce qu nous avons trouvé! Vite!*"

Kenny looked over at me with a puzzled expression.

"He wants you to go see what he found," I translated. "Quickly."

With a nod, the young man allowed himself to be dragged to the front door, while Etienne continued to mutter pitifully, "*O, pas encore! Pas encore!*"

"What do you mean, not again?" I called, but they were already too far away to answer. "My goodness—making such a fuss! It's just grass."

I followed them out into the humid spring sunshine and across the front porch. Enthusiastic salsa music poured from a battered boom box on the top step. We made our way carefully over the saturated sod to where Manuel Esperanza and two other workers stood, staring uneasily down at the ground

"*Ici!* 'Ere!" Etienne loosened his tie with one hand and with the other, pointed at a spot next to the driveway, where a section of sod had been flipped back. There, halfway sunken into the mud below, was a large hunting knife. There were ominous dark stains on it.

"Is it—" I gasped. "Could that be—"

Officer Kenny Bedard took over. "Step aside, please. Has anybody touched this?" He pulled a cell phone from his pocket.

He scanned the workers' faces. They all shook their heads.

"No, senor," Manuel said solemnly. "We know what happened here, about the poor lady." He pointed at the house. "Jose finds this and tells me *immediamente*. Then I tell him." He gestured toward Etienne.

Kenny began dialing a number. He jerked his head in the direction of the porch and the blaring boom box. "Turn that thing off, wouldya?"

One of Manuel's men hurried to comply, his heavy boots squishing in the mud.

When Kenny finished his call, I asked, "Couldn't you have used your police radio to report this?"

"If I did, every wannabe cop in the county with a radio scanner would be here in ten minutes." He squinted at the ground. "Not to mention the press—no offense. We learned that long ago, Miss Prentice, the hard way."

At Kenny's request, I'd retreated a little, but still had a clear view of the knife. "It looks like somebody might have rolled back a piece of sod and hidden the thing there." I shivered and pulled the sweater tighter around my shoulders, though the sun was warm on my back.

"*Si.* I know it was not there when we put the grass down. Today Jaime used his shovel to see if the water was so deep in the ground, and he hit this." Manuel took a bandana from his pocket and wiped his hands. He turned to Etienne. "I am sorry for this trouble."

Etienne shook his head. "I do not blame you."

The evil-looking thing was huge, with a sort of curl at the tip. "Isn't that what you call a Bowie knife?" I tried to control the tremble in my voice.

Kenny was talking on the telephone. All at once, he stopped and said, "Miss Prentice and everybody, I'm going to have to ask you to go up on the porch or inside the house while we wait for the squad to get here."

"Certainly." I gestured for everyone to follow me. "Would you all like some lemonade? I believe Hester has made some."

"*Limonada?*" Manuel invited the other men. They nodded and followed me into the kitchen.

Hester reacted with surprise. "What's all this?" she asked as the group filed in and I gestured for them to take seats at the table.

"Tell you in a minute." I pulled the pitcher of lemonade from the refrigerator and began filling glasses.

"Here's some cookies I just finished baking." Hester loaded a large plate with treats and placed it in the center of the table. "Amelia, put out some paper napkins too."

Manuel and his men seemed grateful for the break. "*Gracias, señora.*"

Hester watched as I handed out the napkins, then hauled me by the arm across the kitchen and out onto the back porch.

She glared at me. "Me and Bert are away for one day— okay, three days, because of the snow—and the whole place goes to you-know-where in a handbasket! What's happened this time?"

As succinctly as possible, I explained.

Hester's eyes widened and she wrung her hands. "I heard Etienne hollering, but he's been moaning around all morning about that stupid front yard and how this murder stuff is going to put us out of business. I just thought it was more of the same."

"Well, in a horrible kind of way it is. I have to admit I'll be really glad to get back home to the lake house. Yes?" I said to Manuel, who was timidly peeking around the back door.

"*Señora, su chica,* your baby?" He held out the monitor receiver, which was making definite squawking noises.

"I guess she's finished with her nap. *Gracias,*" I added over my shoulder as I hurried toward the stairs.

A few minutes later, I heard loud voices downstairs and thereafter, heavy footsteps coming up the stairs at a rapid rate. There was a brisk rap at our door. I opened it to Vern Thomas, graduate student, part time taxi driver, and future bridegroom, frowning down at me.

"Amelia! What's been going on here?" He walked into the room and looked around. He took me by the shoulders and squinted at my face. "Are you okay? You look okay." He gazed down at Janet, who stared up at him from her standing position, clinging to an ottoman and drooling on the velvet upholstery. "She looks okay too. I'm so relieved!" He scooped me up in a bear hug, which startled my daughter, who made distressed noises.

"Vern! You scared the baby." I extricated myself and picked her up.

"Gee, I'm sorry. Do you think she'll forgive me?"

He extended his long arms to her, but she was having none of it. She turned away and clung to my body like the baby monkeys I'd seen in nature films.

"She'll be all right in a minute." I sat, clingy burden and all, in one of the wide Victorian armchairs. "You look as though you survived the storm quite well."

Vern took the nearby matching armchair. "Thanks to the LaBombards, I did. But what's this I hear about a murder? That's all they're talking about downstairs."

When I finished telling him, to my embarrassment, I started to cry. "I'm s-sorry, it's just been so—terrible. And the worst part is, I didn't even like the poor woman!"

"Come'ere." Vern began to fold the two of us, Janet and me, into a gentle embrace, which set off an ear-splitting screech from my offspring.

He backed up, holding his palms before him in submission. "Okay, relax, kid."

To my surprise, Janet quieted down.

"Look, how about I tell you about my adventure. I promise it's murder free, but just barely."

I had to smile. "Please." I grabbed a tissue from the dresser and dried off.

"Well, when that storm started, I was heading to pick up a fare. It was this musician guy, a drummer, who wanted me to take him to the auditorium at the community center. They're having a charity concert—at least, they were, until the storm hit."

"Was his name Herbert Edmonds?" I tried to no avail to shift Janet to a more comfortable position.

"That's the dude. And I learned a lot more about him than I ever wanted to, let me tell you."

"What do you mean?"

Vern leaned back and linked his hands behind his head. "Ladies and gentlemen, sit back, relax, and hear the sad saga of How I Spent Two Days with a Disgruntled Percussionist and Managed not to Kill Him."

"Go on."

"Okay, I'm picking up this guy at Mr. Fixit Car Repair out by the edge of town, and he says to take him to the auditorium, but first, stop at Hazen's Music Store, which is two miles in the other direction, almost to the Mall. He says he *has* to be at a rehearsal at one o'clock, and I say, no way, and he says, he absolutely has to get some more drumsticks or something at the music store, and to step on it, so I do. And when we get to the store, nobody was there. It was closed."

"Perhaps they heard about the storm front coming through. Janet, honey, you're choking Mama." I gently loosened her grip, placed her in my lap and handed her a pacifier, which she accepted, all the while sliding suspicious glances in Vern's direction.

"I guess so. But anyway, this Edmonds guy acted like it was all my fault. By this time, it's really starting to come down, so I head back in the direction of the community center, but before we can get there the snow gets so thick I can't see the road. At one point the taxi slid on the ice and clipped the curb. I think that's where I lost a hubcap. And this Edmonds guy was growling at me the whole time."

"Poor Vern."

"You betcha, poor Vern! You haven't heard what happened next! I knew I'd never make it all the way to the community center, so I took a chance and headed—ever so slowly—back to the taxi stand."

"Good thinking."

"I thought so, but this Edmonds guy didn't. Once we got there, he demanded that I keep going, but I got out and said, 'Come on in if you don't want to freeze to death.' And he finally did, but he wasn't very happy about it. And that's where we were the whole rest of the time."

"I imagine Fleur and Marcel took good care of you," I said, referring to the owners of LaBombard's Taxi.

"No kidding. You know what nice people they are. It was kind of cold in there, but they rigged up a sort of a little heating stove using some flower pots and those little church candles?"

"Votives?"

"Yeah. It was the coolest thing you ever saw—or maybe I should say, the warmest, because they kept that room tolerable by just lighting a new candle or two whenever one ran out. We sat around telling awful jokes—at least, Fleur and I did. Marcel's a kind of serious guy. And we ate candy bars and peanuts and chips and soda from the vending machine they have there. Knock-knock," he said suddenly.

"Vern." I gave him the teacher stare.

"Go ahead, humor me."

I sighed. "Who's there?"

"Yodel lady."

"No," I said.

"Come, on."

"No."

He could see that I was adamant. "Okay. That was Fleur's joke. I thought it was pretty good."

"Candy and soda? That wasn't very healthy," I chided.

"That's what the Edmonds guy said, and I wanted to say, 'Well, I can tell you haven't exactly been on a diet lately.' He's really kind of fat, but you would've been proud of me. I kept my mouth shut."

"That was very tactful of you."

"Well, somewhere along in there, he told us that he was a black belt, so I took that into consideration too."

"Where did he go after the snow cleared up? Did you take him back to the music store?"

Vern rose from his seat and jerked his thumb toward the door. "Didn't you know? He's here. I brought him back. The cheapskate refused to pay me because I didn't take him where he wanted to go originally or something." He shrugged. "Marcel told me to not worry about it." He consulted his watch. "I'm going to have to go."

I stood, allowing Janet to slide off. She gripped a nearby table and began cruising around the room. "Oh, dear! How could I forget? How is Melody?"

Vern put his hand on the doorknob. "Oh, she's fine. Camped out at the hospital the whole storm. They had heat and power and everything there. She's there so much, she said, that she hardly noticed the difference."

"I hope your wedding isn't delayed by this terrible murder."

He looked puzzled. "It won't be, Amelia. Don't worry, I'm sure we'll still have the reception here even if the front lawn isn't fixed. This storm hasn't changed anything."

"But the murder victim, Callie Huff—"

The light dawned. "Is that who was murdered? The wedding woman?" He scratched his head. "Golly. I'll have to call Melody. Wonder if she's heard."

"I think it would be wise, Vern."

"Her mother isn't going to like this much."

"I imagine not."

"Her dad and I get along real well, at least," he said pen-sively. "Her brother likes me, too. Guess what his name is: Cade."

"That's a nice name."

"It would be, only it's short for Cadence. Get it? Cadence, Melody, Harmony?"

"Oh. Interesting."

He sighed. "That's the word for it, all right. I'm marrying into an *interesting* family. Pray for me, Amelia."

He thought he was kidding, but I did pray.

# Chapter | Twenty-three

"Yes, at first, I'll admit I was quite outraged at their moving all my worldly goods to the other end of the complex without consulting me," Hugh said the next day as we sat in the lobby of what I had come to think of as the Big House. He sighed. "They pointed out that it was required by their insurance carrier. Though the move was a *fait accompli* before my return, coming as it did on the heels of our shared adventure, the unexpectedness of the thing quite unnerved me."

"Oh, I'm so sorry, Hugh."

"However, the very sight of you two has revived me." He patted my hand. "It was good of you ladies," he leaned toward the stroller where Janet sat chewing on her rabbit, "to come visit me again."

To my surprise, Janet responded, "Boo," aiming her smile directly at him. Adding, "Boo," she waved the well-worn droopy stuffed animal enthusiastically.

"Did you hear that?" Hugh was delighted. "I do believe she said my name. What an intelligent little girl!"

The old man's perception and good taste deepened my affection for him. "I must agree, but I'm a bit prejudiced."

As if on cue, Bing the waitress walked through the front door, carrying a purse and wearing a raincoat and an attitude. She spotted us and came over.

"Well, hello there! How's my boyfriend today? I heard you got stuck somewhere during the storm. Are you okay?" She plopped down on a nearby easy chair and turned a concerned frown toward Hugh.

"I spent two and a half delightful days, well cared for, at this lady's excellent bed and breakfast. And as you can see, I am hale and hearty. As to being your boyfriend, rumor has it your amorous affections lie elsewhere." He waved a wobbly hand in the direction of the dining room.

Bing plucked at her hairdo. "Okay, there's a couple of guys, but I'd drop 'em like a hot potato if you'd only admit you're crazy about me, Doc!"

She leaned forward to pat his cheek as the old man gave her a glowering, sidelong stare and brushed her hand away. She looked over at the chiming grandfather clock that stood against one wall.

"Oops! We'll have to do this another time. Don't want to be late." She was gone, her sturdy sneakers squeaking on the shiny floor.

"Incorrigible," he murmured, watching her leave, "but kind-hearted. I do hope she finds someone worthy of her." He turned back to me. "Amelia, I'm worried about you. Such terrible goings-on!"

He reached for a folded newspaper on a side table and handed it to me. I sighed. The headline didn't need any embellishment to be sensational: Murder Weapon Found in Lawn of B&B.

A catalog photo of the same variety of knife accompanied the article. I could tell that Gil had probably tried to be as restrained as possible, but even the bare facts sent chills down my spine.

"Oh dear. I'm sorry you saw this. They found that knife after you went home."

"I imagine this creates more difficulties for you and the LeBows."

I nodded. "You're right. Furthermore, a newspaper in Lake Placid has started calling the place Slay Prentice, and it's spread like wildfire. It isn't doing the B&B's reputation any good. Two murders within a week! This town is starting to rival Chicago."

Hugh closed his eyes and leaned his head back for a moment. All of a sudden he straightened.

"Of course! It's the same man! It must be!"

"What?"

He tapped the picture sharply. "The perpetrator, Amelia. The killer. The same man committed all three crimes. I can see that now."

"*Three* crimes? What are you talking about? Not the California murder too!"

Hugh leaned forward and said in a harsh whisper, "I've made a study of my son's cases, especially the Rasputin Murder, so called. They found the weapon from that one also, you know, and judging by this photograph, it was identical to the one found in your yard."

"It's possible, I suppose. There are several connections," I admitted, thinking of the blood-stained quilt I found with Callie's body.

"I know there are those who might not agree, but please trust me, I just know."

"Know what?" a pleasant, Southern-inflected voice interrupted, "Whatcha know, Mr. Channing?" It was Jack Travis.

The tall, handsome busboy from the dining room pulled off his jacket. He leaned over and spotted the picture in the newspaper.

"Dang! Not more of that murder business! Y'all shouldn't be talking about awful stuff like that. It's not good for you, Mr. Channing. You should take this little cutie here on a walk around the garden, or something."

He patted Janet on the head. She grinned up at him and clapped her hands.

Hugh gave the young man a frosty stare. "Jack, surely you are aware of the First Amendment?"

"Yeah, of course, but—"

"Then you will kindly allow us our freedom of speech, as we will yours."

Jack didn't seem to take offense. "Right." He executed a two-finger salute as he backed away. "You got it. Gotta run. See you at lunch, sir. Ma'am," he added, giving me a polite nod.

I looked at my friend with a sense of foreboding. "Hugh, I worry about you. Perhaps we could arrange for you to stay at our house on the—"

"Oh, my dear Amelia, what a sweet girl you are, trying so earnestly to take care of me. But don't you see, I mustn't act out of fear and run from this thing. I must see it through to the end."

Tears filled my eyes. "But how? How do you fight this danger, this evil? I'm so afraid for you!"

He patted my hand. "Where is your faith, my dear? Remember, 'Do not be afraid of those who kill the body, but are unable to kill the soul.' And on that note, I must send you on your way. Run along now." He actually made shooing gestures.

I stood and leaned over to kiss his cheek. "Take care of yourself, Hugh. I'll be praying."

He smiled at me. "That's the most powerful help you could possibly give me. Goodbye, dear girl."

As I wheeled the stroller out the doors of Sunset Bluffs and down the handicapped ramp to the parking lot, I had an overwhelming sense of finality. *Why am I so worked up over this?*

An unexpected movement off to the side caught my eye. I turned my head and saw someone tall stalking away from us along the walkway. With an almost military swivel, he turned and disappeared from view.

*Wasn't that Herbert Edmonds? Probably not.*

It was highly unlikely. I'd heard Vern speak of him recently, that's all.

I loaded my sleepy child into the car, climbed in, started the engine, and thought, *So many things have happened in the past few years. And so much of it has involved death. Perhaps that's why I feel so afraid all the time.*

But there was more: *Hugh reminds me of Papa. That's why I want to take care of him.*

When my father had taken ill and had made such a rapid and final decline, my sense of helplessness had been overwhelming. The man who had always taken care of us was beyond our help. There was barely enough time to say goodbye. Now that I was a parent, I better understood what a fine one he had been.

Suddenly I noticed that tears were streaming down my cheeks. At the time of my double loss, first Papa, then my mother, I hadn't done much crying. Now, all at once, as I endeavored to see the road through a film of moisture, I found I was weeping over everything: my parents, the death of the LeBows' daughter, Brigid's incarceration, her daughter's depression, the terrible murder of Hugh's son, and especially the murder of poor, obnoxious Callie Huff.

"And I didn't even like her very much!"

I was almost home. Janet would be waking up soon, and I didn't want her to see me like this. Holding the steering wheel tightly with my left hand, I fished a tissue from my purse with the right and blew my nose.

The noise woke up Janet, who started to whimper.

"We're almost there, sweetie," I said to her, and punched a button on the car radio. "Maybe some nice music—"

"You need not fear the terror of night," said a strong voice, obviously a radio preacher, "nor the arrow that flies by day . . . "

The words were interrupted by loud static, which was typical of radio reception out on the lakeshore. I turned the tuner knob, but the signal was gone.

Once we were in the house and Janet was happily cruising along the coffee table, I pulled out my Bible and found the passage in Psalm 91, the fifth verse.

"You need not fear the terror of night, nor the arrow that flies by day, nor the plague that stalks in darkness, nor the pestilence raging at noon. A thousand may fall at your side, ten thousand at your right hand: but it will not draw near to you."

"I promised Hugh I'd pray for him," I murmured. "Lord, I claim this psalm for Hugh."

# Chapter | Twenty-four

"Hugh says he's sure all three murders were committed by the same man," I told Gil that night as were going to sleep. "What do you think?" We were back in our own house, settling into our own bed.

Gil put down his book, turned off his bedside light, and pulled the covers over his shoulder. "Not according to my sources," he said drowsily. "Good night, honey."

I knew who that source was, and I wasn't convinced. "You mean Renaud?"

"Um-hum," answered his muffled voice.

"Are you sure you trust him? I mean, somebody who would give you confidential information for money? Aren't you afraid he'll just tell you what you want to hear? Has he even given you the pictures he promised?"

Gil sighed and sat up. "Honey, I've been in the news business a long time. I know what I'm doing. No, he hasn't brought me any files yet. But I'm not the only one he's talking to. He told me the police have a new theory on the Channing death. They're thinking suicide."

I had been about to settle down, but this jolted me wide awake. "What?"

Gil stretched and groaned. "According to Renaud, this Conner Channing had a lot more screws loose than his father was willing to admit or even knew about, for that matter."

"But *suicide?*"

"This is strictly confidential, Amelia, but it was common knowledge among the attendants at Sunset Bluffs that Channing's behavior was getting more and more erratic, even dangerous. They were considering moving him for his father's protection."

"How sad! But what kind of behavior are you talking about?"

"Well, according to Renaud, every time he was left alone in a room, Conner would throw things. He would claim it threw itself or that somebody else did it."

"That does sound dangerous."

"What's more, his appetite had diminished to almost nothing. He would claim his food tasted bad or that some-body had poisoned it. One of the waitresses would even take a piece of food off his plate at meals and eat it to prove to him it was okay, but that didn't do any good."

"I wonder if it was Bing. It sounds like her."

"Who? Oh, never mind. They did their best to keep his father from finding out the worst. Anyway, the wounds the victim had could have been self-inflicted. They think he probably stabbed himself repeatedly and crawled into the closet, where he bled to death."

I felt faint. "Ohh." *Poor Hugh!*

"I know, honey, this is a terrible thing, but it's better to face facts than to indulge in idle speculation."

"But what about the Rasputin connection? The fact that he was Rasmussen's defense attorney?"

Gil got out of bed. "Now, that's just what I was talking about. I know you like Hugh Channing—and I like the old guy, too--but honey, the lawyer connection is tenuous at best. And it doesn't help matters that you and the gang over at Chez Prentice are playing amateur detective and trying to connect this tragedy with a newspaper article I wish I'd never published." He stepped into the bathroom and returned carrying a glass of water. "Brr! This floor is cold! I should have put on my slippers!"

I had no interest in footwear. "But Callie Huff told us she knew Rasmussen."

Gil gave me a quizzical look. He set the water on a coaster and climbed back into bed.

"Yes, and Hester and Marie were there too. She said she, um, dated him a couple of times and that she'd know him anywhere."

Gil smiled and shook his head.

"What?" I demanded.

"You told me what kind of a person she was: condescending to the small-town upstate hicks. How better to impress a bunch of women than to say she actually knew the famous guy in the paper?"

He turned on his light and picked up his book.

"I don't know, Gil. She didn't seem all that proud of it."

He turned a page. "I'll bet Hester's eyes were the size of saucers."

"Well . . ."

"What did I tell you?"

# Chapter | Twenty-five

The next morning I had Gil drop me off at Chez Prentice.

"Did you see the paper?" Hester asked me as I opened the big front door. "It says they think that thing out at the old folks' home was a suicide!" She held it up so I could see the headline.

"Don't believe everything you read," I said.

She tucked the paper under her arm. "What do you mean?"

"I don't know, Hester. I just want to reserve judgment for now."

It was such a strange story. It just didn't sound quite right.

While the baby played in her playpen, I made a call. "I don't care what you say, Hugh. I'll be over there this morning in about an hour and we'll talk. Janet will stay with Hester."

"Amelia, I thought we'd already settled this."

"Not to my satisfaction," I said firmly. "Now, tell me where you'll be when I get there."

I borrowed the LeBow's car again and was on my way fifteen minutes later. Spring had returned with enthusiasm, and the sun was bright on the budding scenery as I headed along the highway toward Sunset Bluffs.

Last night after Gil had rolled over and begun to snore, leaving me wide awake, I'd given the situation a lot of thought. I should have been relieved at the new theory which, though tragic, meant that Hugh wasn't in danger anymore—if indeed he had ever been at all. But why was this heavy, foreboding feeling still hanging over me like a veil, darkening everything?

My mother, the wisest woman I'd ever known, had often reminded me that feelings weren't necessarily facts. Nevertheless, even if I was proved spectacularly wrong, I had to do something.

Lying there in bed, I came up with what seemed a viable plan. Hugh and I would pool what information we had and work out a way to make sure he was safe.

"I have other sources of information too," I said aloud as I drove, thinking of Dennis O'Brien, my reluctant police contact.

The more I planned this proactive approach, the further the dark sense of foreboding and fear receded. *Why, it's even therapeutic*, I thought and laughed at my own rationalization.

Hugh wasn't in the lobby as he'd promised and nobody there had seen him.

I approached Jess Renaud as he wheeled a cart down the hall, but he frowned and waved me away. "Sorry, I'm busy right now." He went into the door marked Pharmacy and closed it behind him.

The lady at the front desk rang the phone in Hugh's room and paged him, but there was no answer. "He's probably out in the garden, dear," she said. "It's such a beautiful day and he so enjoys looking out at the lake."

Her soothing tone did nothing to reassure me. I checked outside, but his favorite bench was empty.

As I returned to the front reception hall, I saw Bing coming out of the dining room, laughing over her shoulder at Jack Travis, who was again in his full busboy uniform: long apron, hairnet, and all.

"Have you seen Mr. Channing?" I asked them.

They both shook their heads.

Travis frowned. "He wasn't at breakfast. We just thought he'd probably gone somewhere with you."

"Did you check his room?" Bing's alarmed expression made me even more uneasy.

I shook my head. "I don't know where it is."

She took my arm. "C'mon."

We took the lobby elevator to the lower floor and hurried through the back exit, across the sidewalk, past the rock garden, and through the automatic doors of the annex. As we walked briskly together along the corridor, my mind registered the different decorations that graced the front doors of the various rooms, much like those in a college dorm.

On one was a framed black-and-white picture of a young woman in a cap and gown. Another had a basket of artificial flowers hanging on a plastic hook. The one next to Hugh's was decorated with children's drawings taped to the door panels. One of them read "I lov Grandma" in a crayoned scrawl.

Apparently Hugh hadn't had time to personalize his door or chose not to because it was pristine, with only the number 17A on it.

Bing reached for the doorknob, but Jack restrained her. "Y'all, it's the man's private room. We can't just barge in there. Hang on."

He stepped forward and knocked sharply. There was no answer.

Bing put her cheek to the door and called, "Mr. Channing?"

My heart was pounding out of my chest. "Hugh?" I called, "It's Amelia. May I come in?"

Our answer was a muffled thump.

"Did you hear that? Now let's barge in!" Bing didn't wait for Jack's permission, but pushed open the door, which was apparently unlocked.

I had never actually been in Hugh's living quarters. My initial impression was that his tastes tended to be Spartan and scholarly. There were two huge mahogany bookshelves lining one wall and a large, round schoolroom-style clock hung between them. On another wall were several diplomas above a desk that held a notebook computer and several family photos in frames. The third wall had a window with floor-to-ceiling drapes and a double bed, where the man in question lay, face up, atop the taut bedspread, fully dressed and apparently asleep.

One arm hung down and a large book lay splayed on the floor. Perhaps this was what had made the noise. Jack knelt down and picked it up, while I picked up Hugh's limp hand and patted it.

"Hugh? Hugh? Mr. Channing?"

The hand stirred slightly. Hugh's eyelids fluttered and closed. He murmured something.

"I . . . feel so . . . bad, Amelia." The words came out slowly and were faint, as if speaking took tremendous effort.

Bing went to the telephone on the desk and punched O. "There's a medical emergency in room 17A. We need help, stat."

To my surprise, two paramedics arrived in the room within two or three minutes. They checked Hugh's vital signs, administered oxygen, and lifted him onto a gurney, which they rolled away down the corridor.

"Where are they taking him?"

"To the hospital wing," Bing said. "Don't worry, sweetie, they'll take good care of him."

*They've done a pretty lousy job so far!* I thought. Instead I said, "Can't I go with him?"

"Family only, I'm afraid. I'm sorry, hon."

"But his family is all gone!"

Bing and Jack exchanged glances. "Look," he said, "we gotta get back to work, but we'll keep track of him for you." He pulled a ballpoint from behind his ear. "What's your number?"

I gave it to him and he wrote it on his palm. "We'll call as soon as we find out anything, okay?"

Bing nodded agreement.

On the drive home, my mind was swirling. *What happened? Was it a stroke?*

The bright spring sunshine suddenly dimmed as clouds closed in. Gray skies were often the order of the day in the North Country, but knowing that did nothing to relieve my anxious mood.

*What do I do now?* I wondered as I turned into the driveway at Chez Prentice.

In times past, in similar situations Lily Burns and I had joined forces as a sort of Lucy and Ethel team. I called Lily's number. There was no answer, only voice mail.

Impatiently I hung up without leaving a message. I needed to talk this over with somebody right away. I needed a keen intellect and the unbounded enthusiasm of youth.

What I needed now was a taxi.

## Chapter Twenty-six

"We'll send a cab right over, Miss, um, Amelia," said Fleur LaBombard, dispatcher and co-owner of LaBombard Taxi.

"How's Yvonne doing?" I asked, referring to the LaBombards' daughter.

"Oh, I'm so glad you asked. She's finished her sophomore year, and she's got a full scholarship for the last two."

"I'm so proud of her."

"Swell! I'll tell her. She allus tells me to send you her love. We can never thank you enough for what all you done for her."

"She's a sweet girl, Fleur. No thanks necessary. Oh, about the taxi: Would you make sure that Vern's the driver?"

"Sure! He'll be there in a jif!"

I would have called it two jifs, but in about twenty minutes, the car with the little lighted crest on top and the words "LaBombard Taxi" followed by a telephone number pulled up in front of the B&B. Vern was driving. I climbed in the back seat with Janet in my arms.

"Amelia," he informed me over his shoulder, "you need a carrier or car seat for the baby."

"It's okay; we're not going anywhere. I just needed to get in and talk to you."

"You mean just sit here?"

"That's right."

I set Janet on the back seat, where she proceeded to crawl around. I wasn't worried. If there was one thing I knew, it was that a LaBombard Taxi was a clean taxi. Fleur's husband was a bit obsessive on the subject.

"I wanted to talk to you, but I know you're busy, so I thought—"

"Got that right! Maybe the bride's family's supposed to pay for most of the wedding, but it's not cheap for me either. At least the kind of wedding the Branch family wants. And everything seems even more expensive after this wedding planner setback. I'm just slammed, Amelia. When I'm not working overtime, I'm studying for exams."

"Setback" was a rather casual way to refer to a murder, but I let it go. "I understand, but you have my word that this is important." I tried buttering him up, "Vern, I really need your sage insight and—"

"Look, this meter goes by time and mileage. Marcel does-n't like it when the hack just idles."

"All right, then could we run around the block a few times?"

"If you use a baby seat."

I sighed. "Give me a minute."

Janet didn't like it much, but soon, buckled and restrained, we were in the slowly-moving vehicle, headed up

Jury Street. At the intersection, Vern turned right at Samuel and continued making right turns as I outlined the situation and my concerns about Hugh. He seemed to listen intently, glancing back at me from time to time in the rearview mirror.

"I don't know how you think I can help," he said with a shrug and a flick of the turn signal. "You should get Gil or the Professor or Mrs. Burns to—"

"They're all unavailable to me for various reasons, Vern. Besides, you have a stake in this. It was your wedding planner who was murdered."

"Correction," he interrupted, taking on a mocking, high-pitched tone, "it was *Allegretta's* wedding planner who was murdered, but I get it. Okay, let's look at this rationally. Who—I mean, whom do you suspect?"

"Suspect?"

"Yeah, if the killer is here, he could be somebody you know, somebody you've met."

I swallowed hard. "You're right, of course. It's just such an unpleasant thought."

Vern flicked the turn signal and made a right. "Come on, you gotta man up, if you want to get to the bottom of this thing." He gestured over his shoulder. "Okay, let's make a virtual lineup. Who's in it? It'd have to be somebody who hasn't been here very long, right?"

"I suppose so. There are the two musicians, both of them guests at Chez Prentice: Ev Holland and Herbert Edmonds."

"Good. I like that Edmonds guy for the crime. He's a real jerk. Hey, aren't you writing this down?"

"I don't have any paper."

He sighed, reached for his clipboard, tore a strip off the bottom of the pad and handed it back over his shoulder. "Here."

"Do you have a pen?"

"Do I have to do everything? Here." He tossed the stub of a pencil back over the seat.

To my surprise, I caught it. Placing the strip of paper across my knee, I wrote down the two names.

"Now, who else?"

"Well, there's the new busboy at Sunset Bluffs, Jack Travis. But he's from Texas. He couldn't be Gregory Rasmussen."

Vern chuckled. "Maybe not, but Amelia, honey, even ah can fayke a Suthin ak-see-ent."

"All right, he's on the list. Oh, and there's that Jess Renaud character."

"Who's that?"

I hesitated. Vern was a journalism major, largely due to Gil's influence. I didn't want to tarnish his uncle's reputation.

"He's, um, he's an orderly at Sunset Bluffs. He seems kind of, um, shady."

"Put him down! Now, how about the women?"

"Women?"

"Sure. You don't think a woman could commit a murder? You of all people should know better than that."

"Yes, but as I told you, Hugh thinks that all three murders were committed—"

"—by the same man, yeah, yeah, yeah. All I can say, Amelia, is that he might be right and he might not. We don't need to leave any stone unturned, as it were."

I shrugged. "In that case, I nominate Allegretta Branch."

Vern barked a surprised laugh that jolted Janet out of her ride-induced stupor. She started to whimper.

"I'm sorry, you just surprised me there. Hey, can she have a lollipop?" Vern fumbled in the glove compartment and retrieved a bag of candies. "I keep 'em for the kids."

"No, she can't. Sorry." I reached in my diaper bag and fetched a graham cracker, which Janet cheerfully accepted.

"Okay, put down Alegretta. I wouldn't put it past her, though I can't see where she'd have a motive." Vern navigated the taxi around another corner. "Seriously, though, can you think of anybody else—man or woman—who belongs on our list?"

"Well, if you insist on adding women, there's Bing." I explained who she was as well as her nickname.

"Okay, so far, so good." He glanced back over his shoulder again. "Look, Amelia, by my figuring, we've gone around the block at a snail's pace twelve times. The fare is mounting. If we keep going, this could cost you a fortune. What do you say we talk more about this on the phone?"

"Good idea." Janet and I were both getting restless. "But let's make it soon. I'm very worried about Hugh Channing's safety."

Vern rubbed the back of his neck as he turned into the Chez Prentice driveway and killed the motor. He turned around in his seat and wrapped his long arms around it. "Look, let me think about this and I'll call you if—make that when—I get a brilliant idea."

"That's all I can ask."

He began to resume his seat, but stopped. "And, Amelia, as you were talking, another aspect of this thing occurred to me."

"What's that?"

"Mr. Channing isn't the only person who might be in danger." He aimed a finger at me and made a clicking noise.

I had paid Vern, including a tip, and was heading up the walk with Janet in one arm and my purse and the baby seat in the other when my cell phone rang. By the time I reached the vestibule of Chez Prentice, it had stopped.

I dropped the car seat on the floor and reached into my purse. The call had been from J. Travis, and it was curiously tagged Waco, Texas.

I pressed the call back button. Jack Travis answered, "Hello, ma'am, I just called to let you know that Mr. Channing's outa danger. Turns out he got kind of confused about his various medicines. He took 'em once, forgot he did, then took 'em again. They got him stabilized now."

"Thank God!"

"I gotta agree with you there, ma'am."

"But what a terrible thing to happen!"

"Yeah, well, it's the kind of mistake that these folks around here can make, but they're going to fix the situation and start monitorin' him closer now."

"And they hadn't been already?" I asked, impatiently.

I heard a clash of metal and the sound of running water. Jack Travis was probably washing pans. "You know that Mr. Channing, ma'am, he's a stubborn kinda coot and he was handlin' his own meds—till now."

"I see. Listen, I'd better let you get back to work. I'm sorry I was so sharp. I know this isn't your fault. It was kind of you to let me know."

I was beginning to alter my opinion of this fellow. Surely he couldn't be the murderer; he was too polite!

"I was real glad to do it."

*But wasn't Rasmussen so charming, he was able to con his way out of a jail sentence?* I remembered all of a sudden.

"Oh, Jack," I called as we were about to hang up. "When would I be allowed to come see Mr. Channing?"

"Tomorrow should be good, ma'am. Yew take care now."

# Chapter | Twenty-seven

"Well, now maybe we can finally get back to normal around here." Hester wiped her hands on her apron as we watched the police van back out of the driveway.

I heard a low growl. Etienne came up behind us on the front porch, waving an envelope in one hand and a letter in the other. "Do you know what this is?" Without waiting for an answer, he said, "I will tell you. It is a letter from the mother of the bride, Mrs. Branch."

"Yes?"

"She 'as made other arrangements for the wedding of her daughter."

"But there was a contract!"

He pulled a piece of the paper from the envelope. It was a check.

"The cancellation fee. It will pay for maybe five squares of the new sod. And to make matters even worse, she's ordering the cake from MacGuire's Bakery."

"Oh, dear," was all I could think to say.

"So I ask you, what is this 'normal' you speak of, *hien?*" He waved his hand towards the still choppy-looking front lawn.

"*C'est ca?*" He turned and headed back into the house. "*Et maintenant* we are called 'Slay Prentice'!" he said, crooking his fingers in air quotation marks. "*Qu'est ce c'cest, le* 'normal,' eh?" He marched back into the house and we followed like a line of domesticated ducks.

Marie caught up with him. "Normal is today, normal is now, normal is all of us together," she said in a soothing tone. "Normal is *le bon Dieu*, Etienne." She pulled him into the kitchen and led him to a chair, where he slumped in a pout.

"Marie's right," I agreed. "Surely in all your years building up various businesses you've encountered setbacks, but you came out all right in the end, didn't you?"

He waved away Hester's offer of a coffee mug. "*Oui*, but I made my own mistakes and I had *le contrôle* . . . what is the word in English?"

"Control," Hester piped up from the sink, where she was rinsing dishes.

Etienne's cell phone rang and he pulled it from his pocket. " 'Allo?" He stood, his eyes wide. "Yes, this is 'e."

*Good grammar, Etienne,* I thought. *Most people would have said "him."*

We watched as he talked, making dramatic gestures to punctuate his words.

"Ah, yes? Oh, we were very 'appy to 'ave you visit. We 'ope you will—eh? What? Well, no, nobody 'as been arrested. Oh, but you must not—" He was rapidly pacing the kitchen floor now. "I can assure you that—" He turned sharply at the back door and came walking back toward the kitchen table.

"Yes, I 'ave 'eard that nickname. It is slander and I 'ave called my lawyer. We are going to sue. Well, no, I cannot agree. Nobody is in danger. This is a very nice neighborhood and we—" He sighed. "I see. Well, *adieu.*"

He ended the call with a flourish and sank back into his chair. He put his elbows on the table and put his face in his hands.

"*C'est tout,* Marie!"

Hester observed, "That must've been the wedding planner people."

Etienne lifted his head. "Yes, and they were not the 'appy campers."

I ventured to lighten the mood. "We still have our two guests, Mr. Holland and Mr. Edmonds. And surely this terrible nickname will be forgotten soon. Gil says the public has a memory like a sieve."

"That's right," Marie hastened to agree. "Give it a week or two and—"

"*Pardon,* I 'ave other work to do. I will be in the office." Etienne made a rapid exit.

The three of us sat down together at the table. "We can ride this out, can't we, Marie? I mean, he's not called the Millionaire from Montreal for nothing, right?"

Marie pulled a paper napkin from the holder on the table and pleated it absent-mindedly. "Well, I don't know. He told me yesterday that he's trying to sell that warehouse we own on Rue Chabanel in Montreal. He had planned to fix it up and rent it out to retail shops, but the sales projections were discouraging. And the payments are pretty steep, too, not to mention the property taxes." She shrugged and flattened the napkin on the table.

I had to smile. Marie's vocabulary had become vastly more sophisticated since she reunited with her long-absent husband.

"Oh, he has more irons in the fire, but Chez Prentice is the project he truly loves." I saw tears fill Marie's eyes. "In a way it's what brought us back together, y'know." She used the napkin to wipe them away impatiently. "I just hate that there's nothing I can do."

Hester stood and retied her apron strings. "That's not true. That's not true at all!" She put her hands on her hips. "In my sewing room at home I have a six-foot-high stack of cartons. In those cartons are pint jars of Authentic McIntosh Apple Butter that I made in February. And there's more in the garage. Two gross, in fact."

"Between making quilts for the B&B and your housekeeping duties, not to mention taking care of your own home and husband, you must never sleep. Hester, when did you ever have time?" I asked.

She shrugged. "I just did. Anyway, all they need is labels. Marie, I bet you could get some of the round kind to go on the tops and print up something about Chez Prentice on 'em. I already talked to the lady who owns that pretty souvenir shop at the beach, and the people at the Steak au Poivre're interested too. And that's not all the places we could talk to. You'll need to call around some more. I know we can unload 'em pretty quick and we can split the profits. I bet we'd get five bucks a jar. And I can make more."

Marie jumped up. "Hester, you're amazing!" She hugged her.

"It's very generous of you, Hester," I remarked.

She shrugged. "Hey, I don't wanna lose my job here, do I?"

I had a thought. "But what about the health department and—"

Hester stepped back, crossed her arms and frowned at me. "If there's anybody who knows how to run a commercial kitchen, it's yours truly, Amelia."

"Oh, yes." I remembered that Hester had formerly worked at the college cafeteria. Her claim to be worried about employment didn't quite ring true, however, because I knew for a fact that she could resume her previous job any time she wanted.

"This is great!" Marie did a little skip and left the room, saying in a singsong voice, "I gotta go make some phone calls."

# Chapter | Twenty-eight

"Amelia?" said a faint voice on the phone the next morning. I knew right away who it was. "Hugh? How are you?"

"Still a bit somnambulant, I'm afraid, but improving by the minute."

"That's good. I was planning to come over there today. Are you still in the infirmary?"

"For the time being. They've promised me that if I behave myself, they'll release me by suppertime. ''Tis a consummation devoutly to be wished.' "

I smiled into the phone. "Quoting Shakespeare? You must be feeling better."

"I understand I caused quite a bit of concern on your part. I do apologize."

"I'm just glad you're better."

"My dear, there is a favor I must ask of you."

"Anything, Hugh."

A few minutes later, as I was helping Janet feed herself breakfast, Gil came out of the bedroom, fully dressed and redolent of soap and shaving cream. I loved that smell.

"Gil, are you going be very busy tomorrow?" I used Janet's

bib to wipe up some oatmeal she'd managed to get on her nose.

Gil went to the refrigerator and pulled out a carton of milk. "Yes. No. Maybe. It depends. What's up?" He retrieved a box of Cheerios from the cupboard, poured some into a bowl and added sugar and milk.

"Conner Channing's funeral is tomorrow, and I promised Hugh I'd be there. I thought maybe you could keep the baby. I hate to keep asking Hester all the time."

Gil had a spoonful of cereal almost to his mouth. He put it down.

"Tomorrow? Wow, I didn't know they'd released the body. Where's is it going to be?"

"Apparently, it's at the funeral home downtown—you know, that white building on the corner with the historical plaque."

"The Beaton House? Sure. Look, honey, I can't babysit for you, but I can go with you. I'm going to need to cover that funeral for the paper. Why don't you ask the widow Burns?" He had made up that pet name for Lily all by himself.

"She was a little distant with me the last time we spoke, but I do know she adores Janet."

I pulled a few more Cheerios from the cereal box and gave them to the baby. "I'll see if she'll do it."

⌣⌢

Lily could and would sit with Janet during the funeral.

"And you're sure it won't interfere with any, uh, plans you might have?"

"Not at all. We'll have a wonderful time."

I couldn't resist. "About your date with Ev Holland the other night. You said to remind you to tell me about it. Did you enjoy it?"

"Yes, I did."

"And?"

"And nothing."

"So you two didn't hit it off."

"I didn't say that."

"So you did hit it off."

"Didn't say that, either."

I changed the subject. "Have you heard from Alec?"

"Well, he called last night, but when I saw who it was, I didn't answer."

"Lily!"

"Bring her by Chez Prentice tomorrow at ten. All the baby stuff I'll need is there." She hung up.

# Chapter | Twenty-nine

Gil and I were at the funeral home by ten-fifteen the next morning.

Standing sentinel at the door was the funeral director, who spoke in low tones that matched the faint strains of piped-in instrumental hymns. He shook our hands gently and directed us to sign the guest book.

We were acquainted from past sad experience. He had directed both my parents' funerals.

"Mr. Channing said that you would be helping," he murmured.

"Yes, but could you tell me what's going to happen?"

Gil patted my shoulder. "You folks excuse me." He walked toward the discreet sign marked "Gentlemen."

"People will be gathering in the viewing room at eleven," the director said. "Then at twelve, everyone will assemble in the chapel, and the service will begin. Do you know how many we might expect?"

"Since there isn't any other family in the area, I would imagine fewer than a dozen. Just some friends, mostly from Sunset Bluffs. Hugh—Mr. Channing—said they'll all be coming in the facility's bus."

"That's fine. And, of course, we'll make the storage arrangements. We'll be sure to let Mr. Channing know when the time is right for burial."

"After today's service, everyone is invited to Sunset Bluffs for a special buffet."

The man nodded. "That's fine. Now, if you'll just wait for your friends in the viewing room. May I bring you something? Water, coffee, a soft drink?"

I declined with thanks and let myself be ushered into a small, but rather formally appointed room with dark wallpaper and even darker upholstered furniture. Two small tables held lamps that shyly emitted an amber glow. The room was freezing cold and, of course, against one wall, dominating the room was the elevated open coffin. The room smelled like Chuck Nathan's flower shop.

There is a practical reason for this custom of viewing. It's an opportunity for friends and family to say one last goodbye to the deceased, who has presumably been made presentable by the funeral home staff.

I took a seat in an overstuffed loveseat and was lost in my own melancholy thoughts. *This is where I bade my parents goodbye.* I looked around the room. *There were many more flowers at my mother's service.* I took stock. *The big basket spray in the corner is from Chez Prentice and that smaller one is—*

A large warm hand settled on my shoulder. Gil circled around and sat next to me.

"Wow. This place hasn't changed a bit, even the restroom," he said in a stage whisper.

I looked at his face, expecting a twinkle of mischief, but he was serious. "Last time I was here was for my sister . . . " He trailed off and turned his gaze toward the coffin. "Have you taken a look?"

"No, and I don't really want to. Hugh has shown me pictures of his son. That's how I want to think of him."

The funeral director appeared at the door. "The bus from Sunset Bluffs has just arrived."

As the white vehicle pulled to a stop under the porte-cochère at the side entrance, we stood watching.

"Oh, Gil, look," I whispered with just the slightest touch of sarcasm, pointing to Renaud, who was driving, "there's your confidential source."

He nudged me with his shoulder and shook his head.

The doors to the bus folded back and the first one down the steps was Jack Travis, dressed like his colleague Renaud in a white jacket with his name embroidered on the lapel and matching white pants, but sans hairnet. He turned and extended a long arm inside.

"Here you come, ma'am."

One of the ladies I'd seen on the patio at Sunset Bluffs descended slowly and carefully, all in black and wearing a small matching pillbox hat with a veil.

The next lady wore navy blue lace and a hat similarly trimmed.

Gil whispered in my ear, "Another veil? Was there a dress code for this shindig?"

"Shh!" I glanced nervously down at my gray dress with white collar and cuffs. *Is this somber enough? Well, too late now.*

I directed the ladies inside to the guest book.

One by one, the remaining members of the Sunset Bluffs contingent descended, some with canes, some with walkers. Women were definitely in the majority.

At last I spotted Hugh coming along the aisle from the back of the bus, holding Renaud's arm. Ever so gently, he was handed down to Travis, and then to Gil and me.

"Well," said Hugh after kissing my cheek and shaking Gil's hand, "We're all here. Let's go in." He was smartly turned out in a well-cut dark navy blue three-piece suit with a gray tie and white shirt.

"Mr. Channing, sir." Jack Travis tapped him on the shoulder and handed him his cane.

While Gil escorted Hugh inside, I gestured to the attendants. "Are you two staying for the service?"

Renaud said, "We'll park the bus and wait outside. This kind of thing is depressing."

"I don't mind it," Jack Travis said, "I'd kind of like to support Mr. Channing. I've seen enough funerals back home. When the service starts, I'll just slip into the back row of the chapel, if it's okay."

Renaud shrugged. "Suit yourself."

"That's fine. See you later." I turned to go inside when I caught a glimpse of someone at the far end of the parking lot, emerging from a car.

*Mr. Edmonds? Why is he here?*

I lifted my hand in a wave, but he apparently didn't see me. The man was turning up everywhere.

I joined the group in the viewing room and kept my eye on the door, expecting to see Edmonds enter, but he never did.

For a small group, it was certainly talkative. Most of those present had at least been acquainted with Conner Channing.

"He looks wonderful, considering," someone said.

"So peaceful."

"They really did a good job, didn't they? You'd never know he'd been murdered."

Gil leaned down and whispered, "Is there a script that people use at funerals? Except for that last bit about murder, this is the exact same thing they said at my sister's."

"They're just trying to be nice."

The director came to the door and beckoned to Hugh.

"Excuse me, my friends." Hugh struggled out of the low easy chair with Gil's help and made his way from the viewing room across the hall to the chapel.

It was a small place with ten long, padded pew benches on either side of a short aisle. At one end was a podium under a stained-glass window depicting white lilies and framed by crimson velvet curtains. Off to one side was an upright piano.

The rest of the group followed. I counted eleven people, not including Gil, Hugh, and me. We all sat quietly in the pews facing a poster-sized photo of Conner Channing.

"He looked like his dad," Gil whispered.

He had been a nice-looking man, having the same blue eyes and hawk nose as his father, but with a rounder face, thinner hair, and ears that stuck out a little.

Someone struck up a hymn—"Be Thou My Vision"—on the piano, and the now-closed casket was rolled down the aisle to the place of honor in the front of the room.

I couldn't help but remember my hymn-humming friend Alec and wondering how he was doing in Scotland. I had a sad thought: *If Lily breaks his heart, will he ever hum again?*

There was a rustle in the pew. With Gil's help, Hugh stood and slowly advanced to the podium. After waiting patiently for the piano piece to conclude, he adjusted the microphone and pulled a sheet of paper from his jacket pocket.

"Hello and thank you for coming. We're here to say farewell to my son, Conner McCabe Channing. This may be a trifle unorthodox, but I will be leading the service."

He pulled his reading glasses from his pocket, opened the Bible that was on the podium and began, "Luke 15:11: A certain man had two sons: And the younger of them said . . . "

It was the familiar parable of the Prodigal Son, a superficial young fellow who claimed his inheritance early and spent it all on wine, women, and song. Destitute, he came to his senses and trudged home, chastened and humbled.

"But when he was yet a great way off, his father saw him, and had compassion, and ran, and fell on his neck, and kissed him. And the son said unto him, 'Father, I have sinned against heaven, and in thy sight, and am no more worthy to be called thy son.' But the father said to his servants, 'Bring forth the best robe, and put it on him; and put a ring on his hand, and shoes on his feet.' "

At the end of the passage Hugh closed the book and took off his glasses. "This parable is told by Jesus to illustrate how happy the Lord is to welcome us when we finally realize how much we need Him, confess our helplessness, and accept His grace."

He bowed his head for a moment, then continued, "Many of you know the unfortunate circumstances that drove a wedge between my son and me. He, himself, was 'yet a great way off' when I realized—and he admitted—that he was very sick and not going to get better. And some of you have commended me for my willingness to be there for him during the progressive stages of his terrible disease."

Hugh looked up and smiled. "But what you may not realize was the sheer joy—yes, joy—I experienced embracing my son once more and, through tears, speaking words of understanding, love, and forgiveness. I forgave him and he forgave me, because I, too, had allowed bitterness and anger to come between us."

He mopped his nose with his ubiquitous monogrammed handkerchief and replaced it in his pocket. "So I can honestly say I know exactly how that father felt when he saw the boy he loved more than his own life coming home."

My eyes began to sting and I heard a few sniffs from behind us.

"All I can say in conclusion is that despite the horrible circumstances of Conner's departure, I am eagerly looking forward to the time when I am trudging up that road that leads to my heavenly home, and I see my Lord opening His arms in welcome to me, standing next to my beloved wife and son. I live in that sure and certain hope and you should too."

He led us in the Lord's Prayer and after the amen, said, "Jack and Jess will be taking us back to Sunset Bluffs, where there will be a special buffet for friends and family in the Outlook Conference Room."

There was a slow and shaky procession to the bus. Jess Renaud sat behind the wheel, while Jack Travis helped people up the steps.

Gil came over and put his arm around me. "I'm going to run over to the newspaper office for a bit. Why don't you ride out with this gang, and I'll come get you at, say—" he glanced at his watch, "—two-thirty?" He looked over at Travis. "It's okay for her to ride with you, isn't it?"

Travis smiled. "Sure, the more, the merrier, if you can say that about a funeral."

I waited while Hugh consulted with the funeral director once more before leaving.

Travis leaned down and whispered, "Mrs. Dickensen, ma'am, isn't there going to be any graveside service or—" He glanced over his shoulder nervously. "Isn't the guy going to be, um, like, you know?" He pantomimed using a shovel. "Or maybe, whatchacallit, cremated?"

"No, he isn't. They have to wait until the ground finishes thawing out in order to dig the grave," I explained in a low voice.

Travis nodded. "Oh, wow, I see. They'll just have to put him back in the fridge till then, I guess."

"So to speak," I said vaguely, as out of the corner of my eye, I saw a dark car pass by and turn the corner by the funeral home very slowly.

*Isn't that Herbert Edmonds driving?* I seemed to be seeing him everywhere. I watched it disappear behind the building. *He was here earlier, I'm sure of it. Where is he going?*

"Mrs. Dickensen, ma'am, we're leavin'," Travis said, interrupting my speculation. He was helping Hugh mount the bus steps.

"Oh, yes." I followed and found an aisle seat next to Hugh in the front row.

The doors of the bus folded shut. Jess Renaud fiddled with the gear shift, and with a grinding sound the vehicle pulled out of the parking lot and onto the street. We rode for a while in contemplative silence.

Finally Hugh said, "I can't tell you how much it meant to have you both here today. I feel like you're family."

I smiled at him. "We feel the same." Suddenly I leaned toward the window and pointed. "Look at that car. Have you seen it before? At Sunset Bluffs, perhaps?"

Hugh squinted at the dark sedan that was now passing the bus. "I don't know. There are a lot of dark cars like it on the road." He sat back and smiled at me. "And you know, since I no longer drive, I don't notice cars very much. Why should I keep a car when I have such splendid transportation as this at my beck and call?" he added with a faint smile and a wave of his hand as the bus pulled into the Sunset Bluffs parking lot.

The Outlook Conference Room was just off the main dining room. "It's for special family parties and club meetings," Hugh told me as we entered. We were among the last to arrive.

There was a long table down the center and fourteen chairs, by my count, with matching table settings. A buffet table with several steaming chafing dishes had been set up along one wall. Along the other wall stood a salad bar and another table with various desserts in little dishes. My mouth watered at the fragrances.

Hugh called for attention and spoke a blessing in a soft voice, after which a sort of low-key stampede began toward the buffet. Bing stood in the middle of it all, helping with seating and serving beverages.

Hugh had taken a seat at one end of the dining table, leaning his cane against the chair arm. "May I fill a plate for you?" I asked and at his nod, stepped into line behind half-a-dozen ladies who clearly already knew the drill.

"Are you Hugh's granddaughter?" the woman I had come to know as Sadie asked straight out as she helped herself to chicken and dumplings.

"No," I said, "just a family friend." I took a spoonful of mashed potatoes and poured a little gravy on it. *Surely Hugh likes that; everybody does.*

"Well, I must say I was surprised that there weren't more family members at the funeral. Why was that, d'you suppose?"

I looked over my shoulder. Had Hugh heard? I hoped not.

"I don't believe there's anyone else left in the family," I explained in a near-whisper.

"I see." She seemed disappointed, but gave a self-deprecating chuckle. "I have such a big family. I guess I just thought . . . you know, most people . . . I mean, I've got just scads of grandchildren—can't keep track of them all."

She moved down the buffet line and came to a halt in front of a large bowl containing a colorful mixture. "Oh look, Renee, there's some of that processed cheese product in this again," she said to the woman ahead of her. "Why, oh why do they insist on ruining macaroni salad with these revolting lumps of fake cheese?"

"Disgusting," said her companion.

Bing reached in between us to replace the nearly-depleted bread basket. "I heard that, Sadie, and I'll have you know, I made that from my mother's recipe." She winked surreptitiously at me.

"And the chef approved this . . . dish?"

"Sure he did! He's trying to get some protein into you people any way he can."

Sadie wasn't placated. "But what about all the salt?"

Bing shrugged. "So don't eat it then. More for me!" She swiveled on her sneakers with a squeak and sashayed away.

I moved past the macaroni salad and opted for some of the spinach salad with cranberries.

*Spinach has iron. This will be good for him.*

"What a nice plate you've arranged for me, Amelia," Hugh said, but by the time I returned to the table with my own filled plate, he had pushed his aside, virtually untouched. He leaned forward and murmured, "The doctor told me I'd be needing more rest than usual. This seems to be the time for it." He pushed back his chair and struggled to his feet.

I stood too. "I'll go with you."

"No, no, please. Finish your lunch." He beckoned to Jess Renaud, who was standing at the door. "He'll make sure I get there, won't you? I will see you again soon, I hope."

"Sure."

"Then thank you for everything. Tell your husband thanks, also."

Renaud extended his arm and they proceeded slowly out of the small dining room.

Hugh's plate was whisked quickly away by Bing and just as quickly, Sadie took his place, accompanied by a huge slice of apple pie. Raising her hand, she said, "Bing, some coffee here, please," then addressed herself to her pie. "Now this," she said, pointing with her fork and with her mouth still somewhat full, "is what they really know how to make around here."

I smiled, nodded and continued working on my meal.

"I'm glad we have this chance to talk, dear. I wanted to make sure you understand that you're barking up the wrong tree."

I took a sip of my water. "Tree? I beg your pardon?"

"About this thing with Hugh," she said in a low voice.

*Maybe she can give me some information I don't already have.* "Well, anything you can tell me will be a help." I buttered a roll.

She looked at me with a frown. "You don't actually think I approve, do you?"

I waited to take a bite. "I don't understand why. I feel it's important to find out all I can. I've become so fond of him, he—"

"Oh, give it a rest, sister. We all know what you're up to!" Sadie abruptly pushed the remains of her dessert aside and walked away in high dudgeon.

*That's a senior vocabulary word,* the English teacher in the back of my mind observed. *I've always wanted to use it.*

As I sat there, buttered roll in hand, another elderly lady slipped into the chair she'd just vacated. "Don't let Sadie bother you. She's just jealous. We're all rooting for you. It's not often we get to see a May-December romance take place right before our eyes. More power to Hugh, that's what I say." She stood and skittered away before I could respond.

Suddenly acutely self-conscious, I gathered my purse and quickly began my escape. *I can call Gil to pick me up early.*

I was almost out the door when Sadie caught up with me again and put her hand on my arm. "You know," she said in a hoarse whisper, "he doesn't have any money. Once he's gone, that's it, pfft!" She gestured with her hand and, turning quickly, made a dramatic exit.

"But I'm already married," I murmured. But nobody was listening.

# Chapter | Thirty

"Wait a minute," I said on my return to Chez Prentice, "wasn't Lily supposed to be taking care of Janet today? I was just about to head over there to pick her up."

The baby was seated in the kitchen's old-fashioned wooden high chair, happily clacking together two plastic measuring cups, while the housekeeper was once again folding laundry on the kitchen table.

Hester shrugged. "Couple hours ago, she came running in here all out of breath and begged me to take over. Said she didn't have time to explain. There's no tellin' with that woman. Suppose she broke a nail?" She gave me a mischievous grin.

"Well, anyway, how was my offspring?" I asked, "Did she behave herself?"

"Good as gold. She helped me cook, didn't you, honey bunny? Well, pretend to, anyway." She reached for the cups. "I'm going to need these later, sweetie, when I make biscuits. You know, the biscuits you like? With jelly?"

Janet was not willing to surrender her makeshift toys. She gripped them tightly, making a fierce, squinting face.

Retrieving them would be almost impossible without resort-
ing to violence.

Hester retreated. "It's okay. You keep 'em. I'll use my
metal ones." She turned to me. "How was the funeral?"

"About as you'd expect, sad, and a little bit inspiring. But
you'll enjoy this: At lunch, I learned that a number of people
at Sunset Bluffs think I'm a gold-digger after Hugh's nonexist-
ent money."

Hester chuckled. "How about that? I'll bet there's some
woman out there wants him for herself. Am I right?"

"I do believe you are." I took a deep breath. "Well, I think
I'll take Janet downtown for a visit to her daddy's office." I
reached my arms out to receive my daughter. "I'll get these
back to you," I promised in a whisper over the baby's head. I
retrieved the diaper bag from a kitchen chair. "So Lily left—
when?"

"Gosh, about eleven-thirty, I think."

I packed Janet, still tightly gripping the measuring cups,
into her stroller and headed down the street toward town and
the newspaper office.

It was good to get out and walk again. The air was spring-
like once more, and the shrubs that had been frozen by the
storm were beginning to recover. Before moving to the lake
house, I'd walked everywhere. I mentally resolved to have
regular walks with Janet and perhaps with her daddy too.

I was just about to cross the street when someone called,
"Amelia! Ms. Dickensen! Wait up!"

I turned to see Ev jogging up the sidewalk, carrying a zipper file case and his instrument. He was togged out in his usual unconventional style, and his footgear of choice today was a pair of backless leather slippers like the ones my father used to wear with his bathrobe. They slapped his soles as he ran. He gave me a pleasant smile as he approached, but I still couldn't help wondering what Lily had seen in this man.

Ev nodded his greeting to me and bent down to wave at the baby. "Amelia. Janet."

Janet clacked the two plastic cups together at his greeting.

"Look, I hate to bother you, but I wanted to get in touch with Lily, you know, Mrs. Burns? And thought you might be able to help me."

"I'm surprised, Ev; I thought you two were, um . . . "

He nodded. "Seeing each other. Yeah, I know. Well, we were there for a while. Had one date the night before the snowstorm, and I thought she had a good time, but when I called her yesterday, she said she'd have to call me back later." He frowned slightly. "She never did."

"Well, maybe she forgot. She does get distracted sometimes."

"I kind of gathered that. But I called back this morning and she didn't answer, and just now I stopped by her house and rang the doorbell." He shrugged. "Look, I'm making too much of this. I must sound like an idiot. Or a stalker."

I hastened to reassure him. "Not at all, but I wouldn't worry too much if I were you. In my experience, you'll soon be hearing from her, and she'll be asking you where the heck you were."

He chuckled. "That makes sense. Thanks." He glanced at his watch. "I'd better get going. We're having another rehearsal. The concert's been rescheduled. I hope you can make it. The admission is free. Remember, we're doing Handel's *Water Music Suite* and some stuff from *Nutcracker*."

"We might be there. Thanks."

*Such a pleasant man, despite his deplorable fashion sense,* I thought. *I can hardly believe he belongs on our list of suspects. A* dark thought interrupted, *But you can't find Lily. Was he really worried about her, or could it be a clever cover story?*

I pasted a cheery smile on my face as he strode off in the direction of the civic center, but as soon as he turned a corner, I reversed course and headed the stroller around the block to Lily's house.

I had known Lily McKendrick Burns ever since we were grade-schoolers. Our family homes were back to back with each other. As children we'd beat a path between the two houses, playing dolls and making mud pies. That was why I had no qualms about checking the mailbox. She hadn't collected it yet.

I knew the McKendrick house as well as I knew Chez Prentice, but today, as I mounted the three steps to the front porch, it seemed unwelcoming. The windows were dark and the doorbell seemed to echo, unheard.

A few years ago, after her husband died, Lily and I had exchanged house keys. Hers was still on my key ring and turned easily when I tried it. I pushed the door open, listening for the sound of an alarm. There was none. Lily's recently installed security system hadn't been turned on.

Anxious, I lifted Janet from the stroller, hoisted her on one hip, and together we entered the darkened entryway. "Lily? I have your mail here. Are you sleeping?" I called up the staircase. No answer. "Hester told me that you were in a hurry about something. What was it?" Silence.

I moved to the kitchen, turned on the light, set the mail on the table, and lowered the wiggling baby to the impeccably clean floor.

I looked in the dishwasher. It was empty. Every plate and eating utensil was safely stowed in its proper drawer or cupboard. All was in order, as usual. Lily was an excellent cook and housekeeper.

I hoisted the baby and headed upstairs. The bedroom smelled faintly of her favorite perfume, *Toujours Moi*. Her old-fashioned chenille bedspread was tightly stretched across the bed. *Apple pie order*, I thought, remembering an old-fashioned idiom my grandmother had used.

The only anomaly I could find on the second floor was the closet door standing wide open. Everything, I had to admit, was far more orderly than my own house on its best days. I turned off the upstairs lights and prepared to head back down.

As we descended the darkened hardwood staircase, a sharp clatter made me stumble and almost lose my footing. Desperately I grabbed the bannister with one hand and jerked Janet closer to my side with the other, causing her to whimper.

*What was that?* I looked around, up and down, trying to locate the source of the noise. Two small white shapes at the foot of the stairs gave me the answer.

Still shaken, I slowly sat on one of the steps and placed the baby on my lap. "Why did you drop those cups, huh?" I asked her gently.

Her eyes seemed huge in the dark.

I hugged her and looked around. "Never mind. I guess your Aunt Lily isn't home," I told her, trying to keep the anxiety out of my voice.

Toting Janet on my hip, I retrieved the cups and took one more last look around the first floor. In the kitchen near the back door, I noticed something.

"What is that smell?" It seemed to be coming from Lily's mop closet. All it took was one peek inside to realize that something was, indeed, very wrong. My fastidious friend hadn't changed the contents of this litterbox.

I looked around and said aloud, "Wait a minute: where's the cat?"

# Chapter | Thirty-one

As I headed back around the block, pushing the stroller, I called Sergeant Dennis O'Brien on my cell phone.

He didn't seem too concerned. "So when did you last see her?"

"This morning about ten, but something's wrong. I know it, Dennis."

I heard him sigh. "Has anything or anybody been bothering her lately?"

"She had an argument with Alec," I volunteered.

Dennis knew Alec. "Did they make up?"

"No, in fact, he left town and Lily started dating a musician."

"I see." He also knew Lily. "Amelia, it seems to me you have too much on your plate at Chez Prentice to worry about your friend's love life."

"But—but she's missing! I went all over her house—I have a key—and she's really gone. And her cat is too!"

"You need to watch your step going into empty houses alone. I might arrest you for trespassing," he added with a chuckle.

"Please, Dennis, I mean it. I'm really worried. There's a

murderer still out there and—"

"Okay look, I'll make a note of the fact that Ms. Burns hasn't been seen recently. But it's really too early. If you want to take this any further, you'll need to wait a couple of days, and then come by and file a missing persons report."

"I believe I will. Thank you," I said, a bit curtly.

Dennis wasn't taking this seriously enough. Lily had come through for me when I was in danger. It was only fair that I do the same for her.

I was thinking intently while marching along the sidewalk, pushing the stroller as Janet sang one of her baby songs and clacked the plastic cups for accompaniment.

Something large and dark fell into step beside me.

I glanced to the side and jumped. "Oh!" I stopped abruptly, giving the stroller such a jerk that Janet's makeshift toys once more fell from her hands, clattering on the sidewalk.

A large, hairy hand retrieved them and dropped them into the baby's lap. "I'm sorry if I scared you. You were walking so fast I had to hurry to catch up." His tone of voice wasn't exactly friendly, but it wasn't hostile either.

I tilted my head in order to look at his face. "Mr. Edmonds, isn't it?"

The man was even bigger close up than he'd seemed in the hallway. He was wearing a dark brown suit, white shirt, and navy blue tie, but he didn't look comfortable in it. He extended his paw to shake mine.

"That's right. And you're Mrs. Dickensen." With his other hand, he reached into a jacket pocket.

I drew in my breath.

"Special Agent, FBI," he said, flopping open a leather case with some kind of picture ID and flopping it closed again. He replaced the ID in his pocket. "I need to ask a few questions. Mind if we talk as we walk together? We're less likely to be overheard this way."

"Um, all right."

Even though he was an FBI agent, the man still made me uneasy. I reminded myself that it was broad daylight in familiar territory.

"What kind of questions? I thought you were a musician."

He grimaced briefly. "I am, sort of. I really do play the drums. I'm working undercover. I got this gig with the orchestra in order to follow a lead."

I had no patience with riddles. "What lead? What is this all about?"

He seemed a little cowed by my stern teacher voice. "Please, Mrs. Dickensen, keep your voice down," he whispered. "I'm looking for a man whose real name is Gregory Rasmussen, but he is probably living under an alias."

I gasped. "The Rasputin Killer! You think he's here too?"

He nodded. "We have reason to believe he has been living and working in the area. Wait—you said 'too.' Who else has been talking about this case?"

"Everybody. Especially since the television show and the newspaper article came out."

He rolled his eyes. "I know. I wish they hadn't done that. They might've spooked the guy."

"But—" I started to tell him more when I heard my cell phone ringing from the depths of the diaper bag stowed in the stroller. "Excuse me," I said, digging as the phone played a rather metallic-sounding version of "Bonnie Annie Laurie," Alec's signature ring.

"Look, I gotta go," Edmonds said, looking over his shoulder. "I must ask you to keep all I've told you in complete confidence until we've apprehended the unsub." He waved a forefinger at me and frowned. "Remember, it could mean criminal prosecution if you tell anybody about this. We'll talk again." He jogged away before I could say yea or nay.

My first impression of the man hadn't changed. *A rude boor if there ever was one,* I thought redundantly. *I've never met anyone in the FBI before. Surely they're not all like that.*

"Unsub?" I asked Janet, who watched with wide eyes. "What's an unsub?"

Her answer wasn't helpful. "Baga!"

Of course, by the time I reached the telephone in the bottom of my bag, it had stopped ringing. I listened to the message: "Amelia, I have something wonderful to tell ye! Call me back when ye can."

I tried calling but kept getting voicemail. "It's just as well," I told Janet as I resumed walking. "I'd just have to explain to him that Lily is missing, and there's nothing he can do about it over there in Scotland."

As if in response to my frustration, the baby began to cry. "Oh, honey," I said, bending over her. All at once my olfactory senses told me the problem.

I picked up the pace. "You need a new diaper, and you need it immediately," I said, turning up the sidewalk to Chez Prentice.

# Chapter | Thirty-two

As soon as I got Janet down for a nap, curled up in her travel bed in the room behind Marie's office, I called Vern.

"Hold on just a minute, Amelia. Thank you, sir," he said.

I waited, pacing the office floor.

Finally: "Okay, I'm pulled over and nobody wants a taxi at this moment. Shoot."

I told him about Lily's disappearance.

He dismissed it out of hand. "You're being a helicopter friend, Amelia."

"A what?"

"You know, like a helicopter mom. You hover too much. Oh, never mind. Was that why you called?"

"No, there's more if you don't think I'm being some other kind of airplane," I said sharply. I told him about my walk with Edmonds.

"FBI, huh? What did he want to know? And why ask you?"

"I think he's talking to me because of my connection with Hugh Channing. My cell phone rang, and all of a sudden, he had to go but he said we'd speak again. When we do, I'll let you know what he says."

*Oh, oops,* I thought. I had totally forgotten Edmonds' order to keep silent. *Well, too late now!*

The response was a loud blast of static from Vern's end. It was Fleur LaBombard on the walkie-talkie, directing him to another fare.

I heard him say, "Right, I'm on it. Listen, Amelia, I've got to go pick up somebody at the Rip Van Winkle Motel, but I'll put you on speaker till I get there. Okay, let's bench the FBI for a minute and get back to our list of suspects. D'you think we have everybody on there? Can you come up with anybody else?"

I pulled the scrap of paper from my purse. "Not at the moment. But you know, I've been thinking about Callie Huff. If her murder was connected to Rasmussen, then we need to give her a closer look."

"Closer? What d'you mean?"

"She claimed to have known the man long ago. Hester and Marie were there. They heard her too. I've been trying to think what she said. One thing, I remember she implied that they'd had a brief, um, intimate relationship, she and Rasmussen."

"No kidding!"

I ignored his guffaw and continued, "I know she also said he was very attractive to women and charming, but not necessarily handsome . . . and that he had a beautiful singing voice."

"That last one's kind of odd, but it could be helpful. Look, I'm pulling up in front of the motel now, but I think you're on to something: the singing voice. If it is the same person who did all the murders, that's the connection, but—Hello, sir! Where to? Gotta go, Amelia."

After he hung up, I paced some more.

*If Gregory Rasmussen did all the murders, killing not only his girlfriend, but Conner Channing and Callie Huff, too, he's probably someone I've already met.* I suppressed a shudder. *A beautiful singing voice, Callie said.*

All at once, it occurred to me how I could eliminate some of the names on the suspect list that Vern and I had compiled. I didn't relish the idea, but it had to be done, and the place to start was Sunset Bluffs.

# Chapter | Thirty-three

"Don't be silly," Hester had said when I asked her to watch Janet yet again, "I don't mind a bit. Since she's sleepin' now, I'll just carry that little radio thingamabob around in my apron pocket and go get her when she wakes up."

I still felt a little guilty as I pulled once more into the parking lot at Sunset Bluffs. *I'm going to need to think of a suitable thank you for all this babysitting Hester's doing.*

I was at the front door when I looked over my shoulder and spotted Edmonds pulling into a parking space. I hurried inside. No matter how official his business might be, I didn't want to encounter him again today. He made me distinctly uncomfortable, though I couldn't put my finger on why.

I took the elevator down to the ground floor and was about to make my way over to the Annex when a friendly voice said, "Hey, Miz Dickensen!" The tall Texan was carrying a laundry basket full of dishtowels.

"Jack, I was just going to come find you. I heard through the grapevine that you have a wonderful singing voice."

"You heard about that talent show thing?" He shrugged. "I do like to sing a little."

He began walking along the hall back toward the elevator and I followed.

"You see," I began, improvising at a rapid pace, "we have, um, parties and things over at our B&B." This was true. "And we, er, sometimes need to hire people to, uh, entertain." This was also true.

He stopped and looked down at me with a smile. "That sounds nice. I'd be honored to do it, ma'am."

I pressed the elevator's up button. "Would you be willing to audition, sing a little something for me, in the elevator, perhaps?" I added as he looked around uncomfortably.

"Well, I guess so."

The elevator doors opened and we stepped inside. They had no sooner closed than Jack began, "Awl mah exes live in Texas," singing in a deep, slightly scratchy voice that seemed to come from someone else.

I nodded to the rhythm of the song and smiled. While Jack's singing was passable, it was nowhere near as melodious as George Strait's and under no circumstances could be called beautiful. Remembering that Hugh said Jack was a sensation at the talent show, I now suspected that it was his lanky good looks that had put him over the top.

"Very nice. Thanks," I said as the elevator doors opened once more.

"Just let me know when y'all need me." He gestured with his elbow. "C'mon to the kitchen. Bing'll be wanting to see you—say hi 'n all."

I followed him through the empty dining room, where the aforementioned waitress was setting the tables for dinner. A delicious smell wafted from the kitchen. Sunset Bluffs residents were in for a culinary treat of some kind.

"Bing, look who's here," Jack began, but a sound I can only describe as a bellow interrupted him.

"Freeze!" We three turned and beheld Edmonds standing in the doorway in a dramatic stance, feet wide apart and a gun held in both hands, pointed point-blank at Jack. "John Travis, aka Gregory Rasmussen, hold it right there!"

Bing and I stared at the FBI man and craned our heads back around toward Jack. He slammed his burden on a nearby table and snapped, "What the Sam Hill are you talkin' about?"

"Put your hands where I can see 'em!" Edmonds walked cautiously forward, extending his free hand while continuing to hold the other man at gunpoint.

"What is this?" Bing asked. "What's going on?"

I, for the moment, was speechless.

The handsome busboy raised his hands. "Don't worry, Bing honey, this guy is just being an idiot."

Edmonds patted Jack down with his free hand. "Idiot, am I? Ladies, this fugitive right here is worth a cool two hundred and fifty thou in reward money. The police have been looking for this guy for years and years. He's the Rasputin killer!"

Bing gasped. Some of the kitchen workers peeked hesitantly around the kitchen door.

Edmonds reached in his jacket pocket. "Now put your hands behind your back. I'm bringing you in."

Jack rolled his eyes. "Look, Yosemite Sam, cut it out. You're scarin' the women."

Edmonds didn't even glance our way, only gestured with his gun. "It can't be helped. You're coming with me right now, or else." He held the gun at arm's length, inches from the other man's forehead.

I gasped. So did the other kitchen workers, cowering in the entrance with wide eyes.

Jack relented, sighing as he put his hands behind his back and submitted to being handcuffed. "All right, but you're in a peck of trouble, *amigo*."

Edmonds shoved him forward, laughing. "Yeah, a quarter-million bucks' worth! Get going!" They headed for the exit.

All at once, something struck me. I called, "Mr. Edmonds, does the FBI really offer a money reward?"

Over his shoulder, Jack answered me, "Of course not, ma'am. This dingbat is no G-man—he's a bounty hunter. But believe you me, he's gonna get his. I'll be back, ladies, don't you worry!" They disappeared into the hall and presumably headed out of the building.

Bing collapsed on a chair. "What can I do?" Tears filled her eyes. She reached in her pocket for a tissue. "Oh, do you think it's true? That he's a killer? I'm in love with a murderer?"

I pulled a chair over and put my arm around her shoulders. "I don't think Jack's a killer, Bing. In fact, I know so."

She blew her nose. "But how can you be so sure?"

I looked over at the door. "Because I heard him sing."

"You should be relieved," Gil said at home that evening right after Janet had been tucked in. "They've arrested the murderer. That's good news!"

I shook my head. "You weren't there. You didn't see how he reacted. I don't think he's the one, Gil."

My husband took me in his arms and kissed the top of my head. "He's not one of your students, honey. You hardly know the guy. My contact at the police department says they have evidence that says he's possibly Rasmussen."

I pulled back slightly. "What evidence?"

"Something about his being at most of the places they think the killer has been over the years. Plus, they think his identity is bogus."

"But—"

He put a gentle finger over my lips. "Shh. Can we change the subject just for a little while? I have more good news. At least, I think it'll be good news to you. Here, sit down."

I lowered myself onto the sofa and looked up at him. "What?"

He rubbed his hands together. "I did something I almost never do, Amelia. I said a prayer about the problems at the newspaper."

He now had my undivided attention. It wasn't so long ago that my husband was a card-carrying skeptic.

"Oh, Gil."

He took a seat beside me. "I asked what I should do about the paper and about, um, the deal with Renaud," he finished rapidly. "And you know what? A thought popped into my head. It said, *You already know exactly what to do*. And—it's just so weird—but I did know, I mean, I really do know."

"I've had that happen too."

"I won't be dealing with Renaud anymore, honey. I'm going to call him tomorrow; tell him his help is no longer needed."

I took his hand. "I'm so glad."

"And I had another idea: We'll go from being a daily newspaper to three times a week. I'm going to put it to the owners tomorrow too. I'm pretty sure they'll go for it, even though it'll mean some pretty big changes. And if they don't, well, maybe I'll just pray a little more," he added with a slight smile.

"We both will," I said.

# Chapter | Thirty-four

"My mom is learning how to type in that prison school," Serendipity Shea announced to me at the end of her tutoring session the following day. "And stuff about computers, too, so she can get a job when she . . . uh, y'know, gets out."

"That's wonderful!"

The young girl's face brightened. "Plus, Dad and her talked a long time, and I think they might be getting back together, kind of."

"That's really good news, Serry."

I fervently hoped it was true. Brigid Shea's transgressions were many, but I prayed that her husband's forgiveness could help repair that badly fractured family.

We gathered up the worksheets and notebooks and I walked Serry out to the car, where her father waited. "She's doing very well," I assured him through the open window, pleased to notice that the hunted look he'd carried around for months had turned to a hesitant smile. I waved as he pulled away from the curb and whispered a prayer for them.

The baby monitor weighed a bit heavy in my pocket, reminding me that I needed to awaken Janet from her nap. I could hear her faint, snuffling snore.

It was just the two of us today. Edmonds had checked out yesterday, Ev was at a final rehearsal for the symphony concert, Etienne and Marie were meeting at their lawyer's office, and Hester had the day off.

I smiled to myself, reminded of the year I had spent all alone in my family's big house. It had echoed with memories and loneliness until that fateful evening in the public library when my world was turned upside-down.

"Miss—Amelia?" someone called as I was about to enter the old familiar front door.

"Chuck?" The florist's battered van had pulled up into the driveway while I was wool-gathering. "Are you making a flower delivery?"

He frowned and adjusted his baseball cap as he approached. "Nope, just brought some new bushes that Etienne ordered for the front yard." He turned around and gestured at the lawn, which was still in a state of unsightly disarray. "Looks like you guys're gonna need a lot more work done here."

His almost-cheerful tone seemed to indicate he anticipated gleaning more income from the situation. I sighed.

"You're probably right about that."

"Look, Etienne paid me already and I told him I'd put them in ASAP. Is he here?"

I shook my head. "No, I'm manning the fort today."

He scratched his neck under the pony tail. "Listen, I got lots to do today. I'm just gonna go ahead and put 'em in right now. That okay?" He pointed to the strip of ground next to the front porch where a row of dead bushes languished.

"I'm sure it's fine," I agreed. "I'll be inside."

I was about to mount the inside staircase when Chuck knocked on the front door. "Can you unlock that basement door for me? Etienne said I could use his tools."

I hesitated. "The police told us to keep it locked."

"Oh, yeah, I forgot about that. But hey, c'mon, they caught the guy, didn't they? It's all over, and Etienne said he had a post-hole digger down there I could use, no problem."

"All right, I guess."

I fetched the key from the office desk and led Chuck around to the back. After I opened the padlock, Chuck pulled back one of the doors and descended the steps while I waited.

"Gee, it's dark in here," he complained. "Where does he keep his stuff?"

I heard a clunk and the sound of glass breaking. Chuck uttered an oath.

"Wait a minute," I called, pulling open the other basement door. I began to descend, but stepped back. The baby monitor couldn't get any signal in the basement. I turned the volume up all the way and set it in the corner of one of the top steps. I was sure to hear it from there.

I went down the steps slowly, one at a time. The outside light from the open doors now made most of the area navigable.

Chuck had found a ragged whisk broom and was squatted, sweeping the remains of an empty canning jar into a corner. "Sorry," he said.

I dismissed the apology. "It's all right. When the police were here, they got things even messier. By the way, that thing you need should be in a big wooden box over there beyond that alcove." I pointed past the shelves where Callie's body had been and couldn't suppress a shudder.

In the shadows, Chuck's face took on a ghoulish expression. He'd noticed my discomfort.

"Oh, hey, is that where you found that woman's body?" He hunched down on all fours to look into the space beneath the shelf. "I heard she was stuffed way underneath there." He looked over at me. "I bet it makes you feel kind of creepy down here, eh?" He chuckled. "Like one of those slasher movies or something. You see that goblin movie last year? What was theme song?"

"The goblins gonna getcha if you don't watch out," he sang in a pleasant, tuneful voice.

*I didn't know he could sing.*

"I don't watch those," I replied stiffly and took a step back, toward the stairs.

"Y'know, some people would be scared of the dead woman's ghost, and—"

"We're not superstitious in this house," I interrupted sharply.

*Just what do I know about Chuck Nathan anyway?*

He'd been here in town for a long time, but, come to think of it, he never talked about his previous life. He never really talked about anything other than plants. I tried to picture him as a younger man, with a long, bushy beard. Could Chuck Nathan ever in his life have been described as hot?

I pointed. "The toolbox is over there." I took another step back.

He followed my gestures, stood and moved toward a darkened corner. "Oh, yeah, here it is. Kind of beat up, isn't it?"

I heard the squeak of the rusty hinges as he pulled the top open and the clang of metal on metal as he rummaged through it. "I can't find the thing. There's nothing here but some old shears and an axe and stuff."

I hurried forward, stepped in front of him, and squinted into the box, extending my hand to feel the contents. "I know it's there. Etienne told me where all the tools were, because—"

All at once, I heard a clunk and a grunt and the bulk of Chuck's body knocked mine forward, halfway into the box.

*Oh, help me! It's the killer!*

I made an incoherent, atavistic noise and struggled to free myself, but the man was a heavy, dead weight on my back. With one frantic effort, I managed to straighten up, shoving him off me.

To my surprise, he fell backward and collapsed in a heap on the floor and lay there, apparently unconscious. I knelt beside him.

"Chuck? What happened?" *Has he had a stroke?* I touched his head and my hand came away bloody.

"So touching," someone said.

I looked up and saw a man's silhouette framed by the basement door. As my vision adjusted, I could see that he held a large shovel in his hand.

"Who . . . what . . . "

"Shut up," the man growled.

I scooted backward on my hands and knees. "Why did you hit him?" I gestured toward Chuck's recumbent form. "Did you think he was trying to hurt me?"

"Don't worry, I don't think he's dead." He shoved Chuck's arm aside with his foot, tossed the shovel away, and took a step closer to me. "Forget about him. It's just lucky I saw the basement door open. I want to have a little talk with you."

"I don't understand what you're saying." I slowly stood. "I appreciate your coming to my rescue, though I assure you I could have handled the man's, um, unwanted advances by myself."

I'd backed up as far as I could, against the side of the large toolbox.

"Come on, don't pretend you don't know who I really am. Callie Huff told you, didn't she?"

It was then that I knew for sure: I was all alone with the Rasputin killer.

"T-told me? You mean the wedding planner?" *The dead wedding planner?*

I prayed my face didn't betray my thought. My voice trembled, making my valid protest sound false.

"Sh-she didn't tell me anything."

"And then you told your husband, didn't you? That's why he broke off our deal and stopped paying me, isn't it, Mrs. Dickensen?" Jess Renaud said. He moved closer. "Isn't it?"

"No, I didn't. I really didn't. I had no idea—"

My eyes had become accustomed to the darkness by now, and I looked intently at the man, searching for a weapon, but his hands appeared empty.

I pointed at Chuck, showing him the blood on my hand. "I think you'd better call 911, Jess. He's pretty badly injured."

He looked down and said casually, "No, I don't think so." He put his hand to his waist, and then I saw it: a huge Bowie knife in a leather sheath on his belt. "You're alone here, aren't you?"

"No, I'm not, there's—"

"Don't try to kid a kidder. I've worked too hard staying under the radar to let a woman put one over on me. Callie tried it. She tried to act like she didn't remember who I was, but I saw right through her. And as for that lawyer of mine—"

"Conner Channing?" As the British say, that's when the penny dropped. "He didn't commit suicide, did he? Or throw those things?"

I was almost backed up to the wall. *I'll bet he even put something in his food too.*

He laughed and shrugged. "Hey, it's in the newspaper. It must be true!"

He took a step closer. With his thumb, he flicked up the snap closure on the knife.

Pieces of the puzzle began falling into place. "But why kill Conner, Jess? You didn't have to kill him. You'd gotten away. Nobody knew where you were."

"He was a slanderer," he said, hissing the word. "He told everybody he thought I was guilty. On nationwide television, no less." He pulled the knife from its sheaf. "He slandered me. My own lawyer! It wasn't right."

"Conner was sick, out of his mind. He didn't know what he was saying."

The metal blade glinted in the low light. It looked brand-new. A crazy thought darted through my mind: *He uses a new one every time . . .*

"Jess, you can get away right now. I know Gil didn't ask for his money back. You can rent a car, take a bus, get to Canada or—"

He continued moving closer. I was inching backward, away from him, but he was steadily closing the gap.

"It's just us two," he said hoarsely into the clammy silence of the basement, "like with Callie."

Then, incredibly, Greg Rasmussen began to sing.

"We got time, baby," he growled in an excellent imitation of deep-voiced singer Barry White. "Lots and lots of time. Oh, baby . . . "

There it was. Callie was right. The Rasputin Killer really did sing.

He saw the surprise in my face. "Didn't know I could do that, did you? You like it? I can do opera, too."

"*L'amour est un oiseau rebelle . . .* "

I had to give him points for versatility. Even in the midst of my fear, I recognized the tune from the opera *Carmen*. Here in this dank, dark place, sung low in a breathy bass voice, it took on a distinctively sinister tone, even . . .

*Hypnotic . . .*

Still crooning, only about two feet away, moving toward me slowly as though under water. "*Que nul ne peut apprivoiser . . .*"

I stared, transfixed as he slowly, steadily raised the glittering knife above his head. His eyes glittered too. I couldn't make myself look away from the intensity in them.

Trapped, I raised my arm in an instinctive defensive gesture.

As the knife trembled at the apex of his swing, a shriek tore through the air.

It was coming from the steps.

The spell was broken.

Renaud whirled around and I saw my chance. Ducking past him, I stumbled across the basement and scrambled up the stairs, losing a shoe and badly scraping my knee in the process.

The screaming had settled down into the steady rhythm of a baby's cry, coming from the nursery monitor. Janet was awake, hungry, and needed her diaper changed.

I didn't stop to retrieve the source of the noise, just kept running, kicking off my other shoe and heading around the house, where I nearly collided with the front bumper of Etienne's car as it pulled into the driveway.

298 | E. E. Kennedy

Frantically, I ran around it, yanked open the car's back door and jumped in, panting heavily.

"*Mon Dieu!*" Etienne exclaimed. "Amelia, what is it?"

I could barely speak. "Call . . . call . . . 9-1-1," I gasped. "The basement. It's the k-killer . . . he's in . . . the basement." Then I hopped out of the car and staggered across the front yard, onto the front porch, and into the house.

My baby needed me.

# Chapter | Thirty-five

"Here," Gil said, "just sign the card. I've already addressed and put a stamp on it."

I picked up the ballpoint he handed me and scrawled my name. "Why balloons?"

I really didn't care about the answer. I put the pen down. It seemed heavy.

"I don't suppose Chuck Nathan would be all that excited to receive flowers, would he?" Gil smiled and sealed the envelope. "And the good news is that he'll be going home in a few days, so I'd better hand deliver all this to the hospital right away. Why don't you get dressed? You and the baby can come with me. We can visit him together."

I shook my head and tightened the belt of my huge, shapeless bathrobe. "I can't, Gil. I just can't. Besides, there are things I should be doing around the house. The laundry and things . . . " I gestured vaguely.

The truth was, I'd let the laundry go, and we'd been eating sandwiches off paper plates for the past few days. I just couldn't seem to summon up any energy.

He took my hand. "Amelia, you've been cooped up in this house for nearly a week. I'm getting worried about you.

What's wrong, honey? Are you afraid?"

*Afraid* wasn't the word for it. Numbed or exhausted said it better. I didn't answer.

"You don't have to worry about Renaud. Dennis says he's probably in Newfoundland by now." Gil bobbed his eyebrows. "And I have to admit, you were right about that guy from Texas. Turns out he's an oil man, a millionaire. John Chisolm Travis. In fact, he's the one who put up that whopping reward for catching the killer in the first place." He chuckled. "I got an exclusive interview. I scooped everybody, even the TV networks!" He was really trying hard to cheer me up, bless him.

"Then why was somebody like that bussing tables at Sunset Bluffs?"

"He was undercover, so to speak. For years, he's been obsessed with finding the Rasputin Killer. He hired private detectives and followed every lead they could dig up. He even went so far as to become an official deputy sheriff down there in Texas. When Travis learned that Rasmussen's lawyer was moving to Sunset Bluffs, he thought maybe the guy might try to contact his attorney. It never occurred to him that Channing was in danger. He feels really bad that he wasn't able to protect him."

"He certainly went to a lot of trouble moving out here and everything." The way I was feeling, moving into the next room seemed a stretch.

"He didn't think so. You see, Rasmussen's first victim was his fiancée."

Now I understood. "That poor girl. And poor Jack," I murmured. "And poor Bing. She told me she was in love with him." I hugged myself. The world was a sad place, indeed.

Gil went on into town without me.

I sat back down on the sofa. It had been raining all day, a cold, hard rain, and it hadn't let up yet. I hoped we weren't in for another surprise blizzard.

While Janet played with a new toy in her playpen, I watched two Lifetime movies and a quiz show, all the while promising myself I'd get up and take a shower before the sun went down. I'd been speculating about making myself a cup of instant coffee for the past half hour when there was a knock at the door.

It was Hugh, rather formally dressed as usual in a sport coat, tweed pants, and conservative striped necktie. He stood on our tiny front porch under an umbrella and waved his cane at a large, shiny luxury car as it sped away.

"Hello, Amelia. I hope you don't mind the impromptu visit. I hadn't heard from you recently, so took the initiative and got a lift here. They'll be coming back for me in a little while." His gaze took in me, my disheveled hair, rumpled bathrobe, and slippers. "Oh, my dear girl."

I stepped back and ushered him inside. "I'm afraid I haven't had time to pick up around the house today," I said, as he furled the umbrella and leaned it in the corner.

I hurried to pick up the TV remote and turn off the commercial for complexion cream. "Would you like a cup of coffee? It's instant, I'm afraid."

He walked in slowly, leaning heavily on his cane, and paused to greet Janet. "I'd enjoy that. Black will be fine. No sugar." He pulled a small stuffed animal from his pocket and looked at me. "I brought her a little surprise. Is this all right?"

I nodded. Janet was delighted.

In the kitchen, I filled the kettle, put it on the stove, and joined Hugh in the den, which is what we called the biggest room in our rustic little house. He was looking at the wooden plaque above the big fireplace.

"Eighteen-ninety. Fascinating. This is quite a nice place, warm and cozy. *Gemütlich*, the Germans call it." He took a seat next to me on the sofa, using his cane to lower himself gently. "Amelia, I wanted to thank you for all you've done. Ever since you found out who Rasmussen really was, the spring in my step has quite returned."

*You could have fooled me*, whispered the worried voice in the back of my head. *You look frailer than I've ever seen you.*

"No, I didn't figure it out, Hugh. He just showed up at my house. It had nothing to do with anything I did. And because I was so clueless, an innocent man was badly hurt." I put my head in my hands. "Poor Chuck. For a little while, I actually suspected him!"

Hugh patted my shoulder. "I've been to visit him. Please don't worry. He seems to be quite enjoying all the attention he's received at the hospital. His room is utterly filled with balloons."

I managed a faint smile. "They're more appropriate for a florist, Gil says."

"I see. Flowers would be coals to Newcastle, so to speak."

"That's a good reliable idiom. I'd almost forgotten how nice it is to talk to you, Hugh."

"Likewise, I'm sure, my dear." He sat back, looking at me sympathetically.

I was prompted to explain myself. "I know, I know. I'm a mess. Please don't think I don't appreciate your visit, but . . . I don't know how to explain it." I clasped my hands and thought a moment. "It's . . . I mean, these past few days . . . no, these past few years have been rather strange."

He had a puzzled expression.

I hastened to elaborate. "Not bad strange, necessarily—I mean, Gil and the baby are the family of my own I never dared imagine I'd have—but there have been some really bad moments too. Moments I didn't think I'd survive. This last thing—this thing with Renaud—was—" I searched for the right expression "—the last straw, you might say. I'm just tired, Hugh."

He tilted his head. "Tell me about the last few years."

So I did, beginning with how the death of my father and mother left me all alone in the big yellow house and about what happened when I tripped over the corpse of poor young Marguerite LeBow and all that had transpired since.

"And I've testified at two murder trials. Somehow it never occurred to me that they'd call me as a witness for the prosecution, but they did, both times. I don't know why I'm telling you this. I hate talking about it."

Hugh nodded. "I can understand why. I imagine the attorneys for the defense were less than kind."

I grimaced at the memory. "That's an understatement. They were brutal. Everyone says to tell the truth, but when you do they try to make you look like a liar. Oh, yes, of course. You know all about this business, don't you? No offense intended to your profession."

He smiled. "None taken. I am under no illusions as to how some lawyers operate, my dear. But you were telling me about the trials. Please continue."

It took a half hour, at least, and when I finished, to my surprise, I didn't feel exhausted any more. I felt unburdened.

Hugh leaned on his cane. "My, my, you have had some remarkable experiences. But you know what it tells me, Amelia?"

I shook my head.

"It tells me that God has had His hand on you all this time, guiding and protecting and . . . blessing you." He gestured heavenward with his freckled, ropy hand. "Blessing you," he repeated quietly. "My dear, you are practically the embodiment of the Ninety-first Psalm." He quoted it in flawless King James.

*Thou shalt not be afraid for the terror by night;*
*Nor for the arrow that flieth by day . . .*
*For He shall give His angels charge over thee,*
*To keep thee in all thy ways.*
*They shall bear thee up in their hands,*
*Lest thou dash thy foot against a stone . . .*

For the first time since the incident in the basement, the knot in my chest unclenched. I took a deep breath. "That was more appropriate than you know, Hugh." A tear coursed down my cheek and I accepted the proffered monogrammed handkerchief. "Thanks—but you're right. You really are."

"That is what I like to hear. You know, Amelia, we aren't promised ease, but we are promised His presence. I've clung to that through all of this, and it's enabled me to smile."

"Oh, Hugh, how shallow you must think me! After all you've been through, here I am—"

"Hush, my dear. We all have our own tailor-made challenges. No one has the patent on hardship." He groaned a little as he pulled himself up with his cane. "Might I avail myself of your facilities?"

"Oh, sure, right down the hall there, near the front door." I pointed.

He was moving slowly, I noticed, slower than ever before. For all his cheerful talk, I was worried about my new friend.

*He's in his nineties, after all,* I reminded myself. *Wisdom such as his takes time to develop.*

I heard the bathroom door close. I stepped into the kitchen and looked at the kettle, then touched the side. It was cold. I'd never turned the stove on! I clicked the knob to high and returned to the sofa.

To the person coming down the hall I said over my shoulder, "I must apologize, Hugh. I promised you coffee and I—" I turned around and stopped.

Standing in the hallway was Jess Renaud.

# Chapter | Thirty-six

At the sight of me, Renaud stopped and stood frozen in the middle of the hall.

Neither of us said a word. I think we were both surprised. His clothes were filthy and sopping wet. He was dripping, making a dirty puddle on the hardwood floor. His sneakers were covered in mud. The uniform he had worn at Sunset Bluffs was filthy and rumpled, and his hair drooped in strings over his face. There was a long, painful-looking scratch across his stubbled cheek, and the eyes that had seemed so hypnotic were now sunken and blank.

I stumbled backwards, stepped on a toy that emitted a pitiful squeak, and almost tumbled back into the playpen.

The murderer's gaze left me and moved to my child. I hastily stepped between them.

*Don't you even look at my baby!*

All at once, I remembered: Hugh was in the bathroom. I had to warn him. In the loudest voice I could muster, I said, "Jess Renaud! How did you get in here?"

I didn't use his other name. Jess had been, for a time, a caregiver. To call him Gregory Rasmussen would have been to recognize what else he had been. And what he still might do.

He just stood, frowning, looking confused as I trembled.

While I watched, his eyelids lowered, and he swayed slightly to one side. Extending an arm, he braced himself on the wall. This was no longer the seductive, opera-singing villain who had threatened me in the Chez Prentice basement.

*He looks absolutely wrung out. I wonder if I could overpower him, hit him with something.*

He looked around again, blinking, fumbling with the sheath fastening at his belt. He was still wearing the knife.

My heart was beating at an impossible rate. *Oh, Lord, please . . .*

*Ask him if he's hungry.*

I didn't pause to ponder the idea. "Are you hungry, Jess?" I moved backward slowly until I was within reach of a box of graham crackers I'd left on the counter. I held the box out to him. "Here."

He grabbed the box and plunged his hand inside. Pulling out three crackers at once, he quickly demolished them, and reached in for more. At least his hands were away from that knife.

*For I was hungry, and you gave me something to eat. I was thirsty, and you gave me something to drink . . .*

"Would you like some milk to go with that?"

I hurried around the breakfast bar into the kitchen and pulled a carton of milk from the refrigerator. I looked over at the cupboard, thinking of a glass, but Jess was suddenly next to me. He took the carton from my hand and drank as I stood watching.

*As ye have done it unto one of the least of these my brethren, ye have done it unto me.*

Again he wobbled.

A savage, tearing cough from deep in his chest caused him to bend from the waist until it subsided and he wiped his mouth on his sleeve. He hadn't yet said a word.

He turned away and headed back into the den, where Janet stood in her playpen, staring silently at the unusual proceedings.

I followed him, preparing to throw myself between him and my child, but he veered off to the right and headed for the sofa that faced the fireplace. As if he had done this before, he pulled the hand-made quilt that was draped over the back around himself, lay down full-length and closed his eyes.

Janet pointed at him. "Ga!"

"Shh," I said, and picked her up.

I heard the bathroom door open slowly and Hugh emerged, his cane held high above his head, wobbling a little, but ready to strike.

Silently, I shook my head and pointed at the sofa.

Hugh moved forward, stopped, and stared down at his son's murderer.

I pulled my cell phone from my pocket. There was just one bar of reception showing. Our lake cottage was a long way from a tower, and the house phone was on the counter, just a few feet from where our uninvited guest slumbered.

In the off chance it might get through, I hastily texted Gil: "Renaud here. Send police immediately. No sirens!"

Hugh stood there, staring down at the sofa for quite some time. I saw tears drop from his face onto the upholstery and heard a muffled whimper. Suddenly, he again raised the cane, but stopped in mid-air as a loud snore tore through the silence.

Lowering his cane one more time, Hugh turned back toward me. The old man's expression was unreadable.

"Come on," I whispered, beckoning and pointing toward the front door, "Let's get out of here!"

We three silently moved to the hallway.

Hugh handed me his umbrella. He whispered, "It's still raining hard out there. Take the child and go—run! You can go faster without me."

I whispered back, "No sir! Come on!" I gripped his elbow and pushed him toward the front door.

All at once, two things happened.

First, there was a brisk knock at the half-closed front door. Hugh and I gasped.

I looked over at the sofa to see if it had awakened Renaud. To my relief, there seemed to be no movement from that quarter . . .

. . . until the tea kettle began whistling, loud and piercingly shrill.

To my horror, I saw Renaud's dark head pop up and turn. He began untangling himself from the quilt and stood, squinting intently in our direction.

His hand went to his belt . . .

There was no more need for silence. I yelled, "Come on! Run!" Flinging open the door, I immediately collided with the midsection of Jack Chisolm Travis, oil man and millionaire, whose shiny car was idling in front of our house.

"Move! Move! Run!" I shouted frantically, pushing him. "It's Renaud! He's got a knife!"

Janet began to cry. The tea kettle continued to shriek inside.

"Oh, he does, does he?"

Travis seemed almost amused. He tipped back his hat, reached inside his jacket under his arm and pulled out a large pistol. I had a brief glimpse of a gold-colored badge pinned to his vest.

"Go get in the car. Ah'll handle this." He walked into the house and slammed the front door shut.

We hurried through the torrent to the car and opened a back door. I crawled in, tightly clutching Janet to my chest and Hugh followed, closing the door after himself.

"What's going on?" asked a voice from the front seat. "Why, hello, Amelia."

It was Bing. She turned around completely, draping herself over the seat in such a way that we could see her hand, which bore a huge diamond ring.

Janet immediately stopped crying and reached out to examine Bing's hand.

"That's right, kid, diamonds are a girl's best friend." She let the baby touch the ring.

"What are you doing here?"

"Didn't Mr. Hugh tell you who brought him over?" she responded and gestured toward the house. "So what's the holdup? What's Jack doing in there?"

"Just a minute." I turned to Hugh. "What's the matter?"

He was hunched over, staring at his cane, which he held horizontally across his lap. "Amelia, for a split second, I committed murder in my heart. I was about to strike that man. I would have killed him if I could have managed it."

"But you didn't."

He looked at me and smiled. "No, by the grace of God, I didn't. 'Vengeance is mine, sayeth the Lord, I will repay.' I almost forgot that." He shook his white head slowly.

As briefly as possible, I explained to Bing what had happened, concluding, "I just hope your fiancé is all right in there."

"Don't worry about that Texan," Bing assured us. "He can take care of himself. It's Jess Renaud who better be scared!" She looked at me meaningfully.

"Listen!" I said, lowering one of the car windows.

"What?" said Hugh and Bing together.

"The kettle has stopped whistling. I wonder what that means."

# Chapter | Thirty-seven

**W**hat it meant, I learned later, was that Jack Travis had things well in hand.

"That miserable, cowardly piece o' trash took one look at m' gun and did what he was told: unbuckled his belt and dropped his great big ol' honkin' knife on the floor," Jack explained to us as the police took away the handcuffed fugitive. "Then he sat on that stool over yonder, while I turned off your stove and called the police. Turns out, they were already on the way."

His voice deepened. "I told that filthy coward who I really was, y'see, and that I was just itchin' for him to give me an excuse to blow his head . . . clean off." His eyes squeezed into a tight squint. "I really wish he did, but—" He shrugged.

Bing came over and put her arm around his waist.

Jack kissed her and added, "I got something else to live for now, thank the Lord."

"Amelia, honey," Bing said, taking Janet from me, and waving her sparkling hand, "why don't you go, er, get a shower or something and put on something else?" She pointed to my shabby, shapeless bathrobe. "It looks like we'll be here for a while, answering questions." She bounced the baby on her hip. "I'll look after her while you fix yourself up."

A little while later, freshened and properly dressed, I escorted Hugh, Jack, and Bing to the front door. The rain had stopped.

"You saved our lives," I told Jack as he opened the door for Hugh.

He tilted his hat back. "Glad to be of service, ma'am, but it looked like y'all were doin' pretty good when I got here." Ever the gentleman, he went around the car to assist Hugh into the back seat and let Bing in the passenger side.

The back window lowered. Hugh leaned out. "Well, my dear, it really is over, isn't it?"

"The terrible part is," I agreed. "But I hope the good part—our friendship—keeps on going, don't you?"

"Oh, yes, God willing," he said, "as long as possible."

⌒

"How do you do it?" Dennis O'Brien asked me a few minutes later when it was finally my turn to answer police questions. They had taken over the baby's bedroom for their temporary headquarters. He leaned forward and frowned at me. "I'm starting to think you're a trouble magnet, Amelia. Heck, I know you are!"

"That's not fair," I protested. I picked up a pink crocheted blanket from the floor.

"Well, how do you always seem to be in the middle of stuff like this?"

I folded the blanket and set it on the dresser behind me. "I don't know. I certainly don't go looking for trouble." I bent down and retrieved a pacifier from under Dennis' chair.

"Will you cut that out?"

I looked at him blankly.

He waved his pen at me. "Quit picking things up. It distracts me."

"All right." I put the pacifier in my pocket and folded my hands in my lap.

"You say you don't go looking for trouble, but what about that thing a while back with the Rousseau brothers?"

"All right, point taken, but that was because I wanted to help them. You of all people should know that. And it turned out for the best, didn't it?"

"Well . . . the jury's still out on that one, no pun intended." He made a mild grimace.

"I have a question for you, Dennis. I'm still very concerned about Lily Burns. I haven't heard from her at all in f-five days." My lower lip started trembling, despite my best efforts. "Something terrible's happened to her, I know it, and nobody will listen to me." Tears threatened, but I blinked them away, frowning furiously. "Not you, not anybody!"

"Gee, I'm sorry." Dennis hastily replaced the pad and pencil in his jacket pocket and leaned forward, patting me clumsily on the shoulder. "Look, why don't we continue this a little later, maybe tomorrow after you've had some rest. Go take a nap or something while we finish here." He went to the door and gestured for Gil to come in.

"All right." I pointed an accusing finger at him. "But Lily's kitten is missing! She's crazy about that thing! That killer has been around here all this time. I'm so afraid for her, Dennis!"

"I know you are." He looked at his shoes. "Listen, I did look into it, I really did. I can tell you she hasn't used her credit card since Thursday, and her cell phone just goes—"

"—straight to voice mail, I know. I've called it I don't know how many times. Please keep at it, please. I don't dare think about what might have happened." And I didn't dare speak aloud my worst fear: that Lily was Renaud's fourth victim.

"We will, Amelia. I promise we will." His expression was serious as he handed me over to Gil.

I actually did go into the bedroom, turn off the ringer on my phone, and take a short nap while the police wrapped up their interrogations, now using the nursery as a conference room. When I awoke everyone had left, and Gil had already fed and changed Janet and tucked her in for the night.

"I didn't even have help with the diaper," he bragged.

I commended him on his courage and said, "I was worried that we'd have to relocate to Chez Prentice again." I followed him into the kitchen.

Gil shook his head as he opened the door to the freezer. "It's not that much of a crime scene here. Though I don't like to think what could have happened if Renaud hadn't been sort of in shock after living out in the elements all week. The weather's been pretty foul lately." He pulled out a pair of frozen dinners and held them up. "What's yours: meat loaf or turkey?"

I pointed to the turkey. "Is that where he's been all this time?"

"Yep." Gil pulled the dinners from their boxes and put one in the microwave. "After he left Chez Prentice, Renaud hitched a ride out of town, but made the mistake of trying to carjack the driver. The man fought back and managed to shove him out of the car and drive away. He told the police that he left Renaud along that area of thick woods next to the lake. They've been looking for him ever since."

"He was a mess. Obviously, he wasn't an outdoorsman. I remember Callie saying as much." I pulled utensils from a drawer and began to set two places at the breakfast bar. "And we thought he was long-gone in Canada somewhere." I sat suddenly on the bar stool. "Oh, Gil, do you suppose he came here on purpose?"

He shook his head. "The police don't think so. They found evidence that he camped out on the porch of the empty Wilson place, but it's not much shelter in a driving rain. I think he just came inside the first house he could find with an unlocked door."

"I won't make that mistake again," I promised.

The microwave dinged. Gil pulled out the turkey dinner and placed it before me with a flourish. "*Pour toi, Madame. And now I'll cook my pate de boeuf.*"

"I really don't think that's the correct term for meat loaf. It's *viande* something." I watched him put his dinner in the microwave. "By the way, you're suspiciously well-informed about the Renaud situation."

Gil smiled. "Don't worry, honey. No money has exchanged hands. I just took advantage of the latest in infant technology." He reached in his pocket and pulled out the portable monitor receiver. "What?" he said to my disapproving scowl. "The monitor was there in plain sight in Janet's room. They could have asked me to take it away or turn it off at any time." He shrugged.

That reminded me of my cell phone. I pulled it from my pocket. "Oh, no."

Gil was at the sink, filling the glasses. "What is it?"

I held up the phone. "Alec called again. I had the ringer off. Gil, I can't bear to tell him that Lily's missing!"

"Then don't. Let him enjoy his trip. When he gets back will be soon enough."

A ding announced that the meatloaf had finished cooking. Gil sat down on the stool next to me and bowed his head. "Dear Lord, thank You for keeping my dear ones safe and thank You for this lovely meal." He lifted his head, bowed it again and amended, "And please forgive this recalcitrant sinner for his underhanded ways. Amen." He picked up his fork and looked over at me. "How was that?"

# Chapter | Thirty-eight

The next morning, around nine o'clock, there was a fierce pounding on the front door.

Gil had already left for the newspaper office, so I approached the little peephole with trepidation and a baseball bat, grateful that I'd remembered to lock it after he was gone.

After one quick peek, I couldn't believe my eyes. I unlatched the chain and flung the door open. "Lily!"

"Amelia!"

Together, we yelled at one another, "Where have you been!"

The two of us stood for a moment, both scowling and trembling with anger. I couldn't help but notice that Lily looked especially pretty, with a faint, flattering pinkness in her cheeks.

"Hold the phone, ladies," a tenor voice said in a familiar burr. "No need to get off on the wrong fute."

"Alec!"

Gently, the Professor herded the two of us into the house and down the hall. "I believe someone else heard the ruckus," he said, cupping his hand around one ear. "Better go see to her, Amelia."

Janet was indeed awake, rubbing her eyes and insisting on being freed from her crib. I changed her diaper and carried her into the kitchen.

Alec and Lily had chosen to sit on the little stools at the bar, which looked into our tiny kitchen. Alec was whistling "Blest Be the Tie that Binds."

"She's going to need breakfast," I announced. My tone was just the teensiest bit curt.

After situating Janet in her high chair, I filled a sippy cup with milk and poured a bowl of dry Cheerios, her preferred cereal. She liked to pick up the little o's herself. It was a tossup—pun intended—as to how many of them made it to her mouth rather than on the floor.

I filled the kettle and put it on the stove. "Would you like some coffee?"

Lily shook her head. "No, thank you, not if it's instant," she added sharply, "but we would appreciate an explanation about where you've been keeping yourself this past week."

"Me!" It was all I could manage to say. "Me?"

She swiveled a little on the bar stool and linked her arm through Alec's. "We've been trying to call you—"

"And I've been trying to call you!"

Lily shrugged. "I forgot and left my phone charger at the house, but I happen to know your phone is practically grafted to your side, so what's the story?"

"Haven't you been reading the newspaper or watching the news?"

Lily and Alec exchanged shy glances. "Noo, I'm afraid not lately, Amelia," Alec said. "We've been ratherr busy."

*We?* I suddenly realized they'd both used the pronoun several times. "Oh, Alec," I said breathlessly, "did you finally propose?"

"Perhaps we do owe her a wee explanation," he murmured to Lily.

She nodded.

"Y'see, I returrned from Scotland early," he said, "and must admit, I'd been pining the whole time." He gazed down into Lily's smiling face. "I couldn't wait another moment, so—"

"He rang my doorbell and when I answered, he swept me into his arms and . . . " Lily actually blushed. "Well, we decided then and there that life was too short to wait around—"

"—and I had heard the news about that poor woman killed at your house, just a few feet away from hers," Alec interrupted. "I wanted to be where I could protect this little lady twenty-four seven, so I finally . . . made an honest woman of her. Didn't little Janet tell ye? She was there when I arrived." He winked at the baby.

"So I brought Janet back over to Hester at Chez Prentice and then—"

Lily held up her left hand. She was wearing both a diamond engagement ring and a wedding band. She was beaming.

"We went out and found a justice of the peace!"

"And had a short honeymoon at the VonTrapp Lodge, over in Stowe," Alec added, blushing to the roots of his now well-trimmed beard.

"You eloped!" I walked around the bar and hugged them each in turn. "That's the most romantic thing I ever heard." A thought struck me.

"But where's the cat?"

# Chapter | Thirty-nine

"And *I* said, 'We dropped him off at the veterinarian's, you dumb bunny. Did you think I was going to carry him around in my purse?' " Lily's bell-like laughter floated above the murmur of the crowd. "It turned out that she'd never even thought of that!"

"I'm getting awfully tired of that story," I said to Gil as I dipped out another cup of punch at the happy couple's wedding reception. "By my count, she's repeated it at least six times since the party started this afternoon."

"Cut the Blushing Bride a little slack," Gil said, using his new nickname for Lily. "It's her turn to be the center of attention."

"Lily has always been the center of attention," I muttered under my breath.

I was feeling a little cranky. After all the emotion and effort I'd put into worrying about my friend, she'd managed to turn my concern into a shaggy dog story.

"Or maybe a shaggy cat story," I amended.

Gil paid not the slightest attention to my dour mood. "I'm glad these two finally got together, but the last thing I heard was that she was dating that flute player."

"I asked her about him. She said the relationship was doomed the moment he told her that, in his opinion, the only good cat was a dead cat."

Gil chuckled. "That'll do it, all right. Hold on, I need to find . . . " He patted his jacket and pulled an envelope from his pocket. "No, this isn't it," he muttered. "These are the concert tickets for tomorrow night. Ah, here it is." He held up a small file card. "Excuse me a second. I need to go over my toast one more time." He melted into the crowd and out of sight.

Weaving her way carefully among the guests, Hester approached the punch table with a loaded tray in her arms. "Bert got Mr. Channing a place to sit down over there," she said, jerking her head in the direction of a pair of wing chairs by the front window. "He was looking a little peaked."

I stood on tiptoe and spotted Hugh, smiling wanly as he watched the milling crowd and sipped from a cup of tea. Today, his whole personality seemed somehow pale and faded. He saw me and waved. I waved back.

"How're the finger sandwiches holding up over there?" Hester asked.

I looked to my right. "There are plenty of them left, but we do need a refill on those little meatballs in the chafing dish."

"Whew! When they say heavy *h'ors doevres*, they do mean heavy!" she said. "This tray weighs a ton!" She refilled various plates and retired to the kitchen.

A dinging sound interrupted the flow of cheerful conversation, and all eyes turned to the fireplace of Chez Prentice's front parlor, where Gil stood, rapping a spoon against a glass.

"I'd like to ask for your attention, please. I want everyone to hear this. Bert, would you go get the ladies from the kitchen? Thanks. Make sure everyone has a cup or glass in hand. That's it."

He glanced at the crumpled scrap of paper in his fist and tucked it in his front pocket. "This is such a special occasion, and it's my privilege to honor Lily and Alec at this wonderful time. I've known the bride for many, many, *many* years."

He grinned as Lily gave him a look from under arched eyebrows. There was general laughter.

"And she has been a true friend to me and to my wife." He waved at me. "Hi, honey!"

I waved back, nodding and holding up my cup of punch.

"Alec, I've known a little while less, but he's a fine man and, doggone it, you two kids deserve each other."

Another round of laughter.

Gil rolled his shoulders uncomfortably. "I didn't know this vow when Amelia and I were married—wish I had—from the book of Ruth. I'm using it in a different context from the original, but it's what I hope for Alec and for Lily and for all of us married folk."

He took on a serious expression and quoted, " 'Whither thou goest, I will go; and where thou lodgest, I will lodge: thy people shall be my people, and thy God my God.' Lily and Alec, may you always be united in the way that these words describe. Ladies and gentlemen, the bride and groom!"

Everybody raised their glasses and the entire room echoed back, "The bride and groom!"

A few minutes later, Gil found me in Marie's office, trying to repair my special-occasion makeup.

"Honey, you've been crying. What's the matter?"

I put a final pat of powder on my reddened nose and clicked the compact shut. "That was a beautiful toast you gave."

"I meant it."

"Quoting the Bible and all."

"I meant that too." He looked at my doubtful expression and hugged me. "Honey, we both know that without some divine intervention, you and I wouldn't stand a chance!"

Bert and Hester appeared at the office door, arm in arm. Each of them held a tissue in their free hand. The housekeeper was wiping eyes that were even redder than mine and her husband was blowing his nose.

"Etienne just told us," Hester said. "He said it was your idea." The couple came into the room.

Gil looked at me. "Told them what, honey?"

Bert said, "That they're givin' us ten percent of Chez Prentice. We'll be part owners!"

Gil chuckled. "Oh, that."

"You two deserve it, after all you've done," I declared.

Hester took me into her buxom embrace. "I just can't believe it! We're partners now, you guys. Thanks!"

"Gil, Amelia, here you are! Come quickly!" It was Etienne, beckoning from the hallway.

We hurried to follow him to the front porch, where most of the party had assembled, watching something that was going on along the newly-sodded, beautifully planted front lawn of the B&B. It was dusk, and the porch lights were on. A perfect spring night.

"Look!" Marie stage-whispered to me, "and listen!"

A small crowd of about a dozen people was arrayed on the sidewalk, listening to a man in a tall top hat and frock coat holding aloft a lantern, speaking loudly and gesturing toward us.

" . . . and this is Chez Prentice, better known in the tabloids as Slay Prentice, where Gregory Rasmussen, the infamous Rasputin Killer, committed the last of his three brutal murders. It was to the root cellar of this hundred-year-old family house that a poor woman was lured to her doom, right before this city was struck by a record-breaking spring blizzard. Due to the snow, the body wasn't discovered until hours later, when the owner descended the steps to fetch a bellows for the fireplace. Later, the murder weapon, a large Bowie knife, was found buried in the inn's front yard, right over there. It's said that the woman's ghost . . . "

"Wasn't that wonderful?" Marie said after the tour had concluded, been applauded by our guests, and departed down the street. "That's the Greater Adirondack Ghost and Tour Company! Etienne says that ever since they've included us on their ghost tours our reservations have been coming in so fast, he can hardly keep up!"

"Do people really want to stay in a place they think is haunted?" I asked, suppressing a shudder.

Gil chuckled. "Sure they do. Whatever's clever. Gives 'em bragging rights: 'I spent two whole nights at Slay Prentice—' " he said, hunching over and adopting a Boris Karloff accent, " 'and lived to tell about it!' "

# The Press-Advertiser

## Obituaries

<u>Hugh Vincent Channing</u>, 93, of this city, died Sunday after a brief illness. Dr. Channing taught for 39 years at Bickerstaff University Law School, including courses in criminal law, torts, and property, retiring eighteen years ago. Two years ago, he returned to his hometown, taking up residence at Sunset Bluffs Retirement Community.

"Hugh related so well to his students," said former B. U. Law School Dean Clifford Clements. "He always said that his job was to impart the information and proper legal techniques to the students, not to tease and taunt them with it. This made him a faculty standout and a favorite among the students."

After serving in the U.S. Navy during the Korean War, Channing earned a B.A. in 1957 from Bickerstaff College and a J.D. in 1972 from the University Law School. He clerked for the NY State Circuit of the U.S. Court of Appeals. After several years in private practice in New York City, he began his teaching career at his alma mater's newly-formed law school in 1970.

"I only knew Hugh for a few months," said local teacher Amelia Prentice Dickensen, "but I came to appreciate him as a kindly and devout person with a keen intelligence. As a teacher myself, I can imagine that he was a great blessing to his students. I know he is now enjoying the reunion he spoke of in his son's eulogy."

Channing's name had recently been in the news due to the brutal murder of his son, attorney Conner Channing, at Sunset Bluffs Retirement Community in late March. The perpetrator, Gregory Rasmussen, aka Jess Renaud, was apprehended and will stand trial for multiple counts of murder this fall.

Channing will be buried at the local Presbyterian cemetery, near his wife and son. Funeral arrangements are pending.

# Worldwide Buzz
## Opera on Death Row!
### Serial killer sings a new song.

Gregory Rasmussen, aka the Rasputin Killer, who has been sentenced to death for the murders of his girlfriend, his former defense attorney, and a former lover, and who managed to elude capture for the first murder for almost two decades, is putting his other talents to use while his current publically funded defense team works on an appeal. He's singing opera.

"He has a surprisingly good voice," says Warden Frederick Keyes. "We don't mind his singing if it keeps him out of trouble. Some of the other inmates actually look forward to his nightly a capella concerts."

Rasmussen's guards agree. "I actually like it when he sings Humperdinck—you know, *Hansel and Gretel* and stuff. That 'Lullaby' song really calms the inmates down."

The chances of success for the convicted murder's appeals have the same prospect as, according to a *Worldwide Buzz* confidential source, "a snowball in hell." In the meantime, however, the prison population can enjoy a little culture.

"*Faust* is really his favorite," says the warden.

# Appendix

*Note:* The Greater Adirondack Ghost and Tour Company really exists! They bring guests on guided walking tours of historic Plattsburgh, New York. These tours are tailored to encompass a broad array of interests so there's fun for everyone! They're justifiably famous for their lantern-lit ghost walks featuring the area's most haunting locations.

Their website at https://www.facebook.com/Ghostand-TourCo also offers up vintage photos and bits of the history of this beautiful region. You can telephone them at 518-645-1577.

# Beef Stew Aristocrat

## Serves 4-6

It's a mystery how such a simple and homely dish got such a high-falutin' name. A version of this recipe was published in 1948 in *Cooking—The Modern Way*, a cookbook published by The Planters Edible Oil Company, later Planter's Peanuts.

The original recipe suggested serving the meat and vegetables in "bowls" of cabbage leaves. Every recipe in this cookbook features peanut oil. Hester prefers to use olive oil, and obviously, she makes a much bigger batch than this. It is so easy and quick, even Amelia can prepare it (after a few false starts).

## Ingredients

3 Tbsps. olive oil

1 lb beef cubes or strips (available in the supermarket for fajitas)

3-4 carrots, peeled and cut in chunks

1-2 onions, peeled and cut in wedges

4 potatoes, peeled and cut in chunks (red-skinned potatoes are good)

1 15-oz can cut green beans, with juice

½ head of cabbage cut in diagonal wedges

## Directions

In a deep saucepan or pot, brown the beef in the oil and once browned, turn to medium heat.

Put the carrots, onions and potatoes in the pot on top of the meat. Pour the canned green beans (including juice) over the vegetables. Top the contents of the pot with a "roof" of cabbage so that it completely covers them.

Hester likes to put a lid over the top to retain the heat. Allow to simmer until the cabbage is tender, roughly 15-20 minutes.

Serve the vegetables and meat on a large platter with the light broth in a gravy boat or ladle the stew, broth and all, into bowls. You can thicken the broth, but we like it the way it is.

COMING SPRING 2017

# Village Idiom

## Prologue

She had considered bringing something to make her eyes run, but finally dismissed it as impractical, too obvious. It would be enough to wear her carefully-practiced stricken look: eyebrows raised, head bowed, lips tight but trembling. She had added the crumpled, shredded tissue at the last minute. She flattered herself that she was the very image of barely controlled grief.

Her lawyer had parked her outside the courtroom labeled Grand Jury.

"It won't take long," he'd said. "I heard their case against you last week." He shook his head. "Pathetic." He'd patted her hand. "They have no hard evidence, none at all, just speculation. I don't know why they're wasting our time like this. Don't you worry."

She'd been right about the weapon. It had to be something that belonged in the room, something that didn't present itself as deadly. In this case, it had been the edge of the tub, which did the job quite nicely.

She glanced at her watch. It had only been five minutes. She ran her finger over the diamond-encrusted face. The expensive watch had been the original bone of contention between them.

If only Sibyl hadn't been such a miser, more concerned about having money in her old age than taking care of her only daughter. *Okay, her stepdaughter. But we were family, weren't we? Aren't parents supposed to keep their children happy? That's what Daddy always said.*

Well, she was an orphan now, with both parents dead in the space of a year. She thought about her future, that of an heiress with a million in the bank.

*They'll pay attention to me now, for sure.*

The courtroom doors opened and her lawyer emerged, smiling.

She stood, shouldered her backpack and gazed at him with a sad question in her eyes: *Is it over?*

He nodded and stepped forward to escort her down the hall. "Let's get going, young lady. I promised that this wouldn't make you late for your next class. We want you to graduate from high school on time."